INTIMATE FRACTURES

The Aftermath of a Rape

INTIMATE FRACTURES

A NOVEL

WAGIH ABU-RISH

Published by Kirkland Publishing House in the United States.

Cover design: Riley Quinn

ISBN: 979-8-9859152-3-5 Paperback

ISBN: 979-8-9859152-4-2 Hardcover

ISBN: 979-8-9859152-5-9 eBook

979-8-9859152-6-6 Audio Book

First Edition

www.wagihaburish.com

In memory of my brother, Munif, 1946-2023,
who passed away before publishing his novel
and while I was finishing this, my current novel.

MAIN CHARACTERS

MUSTAFA MAKRAM—Palestinian Student at Duke

ZEINA ABERCROMBIE—Mustafa's First Love

RAMZI—Mustafa's Father

ZEINA, JR—Mustafa's and Zeina's Daughter

COL. SAMY ABERCROMBIE—Zeina's Father

GEN. JONATHAN ADAMS—Two-Star General

FARIS—Mustafa's Best Friend

WILLIE KUEHN—Mustafa's New Friend at Duke

MONA—Willie's Sister

MICHELLE PARKER—Mustafa's Second Love

ROSE—Michelle's Paternal Aunt

WILLIAM PARKER—Michelle's Father

JOHN CARPENTER—William's Criminal Attorney

AMANDA SUMMERFIELD—Mustafa's Sexy Professor

NIJAD MAKRAM—Mustafa's Chicago Cousin

CARLOS MAKRAM—Mustafa's Argentine Cousin

SHAWKI ZURZUR—Palestinian American Attorney

FAROUK FAKHRY—Qatari Ambassador in U.S.

HASSAN—Qatari Ambassador's Brother

THE STANDARD OF RAPE

*Religion and Culture are platforms
of varied dogmatic indoctrinations.
To the victim, rape carries a standard
aftermath, of a deep-seated trauma,
regardless of the venue.*

Physical rape in the scheme of traumas

is a most dislocating experience.

Its aftermath is usually more

traumatic than the act itself.

Reconciling with such an aftermath

is a life-long challenge

which keeps the victim pondering:

> *I am the wonderer of my mind*
>
> *I am the seeker of my truth*
>
> *I am the wiseman of my kind*
>
> *I seek to know why fate is so*

CHAPTER 1

1960

Amman

The reason Mustafa Makram chose to go to the University of London was simple. His father, Ramzi, thought highly of the British university educational system, and he thought just the opposite of America's. Mustafa believed otherwise but could not get his way to accompany his friend, Faris, to the United States. Even though Duke University, in Durham, North Carolina, had offered Mustafa a most generous scholarship, Ramzi persisted.

Going to the University of London would cost him $1,500 more per year, but that's where Mustafa's attempts ended. His father would not sell a parcel of land in Palestine to partially finance his education in the US.

Nothing was more delightful to Mustafa than writing to and receiving letters from Faris, who had chosen Duke. They compared courses all the time, as they were both studying business. True to their high school performances, both maintained A averages.

One year later, Ramzi started changing his mind about the American higher educational system. His new boss at the CPA firm was an American university graduate who managed to pass his CPA exam in the United States before returning to Amman, Jordan, where many of the Markram family lived. Ramzi was most impressed with his new boss and decided that he was more qualified than the other two department heads, both chartered accountants who had studied in England.

Ramzi did not mind repeatedly sharing his newly developed appreciation for the American educational system with Mustafa. As Mustafa finished his second year of college, he felt it was a good time to test if he could transfer to Duke, where Faris was excelling academically, financially, and romantically. Mustafa did not much care for London's weather and Faris didn't miss an occasion to tease Mustafa about how well he had it, and how challenging it was for Mustafa. Faris was dating three different girls at the same time.

With Mustafa maintaining an A average at the University of London, Faris went to work to obtain a similar scholarship as the one Mustafa was offered two years earlier. Faris was exceedingly successful, securing a better deal for Mustafa than he did for himself. Not only that, but Duke managed to reserve for Mustafa a London–Durham ticket for a mere $160.

The day Mustafa and Faris reunited in 1963 was a celebrated one. Faris invited twelve male and female students, throwing a small party in Mustafa's honor. He made sure that three of the five girls that showed up were uncommitted. One of them showed a keen interest in the very handsome Mustafa.

The party was fun, but Mustafa was not in the mood, especially since the gathering did not result in anything worth pursuing. The following day, Faris told Mustafa that he was lucky, in the sense that "Faris" was easy to pronounce by Americans. He added that "Mustafa" sounded too foreign for the average American, especially for interacting with exciting American girls. He insisted that Mustafa start calling himself Steve, as many Middle Eastern Mustafas did. Mustafa was resistant at first, but grudgingly agreed after some prodding by Faris.

Even though it had been a small party, Mustafa had concentrated on reconnecting with Faris and was much less interested in hooking up with one of the three female students. Faris was surprised, as one very pretty and sociable student, Anne, showed keen interest in Mustafa.

That prompted Faris to open the subject of girls and sex. After he briefed Mustafa about his own accomplishments in the field, he asked his friend to tell him about his romantic experiences in London. Mustafa was open, telling Faris that in Amman he had dated half a dozen girls, but none involved real sex. He added that in London, in two years, he had sex four times—twice with one student and twice with his physician's secretary. Otherwise, he told Faris that he did not like having sex for sex's sake. He wanted to have it with someone he loved.

Faris tried hard to convince Mustafa that he was misdirected and that sex for love's sake came later in life, and not while they were just twenty years old. He looked his friend in the eye. "At any rate, you are not going to get many dates if we stick to your Arabic name. From now on I will start calling you Steve so that you will get used to it and answer automatically."

Mustafa finally agreed. "This is Steve responding to your advice—the same kind of advice you used to dish out to me while we were in high school."

Mustafa was in good spirits. In the mirror, he practiced calling himself Steve. He was okay with the sound and the feeling of his newly acquired nickname. He went to the student union, hoping to meet someone who would give him the opportunity to use his Americanized name. He sat near and across from two students. One of them introduced himself.

"Hi, my name is Steve," he said, feeling comfortable with the transformation.

Another girl was sitting by herself at another table. Mustafa moved over and asked a few questions about the campus, after which he introduced himself as Steve. Neither party seemed to notice anything wrong with the name.

The following day, Faris took Mustafa around to places he routinely visited. The introductions proceeded smoothly as Steve replaced Mustafa.

CHAPTER 2

September 1963

Durham, North Carolina

Mustafa got to his first class five minutes to ten and sat in the second seat in the third row on the left. He kept the aisle seat empty, expecting at least one more student to share in the row's remaining six empty seats.

At exactly 10 a.m., a tall, beautiful, and slightly lanky girl entered the statistics classroom. The professor had not arrived yet. She took one step into the room and looked around for a whole minute while being noticed by many of the male students. She then proceeded to walk further in, looking at no one in particular. As she got to the third row, she stopped, set her binder on the aisle seat, and remained standing. She took a 360-degree look around the classroom, picked her binder up, and then sat down.

As she set her elbows on the desk, she turned left and looked at Mustafa. "I am Zeina. What is your name?"

It took him a few seconds to answer, as *Zeina*, an Arabic name, fascinated him. "I am Steve."

She gave him a more surprised look than the one he'd given her. "Steve?! Is that your real name?"

He smiled but paused for a few seconds. "What do you think?"

"I think your name is Suhail."

That was another Arab name. "Where did you get this Suhail from? How come you know the name Suhail? Are you of Arab extraction?"

"No, but I lived in Kuwait for four years," she answered.

"So, you speak Arabic."

"No, I don't. I was eight when I left Kuwait. My father was the US military attaché there. And yes, this is why I'm called Zeina. He loves the name and so do I, very, very much."

"This is funny—this is really funny. You have an Arabic name, and you like it and use it, and I have an Arabic name and I do not use it, although I like it," said Mustafa. "I feel like I should keep Steve. My real name is Mustafa. My friend Faris tells me that the girls will stay away, as they are not able to pronounce my name."

"Look at me, Mustafa—look at me. I'm a girl and I love the name Mustafa. I hope you revert to Mustafa and forget about Steve, which is so plain and common. Mustafa is great. I always liked that name. The brother of our last house cleaner in Kuwait was called Mustafa. He was Palestinian."

The professor arrived ten minutes late. Zeina hurriedly said to Mustafa that she wanted to see him afterward, outside the classroom, to discuss the name issue. After class, Mustafa told her that he planned to bounce the name off a few more students before he made his final decision on which one to use.

"OK, I'll do the same. I'll bounce it off my boyfriend and see how he reacts. I'm not going to ask my father, because he loves Arabic names."

The implication did not escape Mustafa, who figured that Zeina was signaling that he would not be the object of her romantic interest. He did not mind, as he was not in that state of mind, although he liked Zeina's attitude and admired her looks.

The following statistics class, Mustafa sat in the same seat. Zeina was there within seconds and followed suit, next to Mustafa. She continued with their prior conversation. "What did you find out?"

"Find out about what?"

"What do you mean? You've already forgotten. You were supposed to find out which name to use!"

"Oh, that! What about you—what did you find out from your boyfriend?"

She hesitated. "Well, my boyfriend likes Steve. But you know, he has never been outside North Carolina."

Mustafa then told her that he checked it out with two different girls and one male student, and they all agreed that using Steve was more practical.

Zeina looked at him without saying anything, exhibiting regret at his decision. "Well, I'm overruled. I would have chosen Mustafa. You can go with the overwhelming majority and call yourself Steve from now on, but I will never use any name besides your own." She extended her hand. "Welcome to America. I think we can celebrate by having a pecan pie together. You're here in North Carolina, which is near Georgia, famous for pecans and pecan pies."

"Great, pecan pie! How about including your boyfriend—what is his name?"

Again, Zeina paused. "His name is Randall. He's studying sociology, but let's not involve him. We're just classmates, and he knows about you. That's what counts."

Before the following class, Mustafa and Zeina met at the student union and shared an early pecan pie, she with whipped cream and he without it. Over coffee, they had a lengthy conversation. Zeina told Mustafa that she had told her father about him. She asked if she could invite him to visit with her father because he wanted to practice his Arabic. Mustafa said if her father extended an invitation, could the visit not take place for a few weeks? The timing was OK with Zeina.

For the following three weeks, the two saw each other three times a week, in class and after class. During those get-togethers, Zeina intentionally avoided calling him by either name. Their conversations grew deeper, and she told him that she did not mind discussing any subject with him except religion and politics. She added that she developed this approach while going out with her boyfriend because he belonged to a sect that did not believe in going to a doctor.

When Mustafa asked Zeina about the name of the sect, she answered, "The less I say about religion, the better. I think I know what religion you are, but I wouldn't mention the name in this case too. It's a clean break with this subject. I also will not comment on what the president of the United States or any other politician says. This way, personal relations are better maintained. It's our individual, ethical, and social habits that count and cement such relations. Politics and religion tend to disrupt relations, don't you think so, Mustafa?"

"Zeina, it is all the same. I think you can propose this exclusion and the other party can accept it or turn it down. In this case, it is all right with me. I am not a religious person, and if I start talking about politics, it always ends in discussing the situation in Palestine. It's a subject I usually do not want to set aside, but I can for the coming three months," he said.

"Three months—why three months?"

Mustafa then reminded her that they had three months left before the semester was over.

"You mean you don't want to be friends—just friends—after the semester is over?" Zeina looked disappointed.

"Why not? We can stay friends. I have an uncle back home who loves the company of women. He thinks they dish out better advice, since society does not provide them with the opportunity to give it routinely. He thinks men are advice poor."

"Well, how about next Saturday to meet my father? I'll cook chicken pot pie and I'll fix the best pecan pie in the whole southeast, with ice cream. Is vanilla OK?"

"How about Randall?"

"Oh, Randall…he'll be with his parents upstate."

————

The following Saturday, Mustafa arrived at Zeina's house. Her father opened the door and said in Arabic, "I'm retired Colonel Sammy Abercrombie." He shook hands with Mustafa firmly.

Mustafa introduced himself by his real name, never having gotten used to his American name. He must have subconsciously been influenced by Zeina's preference.

As Mustafa walked into a spacious and tastefully decorated living room, he saw Zeina, smartly dressed, with an apron around her waist. At that point, it dawned on him that he had never asked about Zeina's mother. He did not know if she was alive or dead.

To conceal what was on his mind about her mother, he said to Sammy, "You don't realize how much it pleases me that you chose an Arabic name for Zeina."

"What do you mean? Not only did I choose the name Zeina

against the wishes of my ex-wife, but I also changed my name from Andrew to Sammy. You see, Sammy is common to both the Arabs and the Americans. I even changed my religion after I served in the Middle East."

Mustafa looked at Sammy, thinking that he had converted to Islam. "Both Zeina and I are now Unitarians. I still can believe in some particulars of Christianity and other particulars of Islam."

"Wow. Before I finish my thoughts, let me go and say hello to Zeina. We cannot neglect her just because the subject matter is particularly of great interest to both of us!" said Mustafa.

"Zeina doesn't have much to say," said Sammy. "She refuses to discuss religion or politics. I really don't know whether she is a Republican or Democrat."

Mustafa proceeded to the kitchen, catching Zeina sticking the chicken pot pie in the oven. He apologized and said that he had not expected her to prepare all this food, and instead, he anticipated she would be helping her mother, trying to confirm what he had heard from Sammy.

"My parents have been divorced since my father and I changed our religion from Southern Baptist to Unitarian. My mother remarried another Southern Baptist, and she refuses to acknowledge either of us. Still, I don't like to talk about religion and politics."

Suddenly, Mustafa said, "Oh my God, I set the baklava on the deck and forgot about it as I took off my shoes."

As Mustafa ran out to fetch the baklava, he overheard Zeina asking her father to stay away from discussing politics or religion. Sammy replied that she was missing out, as those subjects represented the most interesting and animated discussions, and without them, potential conversations were too limited for him.

During dinner, Mustafa talked more about his background,

explaining that his mother had died and that his father provided well for him and his sister. His father took accounting courses for two years, gained a middle management position, and was well-remunerated at the accounting firm. He took care of the financial affairs of many rich orphans, and in due course, some of them rewarded him generously after they grew up.

Mustafa wanted to change the subject of the conversation from him to Zeina. He asked her how she liked her industrial management class.

"It's an industrial management seminar, and I like the fact that Dr. Randall Miller has the ten-student course at his house, in a very informal setting."

"Where is Dr. Miller from?"

Without much thought, she quickly answered that he was from upstate.

Mustafa thought that it was strange that Dr. Randall Miller was from upstate, just as her boyfriend Randall was. He wanted to test his suspicion that she was using particulars about Dr. Randall Miller to create a fictitious boyfriend, but in the end, he decided against it.

As they finished dinner, Mustafa praised Zeina for her cooking and efforts while wondering why she may not have been on the level. It must have been for an unknown reason, as far as he was concerned.

Sammy led Mustafa to a special room full of Middle Eastern artifacts. The older man started speaking of one antique after another and paused when he got to a gold piece, an intricate set of Ottoman gold coins, all arranged and hooked up to be worn over a woman's head, to show off her wealth. This type of head covering was popular in greater Syria up till the end of the nineteenth century. Sammy bought it from his Palestinian housekeeper's family in

Kuwait. Mustafa was not familiar with the piece.

"It is called *saffa* in Arabic, which means setup, as in a jewelry setup," said Sammy. Still, Mustafa was not familiar with that specific term.

Sammy wanted to open a conversation about the Palestinian "calamity." Mustafa told him that he would love to, but once such a subject was open, it would take hours to conclude, and he had to leave to do some reading. Mustafa and Sammy went back to the living room. Mustafa said goodbye and thanked Zeina for her invitation. He felt that her attitude, in the end, became slightly tepid toward him. She did not ask him to stay longer and proceeded to tell him how happy she was that he could come. Sammy said the same.

CHAPTER 3

Once home, Mustafa confided in Faris that he was sure Zeina was trying to convey a particular message to him: that she liked him, but not as a potential boyfriend—only as an interesting friend. He told Faris that he had no romantic feelings toward her but felt offended she had to resort to lying to make her point. Unsettled, he skipped the first class of the following week.

At the next class, Mustafa was there first and sat across from Zeina's usual desk. When she walked next to him, she stood up straight, tilting her head with a scolding look. She then silently proceeded to point her index finger to his regular seat, as if she was guiding him to sit in it. He hesitated at first but moved across the aisle to sit there.

She sat in her regular seat. "I missed you last time. Where were you? I was here first and put my binder on your chair to save it for you. You know, when a friend disappears without notice, one starts to think of all kinds of things, some of them bad. I wanted you to help me out. I really felt let down and disappointed."

"Help you? You are an A student! You don't need any help," said Mustafa dismissively.

"I'm not talking about statistics; I'm talking about my trail ride. I'm supposed to go on a fifty-mile horse trail ride in two weeks and I wanted to visit this new trail with somebody since the trail was too isolated for me to be alone. I thought of you. Have you ever gone horseback riding before?"

"No, I have been on a donkey and a mule, but never on a horse."

"It is very simple—I will teach you how. Would you be willing to accompany me? It will not take long—just three hours."

Mustafa said nothing for a while, pondering what to say. He then said, "What are friends for, except a friendly dinner, a friendly horseback ride, and friendly exchanges?"

"Can you be at my place at 8 a.m. this coming Saturday? Oh, I forgot, you don't have a car! How about if I pick you up from the dorms at 7:30?"

He agreed.

———

On Saturday, all went according to plan, even though at their last meeting, Zeina had sensed that Mustafa was trying to tell her something. She could not figure out whether he was talking about her or about something that might have transpired with her dad.

She packed water and sandwiches for the trip and told Mustafa that the first three miles were the most dangerous. The trail went through a heavily wooded and totally uninhabited area.

"Everything after that point will get easier. But watch for the tree branches once we get into the forest," said Zeina.

She was guiding him through and barely paying attention to her own route. Minutes into the forest, Mustafa's horse stepped on something and bolted. As Zeina tried to control his horse, hers unexpectedly stopped and threw her forward. His horse got agitated, but Mustafa managed to grab a solid tree limb and jump off. As he dropped down from the tree, he could see that Zeina's inner thigh had been pierced by a dry branch as she fell.

Mustafa held on to the twig to stabilize it. Zeina told him not to pull it out yet and first to see how it entered the flesh. She directed him to her saddlebag, from which he could fetch a pair of scissors and some bandages. When he returned, she asked him to cut open her jeans from the bottom of the twig all the way down. He followed her instructions but could see nothing, looking at her smudged and bleeding thigh. She then advised him to loosen her belt and cut her jeans upward, all the way to the waist.

Mustafa hesitated at first.

"This is not the time to be a prude. I don't care if you see my panties. I want you to help me remove this twig."

After Mustafa obeyed, Zeina finished the rest by slipping off her jeans slowly and assessing the situation. Her partially seethrough panties were smothered with blood, although not over her genitalia.

Mustafa took off his jacket and tried to cover her crotch.

"What are you doing? This isn't the time for modesty. You need to see everything to be able to remove the twig. Now, find which way the twig went in and then try to remove it by twisting it opposite to its entry rotation. Are you reading me, Mustafa?!"

"I am reading you. Don't shout—I am reading you."

He followed her instructions and removed the twig cleanly. The bleeding intensified as Mustafa tried to apply pressure to her thigh. Zeina told him to get a towel from the saddle, but he did not.

Instead, he looked at her thigh and prepared a large new bandage. Surprisingly, he spread her legs, put his mouth to the cut and sucked all the spewing blood, and then crisply applied the bandage, all before he spit the blood out. The bandage took and stopped the bleeding while Zeina was looking at him with some admiration. He fetched the towel from the saddle and wrapped it over the bandage. She noticed her see-through panties were now showing her genitalia.

"Under the proper circumstances, Randall should be the one to carry out first aid to his girlfriend's thigh, not a simple friend," he said, to Zeina's utter surprise.

She said nothing, not knowing exactly what to say. She could not tell if he had figured out that there was no Randall, or if he genuinely believed that Randall was the one to be privy to her marble-like thighs.

He surprised her again with his next revelation. "I know that there is no Randall. You used your industrial management professor's particulars to create a convenient boyfriend. I did not hit on you, so why should you resort to this devious method? You could have said that you wanted to be just a friend and that would have settled everything."

Zeina bit her lip and kept silent for a while. "Why don't you cover me with your jacket, and I will tell you everything." He obliged as she looked at him intently. "You know, Mustafa, what I did was to follow a bad high school tradition. Just about every girl pretends to have a boyfriend to up the ante when she is interested in the real one. My friend, Dorothy, works at the International Students Adviser's office, and she is the one who told me about you. It turned out to be very convenient that both of us are studying business. I chose Statistics since it is one of the required courses. Dorothy showed me your schedule, and I chose that class to approach you."

Mustafa looked at her, almost dumbfounded.

She continued. "Needless to say, with my father having served in Kuwait and my having lived there, it was a natural platform to be more interested in someone like you than other girls might have been. End of story. Now let me slip my jeans back on, blood and all, and let's head back home. We can continue to be friends…if you're not totally insulted by my stupid approach."

"Why would someone beautiful like you want to resort to such a game?" asked Mustafa. "Instead of turning me on, you turned me off. I don't understand, but I will take you home."

"Look at you. Look at your reaction! I think an apple-pie American boy would have appreciated my trying hard to hook up with him. You don't. They say that cultures aren't logical. It is a custom that gets established over the years and seems to conflict with traditions of other groups."

"You can shine in reciting words of wisdom, but it is hard to act wisely when emotions are involved," said Mustafa.

"I know. It's kind of ironic." Zeina grabbed him and gave him a mouth-to-mouth kiss, followed by another on his cheek. "I'll leave it up to you from here forward. Let's go home."

———

Zeina's wound could have managed with two stitches; Sammy's army experience more than sufficed for the needed remedial action. On Monday, Zeina was sitting next to Mustafa with a glow to her looks and a smirk on his face. After class, he led Zeina outside the business school building, took shelter behind a bush, and kissed her.

"I think I owe you this. It did not feel good with you having kissed me twice and without my having kissed you at all. I want you to get exactly the right idea. Unlike you, I don't want to relay the opposite idea."

Mustafa told her that he had spoken to Faris and to his new friend at the dorms, Willie Kuehn. "I told them that since you succeeded in confusing me, I did not want to admit having feelings for you. But ever since you showed your true feelings, I stopped being confused and have admitted that I have been attracted to you from the very start."

Zeina said nothing at first, then added, "You could have said what you just said now in one short sentence. You like to use many *ifs* and *buts*." She held Mustafa's hand and led him out from behind the bush. She wanted to declare openly, mostly to herself, that they were falling in love. Mustafa preferred to hold her around the waist, as he shortly chose to do, so he could look into her eyes.

Weeks went by and their love flourished with a lot of affection and caring, much to the adoration of their friends but of some concern to Sammy's psyche. As much as he cared for Mustafa, he was concerned that should this love affair end, it would be devastating to both, but above all, to his daughter. The intensity of the relationship was somewhat unreal. Sammy did not know what to do. In the end, he let the situation proceed without any input on his part.

Having educated herself on Arab cultural traits and psyche, Zeina was aware that virginity and its lack thereof was a critical refrain for many Arabs. She wanted to have sex with Mustafa but was afraid of his reaction when he would realize that she was not a virgin. Mustafa was not pushing to have intercourse with her. He was enamored with the fact that he'd found a real lover, a special lover who was full of care and admiration toward him.

Zeina intentionally allowed Mustafa to guide their sexual interactions. They had frequent sex, but short of penetration by Mustafa. That aspect was of serious concern to Zeina. She thought that if he had figured she was not a virgin, he would not have refrained from penetrating her.

Late during the first semester, Mustafa received an unexpected and belated response from Stanford University, in California, to his application—one that he had filled out cavalierly just to compare Duke against Stanford. Now Stanford was offering Mustafa a hefty scholarship, superior to that of Duke. He shared the response with Zeina and informed her immediately that he was turning the offer down, simply because he could not think of a situation in which he would not be with her. She shared the same with Sammy, who liked what he heard, but it aroused further concerns about the result of an unlikely break between the two mutually mesmerized lovers.

The second semester started with the two taking identical courses. Zeina was maturing so gracefully and was glowing as her looks progressed toward womanhood. She also improved her application of makeup and her choice of more fashionable attire, all courtesy of her father's largess. He extended it admirably but with mixed feelings.

It was a trip to a North Carolina beach that raised Mustafa's level of sexual attraction. After enjoying the sun and surf, they returned to their hotel. As he lay down with his head resting within inches from Zeina's crotch, she stroked a birthmark down his neck and jokingly said, "You can't hide from me—you have this unique and charming birthmark. I can find you anywhere in the world."

He'd never thought twice about the birthmark. It was mostly not visible to him, only when looking through two opposing mirrors. "You, on the other hand, can be recognized because you look unique and special. You don't need a birthmark—I can locate you anywhere in the world."

The exchange worked as a potent aphrodisiac. Slowly, Zeina put aside her wine glass. She started breathing heavily, got up after she set his head on the couch, and pulled his polo shirt off. She then slipped his slacks and shorts off and took off her own clothes. Mustafa looked at her and got sexually excited, as he could feel the desire and passion in her widening eyes. She mounted him and helped him penetrate her in an almost volcanic exchange.

The two had sex for three hours nonstop. It was an emotional and sexual experience to savor. That night they spent the whole time in each other's arms, naked. They did not want to wake up and let go of each other. But they did after another course of sex at dawn.

Zeina was apprehensive that he would be brazen enough to ask her about her virginity. For one or more unknown reasons, Mustafa never asked, and the interludes continued. But unlike the first time, future rounds of intercourse used proper precautions against any potential pregnancy.

The second semester was over, except for Mustafa and Zeina to submit research papers for their advanced marketing class. They decided to separate for two days so they could concentrate on finishing their papers.

CHAPTER 4

Mustafa managed to finish first after he applied himself for eight straight hours. He told Willie Kuehn that he was not supposed to see Zeina for another day, although he himself was done with his research paper. Willie told him that it was convenient, as there was a rally for Barry Goldwater and he was interested in attending the rally to listen, "If the man makes any sense." Mustafa welcomed the opportunity and agreed to accompany Willie.

At 6 p.m., Willie drove up, telling Mustafa he had to cancel, as his mother and his sister were fighting. His mother found out that his sister was going out with a Black classmate. Willie added, "I am never going to convince my mother that it is OK to date a Black person or, God forbid, marry one. She is hung up on being Jewish ethnically and religiously. My sister may not even like the guy…she may be doing it to spite my mother."

The two drove back to Willie's house. Willie's troublemaking sister, Mona, was waiting outside. She told her brother, "Why don't you bring your handsome friend in? Mustafa has a very sexy tush." That expression of crude admiration toward Mustafa was clearly meant to further challenge Willie's mother.

Mustafa proceeded with Willie's car to the Goldwater rally. It took him over ten minutes to find parking, and then only from a long distance from the site. He turned a corner around some bushes and came face-to-face with two burly white guys who looked intoxicated. A third was urinating in the open.

The encounter was wholly unexpected on both sides. Without covering himself, the man who was urinating looked at Mustafa, paused, took his hand off his penis, and extended it for a handshake. Mustafa did not reciprocate, not wanting to touch a contaminated hand, and kept walking. His reaction did not sit well with the urinating man.

Still exposed, he yelled, "Stop!" Mustafa kept going.

One of the other two said, "Peter, that's OK. Let him go. Look how he is dressed—real fancy."

From behind him, Mustafa heard Peter yell, "Tom, Kevin, stop him! Let me show you what I'm going to do with this fag." Mustafa instinctively knew the man was approaching him even before he felt the tug on his shirt. "Where did you get this fancy shirt from?"

The other two men, Tom and Kevin, moved in front of him and winked at each other as if they had gone through this exercise before. Suddenly, all three jumped Mustafa in unison. Each weighed fifty pounds over him. In no time, Mustafa was on the ground, being held down by his extended arms behind his back, and with Kevin and Tom each having one boot on his spine.

Out of the corner of his eye, Mustafa saw Peter, with his penis still dangling out, looked at him and proceeded to slip his slacks down.

"Don't remove my trousers," said Mustafa, words muffled by the ground.

"Trousers—fancy you. You must be a fucking Jew. The 'Hebes'

speak just like that. They speak different."

"No, Willie does not speak like me. I am not Jewish—I am Palestinian. I go to Duke!"

"Palestinian—what's that? You spy for the Jews!" said Peter.

Kevin said, "That's it. He's a Jewish spy. Let's take care of him!"

Peter added his foot to Mustafa's back. Two of them started kicking his rib cage, hard. Peter landed with his knees on either side of his thighs and finished ripping his slacks down to his ankles. Fingers penetrated his rectum, then replaced by Peter's penis, which only partially completed the job. One of the two changed positions to hold Mustafa's ankles firmly so Peter could finish the assault.

———

Two-star General Adams was on his way to the rally, also trying to find parking. He heard a commotion, with a man groaning. He got out of his car and went behind the bushes to see what was happening.

"What in the hell is going on here?" he said in a loud voice.

As soon as he understood the situation, he grabbed the startled Peter with his penis dangling out and pulled him off the man being assaulted. Adams stood him up and used all his six-foot-three-inch, well-built physique to punch him hard. Another of the three men hurried to pull up his own slacks, apparently having intended to follow his pal in raping Mustafa. After the rapist fell hard on the ground, Adams held on to the arms of the other two.

One said, "Let go of my arm! You are attacking a sergeant in the United States Army."

"Oh, yeah," said Adams, "and I am ten ranks your senior, you sonofabitch. I am General Jonathan Adams."

The dumbfounded captives said nothing as he ordered them not to move. He approached Mustafa to help him stand up and fix his clothes. Then he guided him to his car and commanded the three to follow. Adams drove to his house with the silent victim next to him and the three in the back seat. After arriving, he signaled the three to sit down and guided Mustafa to the shower and told him to clean up and come back to the living room.

When the men's victim came into the living room, Adams said, "Can you tell me your name?" When he didn't speak, Adams handed him a pad and pencil and he wrote, "Mustafa Makram."

"Mustafa, son, I'm calling the local police and the military police. The police will take care of your case, I will be your witness, and the military police will take care of those bastards. I cannot tell you how sorry I am and how ashamed I am for what they have done to you—especially soldiers in the US armed forces. I promise you I will take care of them if it is the last thing I do on this earth."

Mustafa did not answer. He just shook his head no.

"What are you trying to say?"

Mustafa kept shaking his head and mouthed silently, "No police."

"No, you have to file a complaint against those perverts, or else I may not be able to help you."

Again, Mustafa tried to speak, shaking his head. "No police." But no sound came out.

After almost ten attempts on the part of Adams, Mustafa was adamant that he was not going to file a complaint or speak to the police. Adams told him not to be ashamed; he had done nothing wrong, and that Mustafa was ten times the man they were.

Mustafa's eyes filled with tears, and he mouthed the words, "I am not a man anymore."

Adams put his hands on his head and said, "No, no! You are, you are! Don't do this to yourself. This will be the worst thing you could do to yourself, son!"

After more than an hour of Adams talking, the three listening, and Mustafa nodding and again mouthing words instead of being able to utter them, Adams realized that they were at an impasse. In the end, Adams asked Mustafa for his wallet. He copied all the information he needed, including the fact that Mustafa was living in the dorms.

Mustafa tapped the pad of paper and wrote, "Please call my friend Willie." He listed two phone numbers: one was Willie's home phone number, and the other in the dorm lobby.

Adams called Willie and impressed upon him that Mustafa needed his help very badly. In no time, Willie was there. Adams took Willie to the side and told him what had transpired.

Willie was utterly shocked. "If it weren't for this bitch, Mona, this would not have happened." When Adams inquired, Willie told him that they were supposed to go to the rally together, but he got distracted by his sister's behavior.

Adams told Willie that he would be in touch with him the following day, and that he did not want to drop the matter. It was too insulting to him and the army for this to go unpunished. Willie agreed and took Mustafa to his home without his friend answering any questions. Willie stopped asking altogether.

At the house, Willie met his mother, Lia, and his sister, where he told them that he and Mustafa were spending the night over at the house and that Mustafa had fallen hard and needed a good night's sleep. His mother accepted the story, with Mona trying to look at Mustafa's behind.

Mustafa, still disoriented and experiencing some rectal bleeding, took another shower and went to bed, not speaking one word.

————

Mona woke up at five in the morning. She tiptoed to where Mustafa was sleeping on his stomach. She slowly removed the covering so she could look at his behind. To her utter surprise, a small pool of blood had flowed down from his crotch, smearing his legs. She kept the cover off and went tiptoeing to her mother's room. She woke up her mother, Lia, and told her that Mustafa was very sick.

When Lia saw the blood, she immediately woke up Willie. He looked at the blood coming from his rectum and was totally shocked and worried that he had not taken Mustafa to the emergency room the previous night. He managed to put his finger to his mouth, asking her to say nothing.

When they got to the kitchen, Willie confided in them and explained what Adams had said. He also told them that Mustafa had refused to say anything since the incident, and that he had refused to go to the police.

Lia said, "Let us wake up your Uncle Arie and have him look at Mustafa first."

Mona hid in the corner to watch when Arie arrived. He looked at Mustafa's rectum as best he could without disturbing him and stepped out of the room with Willie's family following.

"I can do nothing—I'm a dermatologist. This is too serious. You need to take him to the emergency room or call my brother-in-law, Mark, first. He's an emergency room surgeon and will know

much more about this than I do. He should be able to do something, or at least advise you what to do. Let me call him for you."

———

Mustafa was awakened by the conversation that took place outside the door, but chose to pretend he was still sleeping. When they
called Mark, Mustafa listened while Mark's wife answered the
phone and told Arie that her husband had been manning the grave-
yard shift. He'd only gone to bed at four in the morning. She promised to wake him up in a couple of hours.

As the family was considering what else to do, Mustafa managed to get up quietly, dress, and leave. Dazed and despite the gray
shadow of the overcast dawn, he managed to find his way. He was
murmuring to himself in Arabic, "You stupid and decrepit creature."
He repeated it several times before he went completely silent,
lowering his head as if to symbolize his feeling of low self-esteem.
Within half an hour, he was seventy yards from Zeina's house. He
could think of nobody else to bury his grief in other than her, yet
he was confused as to what to say to her.

Mustafa saw that Zeina was already out to get the morning
paper. She had a hat in her hand and casually put the hat on to pick
up the two papers. Mustafa got closer and could see it was the same
kind of Goldwater-Miller campaign hat that his three attackers
wore the night before.

Although demoralized and depressed, he immediately remem-
bered why Zeina said she would not discuss politics or religion. He
jumped to the conclusion that if she were to divulge her political
views, he and she would have a conflict. He immediately stopped
and crouched in disgust, trying not to let Zeina notice his presence.

She did not. Mustafa decided not to proceed to see her, as he felt the whole matter had become so confusing, and even demeaning. *Imagine being in love with a woman who belongs to the same party as those who raped me.*

Instead, he proceeded to the dorms, where he left a note for Willie.

By the time Arie's brother-in-law arrived, it was too late. Mustafa's absence was discovered. Willie sped toward the dorms, only to find Mustafa's note. He read the note to himself, which said:

You know what has happened. General Adams told you everything, although I would have preferred that he would have kept it to himself. Please, I beg you, don't share it with anyone else, especially Zeina. I don't feel that I am the man I was before.

I headed to see Zeina after I left you this morning, but there I saw something most disturbing and most disappointing. She needs to have her space. Give her my love and despite what I saw, I still love her more than anything. Please share this letter with her and with Faris.

I have no idea what I am going to do—I will do something, hopefully reasonable and healing. Currently, I don't feel good. I feel I am having an out-of-body nightmarish experience. I am looking down on my poor real self, and what I see does not look good.

Thank you and your family for everything. Don't forget to give the research paper to my professor. Zeina is also working on her research paper for the same course. Good luck. Tell her that I love her.

Mustafa

———

Willie could not believe what was happening, and he blamed himself for being so careless in monitoring Mustafa. He immediately jumped into his car and headed toward Zeina, after stopping on the way to make copies of Mustafa's letter. She was alarmed at his being there without Mustafa. When he got closer, she had forgotten to take off the Gold-water-Miller hat. At first, Willie was very surprised that she was wearing such a hat, as all else indicated that she was either a liberal or a libertarian.

When she saw the look on Willie's face, she told him that one of the neighbors must have left the hat at the door and that she tried it on and forgot to take it off. "It is not the kind I would wear."

Willie said nothing but handed a copy of the note to Zeina. When she read the note, she yelled at Willie, "What does all this mean? You mean he's leaving? He's my love—my life! What exactly happened? What does it all mean? Has he gone mad? This makes no sense… Does it to you, Willie?"

Willie looked at her and said, "It's not normal, but under the circumstances, it makes sense. I know what happened, and it has nothing to do with you. He's traumatized. Give him some time to come to his senses. As you can see from the letter, he pleads with me not to share what happened to him with anyone, including you."

At that point, Zeina called her father. When he arrived, she handed him the letter. After Sammy read it, he looked at Willie. "No, you cannot keep this from Zeina. I was afraid something like this could happen. She cannot live without knowing what has transpired, and even if she did, she may not be able to take it. This is too much. They are soulmates. No, no, you must tell her."

Under pressure, Willie asked Sammy if he knew General Adams, and when Sammy confirmed that he did, Willie told him to check with General Adams, as he was a witness to what had happened. Willie wanted to leave right away to see Faris, per Mustafa's request. But before he could get away, Zeina sat on a chair in the foyer of the house and started crying.

Sammy tried to console her, but she continued. "Mustafa is a great guy, but these cultural and religious considerations scare the hell out of me. You know what happened to us when we quit the Baptist church—your mother left us both."

Willie was able to slip away amidst the confusion and drive to Faris's house, who became openly agitated upon reading the letter. He cursed the day he convinced Mustafa to transfer from London. He blamed himself and said that he would spend all his time look-ing for him if he did not surface within the coming forty-eight hours. He wondered how he was going to reveal this to his parents if Mustafa had not already informed them.

In the end, he looked at Willie and said, "Listen, isn't the Chief of Police in Charleston your cousin? You think if Mustafa disap-pears, he can be of help?"

Willie was more than willing to try any way he could to find his friend, feeling guilty for sending Mustafa to the rally by himself. He promised to specifically call his cousin in Charleston.

CHAPTER 5

Zeina was inconsolable. "How could he do this to me? He's not only my love, he's my soulmate! This is so strange! I know him—something must have happened to traumatize him. Something must have."

Her father told her he knew where the general lived and that he was heading there unannounced.

"Not without me, Dad. You don't mean it! How could you?"

Sammy looked at her and said, "We are military. We know and trust each other. This could have something to do with national security—who knows? He may want to reveal things that he would hesitate to do in your presence."

When Zeina insisted, Sammy told her to follow him within half an hour. This way it would give Adams time to tell him things he might not have wanted to say in Zeina's presence. Initially, Zeina accepted the compromise, but within thirty seconds, she drove after her father.

Adams was surprised to see Sammy at his door, and before long, Zeina was behind him. Adams thought Sammy's visit may have had to do with programs both participated in, regarding issues of army retirement and the like, but Sammy told him that he was there regarding a man named Mustafa, who was a student at Duke.

"You mean Mustafa Makram?"

"Yes!" Sammy responded.

Adams explained that he could relay his name since he made a copy of his ID. He said that he was planning to go to Duke later in the day to look Mustafa up and talk to him, to convince him to file a police report.

Sammy asked, "A police report about what? What exactly happened?!"

"You mean you don't know? Three guys at the Goldwater rally attacked him severely."

If Adams had any inclination to tell Sammy about the rape, he sure didn't mention it in the presence of Zeina. He suspected she was Mustafa's girlfriend.

"What do you mean, 'attacked him severely'? You mean he is physically injured?" exclaimed Sammy, massaging the side of his head with both his hands.

"Yes, that is exactly what I mean. They beat him all over. His head is bashed up and I think they may have broken two of his ribs. I thought you knew," said Adams.

"Oh God, oh God. Go sit down in the next room, Zeina," he told her, as she seemed she was about to faint.

Adams took Sammy to the side, away from Zeina, and asked as to the seriousness of the relationship between Zeina and Mustafa. Sammy told him that he had not seen anything like it—they were inseparable and cared for each other much more than in a normal boy/girl relationship. Zeina had two relationships in college before Mustafa, and neither had lasted for more than one month.

Adams said, "This is a tough one. I'll be happy to try to handle it if you can't. I can imagine the tough position you are in."

"You're right, Jonathan. I don't think she can handle this one. It's going to devastate her," he said, calling Adams by his first name for the first time. No sooner than Sammy finished asking questions of Adams, with his head down to his knees, than Zeina came over from the other room. She seemed not to be able to wait.

To change the conversation, Jonathan Adams officially introduced himself to Zeina. Then, he described how the three jumped Mustafa and beat him severely, intentionally exaggerating the severity of the beating, as he was struggling to avoid mentioning anything about the rape.

Zeina said, "But was he hurt in the head or something? His behavior is strange." She then took out the copy of Mustafa's letter and read the part that said that he did not feel like a man anymore. "Does that mean anything to you?"

Adams said that it did, but it was not easy to describe. Zeina said, "Don't keep me in limbo. We've had the most gorgeous and almost heavenly relationship. He is mature beyond his years, and I hope I am, too. He is everything to me. He and my dad are my idols. Please don't torture me, General, by withholding anything. I need to know, or I'll go crazy. Nothing makes sense to me!"

"I don't know how to say it any other way," he began. "There were three big guys at the Goldwater rally. After they beat him severely, one of them tortured him. In the end, he was broken and completely demoralized."

"Oh my God, oh my God, my love, my soul! What have they done to you!?" She crouched on the floor and started wailing. "Now I understand—they tortured him. Forgive me, forgive me for not being with you. Forgive me for what my countrymen did to you. Now I know—I am sorry, I was wearing that cap by mistake. Forgive me, for I looked like I joined them, and I ended up adding to your hurt, all unintentionally. Believe me, my love."

Adams went to the other room, fetched Sammy, who was trying to call his attorney, and told him that Zeina was beyond distraught, heartbroken and totally distressed. Sammy tried to control the situation by crouching next to Zeina and hugging her.

She said, "No, now I understand. He came to see me and found me wearing the Goldwater-Miller cap. Probably one of them was wearing the same. How stupid of me! Forgive me, my love, I did not mean it. I did not mean it! Come back to me!"

Zeina then lay down on the floor, crying and moaning in a semiconscious state. Both Adams and Sammy, seasoned war veterans, were shocked. Sammy asked Adams to call an ambulance and Zeina was taken to the emergency room. In no time, Willie and Faris were informed of the situation. They and four other friends showed up at the hospital—two were female students that Faris had tried to fix Mustafa up with, and who later became just friends with him.

At the hospital, Willie, Faris and the other four exchanged ideas. Faris said that something needed to be done to find Mustafa, but he did not have the experience nor the knowledge of the community to propose any concrete ideas. It was one of the two female friends, Samantha, who proposed that a search party needed to be organized.

Nobody at Duke knew of the rape aspect except Willie and Faris. Before long, the foreign students adviser was at the hospital, after Adams had spoken to the university's security department. She was the one who suggested that six churches be contacted— the same ones Mustafa had spoken at and received a positive reception. She further advised that the effort be started after Zeina recovered from her trauma.

The following morning, Zeina was awake, and all her vital signs had returned to normal. Yet she was still slightly disoriented at finding herself in the hospital. The first thing she asked her father was whether anybody had heard from Mustafa. Sammy told her that everyone was waiting for her to get better for the search parties to start looking for him.

Within a couple of days, Zeina, Sammy, Adams, Willie, and Faris visited all six churches and managed to secure their full cooperation. Between Duke and the churches, the search parties came to around 500 people. Sammy and Adams took the lead, organizing thirty separate parties. Some manned phones and others went out searching. On the first day, it was suspected that Mustafa could not have left on a bus or driven himself. They checked every terminal and bus company, and every road leading out of the city. Willie's car was found at the site of the rally.

They were convinced that Mustafa must have walked to a different location in the city or may have walked or hitchhiked out of town. Little did they know that Mustafa chose to take the horse trail where Zeina fell off the horse and injured herself, and where the two of them expressed their initial attraction to each other.

———

By the time Zeina mentioned the possibility that Mustafa may have taken that path, he was seventeen miles from the start. At the entry of the trail, two riders on horseback and a third horse, only wearing a halter and a saddle, were going in the same direction. They stopped and asked Mustafa where he was going. He signaled that he was going forward. When they asked where to, he continued to signal to them without talking.

When one of the riders asked him if he could talk, Mustafa shook his head without saying a word. One rider asked if Mustafa could hear; he nodded. Then the rider asked Mustafa if he would rather ride than walk. Mustafa signaled "No." When the rider told him that they were trying to break the three horses in and he would be doing them a favor if he would ride the third horse with them, Mustafa accepted reluctantly, as he was still in pain.

A mile into the trail, they arrived at the spot where Zeina fell off the horse; Mustafa got down, wrote "I love you, Zeina" on a piece of paper, attached it to a fallen branch, and stuck it in the ground. The two riders looked at each other with some surprise, realizing that there must have been a story behind Mustafa's long trip over the trail.

Ten miles and two hours further ahead, the trail forked left and right, widening for a car to drive through it. Immediately on the right side was a farm, with a large house half a mile in. Mustafa signaled to the riders that he wanted to get off at that spot. They asked him to continue with them but relented after he insisted. One rider tried to hand him a five-dollar bill. Mustafa gave him an angry look and shook his head. They continued after they thanked him but were clearly curious as to his motive in walking the trail, especially after he wrote the "I love you" note.

Mustafa dropped his duffel bag on the ground and sat down against the gate of the farm.

In less than three minutes, a beat-up car came through. Its speed was increasing, but the driver stopped when he noticed Mustafa. One of the two in the car whispered into the other's ear, "I think it is our lucky day."

After they passed where Mustafa was sitting on the ground, they backed up. They stopped right next to him. One of them got out of the car, carrying a beer bottle hidden behind his back. As he looked down at Mustafa, he swung the bottle and hit him on the head, causing him to lose consciousness, with slight bleeding.

CHAPTER 6

Within ten minutes, Michelle Parker—the daughter of William and Amanda Parker, the owners of the farm drove by and got out of her car to open the gate. There she found an unconscious man with traces of semi-dried blood all over his face.

Without trying to help him, she accelerated and headed to her father's home office. There she found her father and Dr. Nelson, who was on one of his three-a-week visits to the 2,600-head dairy farm.

"Thank God you're here, Dr. Nelson. There's a young man unconscious by the gate."

Michelle's father William, Nelson, and Michelle got into the car and headed back to see if the man was still unconscious. Two of his pocket linings were still sticking out. The three figured he had been held up.

Nelson directed Michelle to sit in the back seat while William and Nelson carried the limp figure and placed his head in Michelle's lap. Within minutes, Mustafa was lying down in one of the ten bedrooms of the palatial farmhouse. Nelson repeatedly used smelling salts, which managed to wake him up.

Michelle spoke first. "What's your name? Are you okay? What happened!?"

Dr. Nelson, not liking Michelle's barrage of questions, tried to calm the situation down by introducing himself. All the while, the young man was looking at them, bewildered. Nelson told him to take his time. He felt himself and found out that he was sleeping in his t-shirt and briefs. He hugged himself, looking at Michelle, embarrassed. Nelson, trying to ease Mustafa's anxiety, told him that whoever held him up must have ripped his shirt open and damaged his slacks zipper.

"I think they tried to take off your shirt and pants, but they couldn't, and then they ripped them open."

Mustafa kept looking at Michelle with a slightly piercing look. He signaled to her to bring him a pen and paper. She hurried and got them to him. He wrote, "My name is Mustafa. I cannot speak."

"I'm sorry, we didn't know that. Are you mute?" Michelle asked.

Mustafa wrote again, "No, I cannot speak now. Maybe in the future."

Michelle and William looked at Nelson, seeking an explanation. Nelson looked back at them with the same degree of confusion and said, "Maybe he has an infection of sorts that's taken away his voice. I cannot think of one that would make him temporarily mute. But I know of many reasons that can suppress most of one's voice."

Michelle went out and came back holding Mustafa's slacks and shirt. She pointed at the clothes and said, "I'll go to the store a mile from here and will get you new clothes, a pair of jeans, and a shirt."

He then pointed to his pants and mouthed, "Money." She told him that the thieves must have taken all his money and wallet, and that he had absolutely nothing left on him. "Don't worry. We'll take care of everything."

———

When the tall and stunning twenty-two-year-old Michelle came back, she had bought three pairs of slacks, four shirts, six t-shirts, and briefs. As she got them out of the bag, Mustafa looked at her and gestured that he needed only one of each. She told him not to worry, and that theirs was a dairy farm where the grounds were muddy, requiring frequent changes of clothes. Mustafa signaled that there was no need, and that he would be leaving soon.

"Dr. Nelson said that you need at least one week to heal, so don't be planning to leave anytime sooner than that. And when you do, either I or someone else will drive you home."

Mustafa paused and appeared he was about to indicate something before he stopped, as if he recalled there was no home for him to go back to. Michelle noticed Mustafa's hesitation to describe where home was. She brought him one of William's fancy robes and he gently ushered her out of the room so he could try on his new clothes.

The clothes fit Mustafa well and he looked younger, wearing a pair of jeans and a checkered shirt. His younger robust look was noticed by Michelle, who asked him if he was a college student. He intentionally lied and wrote on a pad of paper that he was a student at the University of North Carolina at Chapel Hill.

Again, Mustafa was not specific as to what he was studying or to the college he was attending. This added to Michelle's suspicions, and he guessed she would try to find out about this foreign stranger sleeping in one of the bedrooms. Since he had written that he could not speak at the time, he sensed that Michelle seemed to have developed some doubts about his temporary inability to speak. She suggested they see Dr. Nelson again. To explain the visit, she told Mustafa that she was setting up an appointment with the doctor to check his voice. Mustafa pulled the pockets out of his new jeans to indicate that he had no money.

"Don't worry about it. We have a great family doctor, and he'll check you out thoroughly. He is also our business doctor. He treats all our employees," she said. Mustafa suspected the visit was mostly for her to investigate his background, with the help of Dr. Nelson.

————

The following morning, Michelle took on the responsibility of taking care of Mustafa without first consulting with her father. Her mother had been deceased for four years, but their housekeeper, Bertha, had served the Parkers since Michelle's birth. She was the one who served Mustafa and Michelle breakfast when they arrived in the kitchen.

The first thing Michelle did after that was to take him on a farm tour. When he got to one barn, Mustafa saw Dr. Nelson examining some cattle and got mad. He thought that Dr. Nelson, who first took care of him and was expected to further examine his voice, was a veterinarian. Mustafa pointed to the cattle first, then himself, and third to Dr. Nelson.

Michelle understood well enough what he was trying to say— that he was being treated by a veterinarian. Michelle slowly explained to him that Dr. Nelson was a regular physician who decided to go to veterinary school for two years, then took the needed exams. He was, at the time, licensed in both. When she noticed his lingering suspicion about Dr. Nelson, she said, "Don't worry. I will take you to another physician who is not a veterinarian."

In the process, Michelle sensed that Mustafa was trying to avoid being seen by any physician. She thought to herself and schemed. She suspected that he must be evading something or someone, and that he was conning them to conceal his identity, pretending not to be able to speak. She could not have imagined the traumatic truth. To her, it seemed like a sham.

Bertha had cleaned Mustafa's room and made up the bed, and in the evening, Michelle brought him a set of pajamas and a robe. Without thinking, before she completely left the room, he slipped his clothes off to put his pajamas on. Michelle turned around to see a nicely built body with an attractive and firmly contoured behind.

She had mixed feelings. On one hand, she suspected that he was not on the level, and on another, she suddenly had a very hand-some and wholesome-looking man in the house, who showed promise. She shared her mixed feelings with Bertha, who suggested that Michelle test him.

"What's wrong with some feminine special care? Why don't you hold him by the arm, or even rub your arm against his? See what kind of reaction you get."

"Bertha, you are a wicked genius. I'm going to do something like that…after I make sure my dad is staying on his side of the house."

CHAPTER 7

That evening, Michelle moved to the bedroom next to Mustafa's. She threw the evening paper between her new room and Mustafa's and then called him to pick it up. The paper was right in front of her bathroom, which had the door open. When he came into the hallway, she knew he could see her in front of the mirror in her slip and bra. He immediately withdrew into his room without picking it up.

Michelle got mad at her failure and then took the audacious step of going into Mustafa's room—after putting on her robe. "Why didn't you pick up the paper? Or would you rather I read it for you?" Michelle said gently, trying to find an opening.

He was looking away all the time, as one of Michelle's breasts was partially showing. She then proceeded to pick up the paper, bring it to him, and start reading the Durham, North Carolina, headlines, leaning forward, showing her breasts further. He looked at her and signaled that he wanted to sleep. Michelle had little choice but to leave him alone.

After discussing it with Bertha in the morning, Michelle decided to continue with her cat-and-mouse game. She told Mustafa that Dr. Ratcliff would see him in two days, but they would spend the time after breakfast swimming in a natural pond on their 3,000-acre farm. To her surprise, Mustafa liked the idea. In no time, Michelle got him some well-fitting swimming trunks and got herself the smallest bikini. She made sure she wore the bikini under her regular clothes to surprise Mustafa. When they got to the pond, he stripped down to his swimming suit and Michelle took off her clothes, down to the bikini. She took Mustafa by the hand and jumped into the shallow pond, making sure that her body and well-endowed breasts rubbed against him. Yet, there was no reaction on the part of Mustafa.

Michelle came out of the pond and looked at Mustafa. "Tell me the truth. Are you interested in boys rather than girls?"

He looked at her with piercing and angry eyes and shook his right index finger to indicate strongly he was not. He looked mad and disturbed.

"Then what is it, Mustafa? I had every other student wanting to go out with me when I was at Yale. So, what's wrong with you—or me, for that matter?! Don't you find me attractive? Tell me."

Mustafa looked at her pensively and mouthed, "I cannot."

"But why not?"

"I don't know."

Michelle said, "Then I know what to do." She climbed up thirty-five feet and stood on a rock above the pond, took both pieces of her bikini off, and pretended to jump into the pond. Mustafa seemed to be amazed at her actions—and her beautiful naked body—and stood up and frantically signaled to Michelle not to jump. They both knew that the pond was very shallow. She balanced herself further and spread her legs, all to challenge Mustafa's senses, giving him a firmer impression that her jump was imminent.

It was then that Mustafa hollered at her and said, "Don't jump! You may kill yourself. I will tell you everything."

Michelle's surprise froze her altogether, totally naked with her crotch looking down on him. She slowly climbed down after she put her bikini back on. Without speaking one word, she sat on the sand next to Mustafa. She took several deep breaths, and he took a few himself. He then took her left hand into both his hands, paused, and then lowered his head. He paused again for a long minute. Michelle was not saying anything, but she could see his face turning green, sallow, and withdrawn. She grew concerned, and she looked as if she wanted to say something to relieve him of his pain. After taking few more breaths, he said:

"I promise to tell you everything if you help me leave peacefully. I have done nothing wrong, and I am not a criminal or a thief. I am a very law-abiding foreign student. You must promise me that you will not stand in my way to leave your generosity. I want to be free—free from everything. You will understand when I tell you my story."

"Oh, God, you're scaring me. And you're suddenly so serious and expressive," said Michelle with an overtone of guilt.

"My story is serious, at least in my eyes. I hope the politics of the story do not offend you, but I must tell it as it is, if I am to tell it at all. You will be the first person I tell it to verbally. My friends at Duke—I don't go to the University of North Carolina—received a note from me, revealing the details of the incident that I could not share face-to-face. You and your father have been so kind to me, and since I did not know you before the incident, I think it is easier to share everything with you."

"Mustafa, you're scaring me. Tell me what happened."

"I will tell you. It is not easy. I was alone in Durham at a Gold-water rally just to watch and observe. Before I got into the big tent, three men with Goldwater-Miller caps attacked me severely. They pinned me down on the ground and one of them managed to rape me. This is my story, and this is why I can say no more." Tears poured down his cheeks.

Michelle stood and said in a slow, vibrating, low voice, "Jesus Christ, Jesus Christ! What have they done to you? Jesus Christ!" She then picked up her towel and wrapped it around her protruding breasts. She continued, "Oh, God, I'm sorry. I am so stupid, so obtuse for thinking you were a con man. I am sorry, so sorry. I ask for your forgiveness. Please forgive me. I had no idea. Let's stay here for a while. I don't know what to say, what to do. This is more than I expected, much more. I feel so stupid. Forgive me. Will you forgive me?"

Mustafa stood up and said, "Michelle, stop it—just stop it. You are making me feel guilty that you are feeling this way. You have done nothing. It was them. Naturally, you thought of all sorts of things about me. All that you knew was that I was unconscious in front of your property. The rest could have been anything! I could have been a killer that happened to have been held up. Look at it this way: without you, I might have refrained from talking for another year. You loosened my emotions and made me talk again. Wait until your father hears me talking. He will be happy. I am less sad than I have been since the incident, and it is all because of you. I could not even say goodbye to Zeina."

"Who is Zeina?"

"Zeina is the air I breathe and the pulse that my doctor detects. She is the love of my life and yes, I fully understand that half of the Yale students were chasing after you. I am wondering what was wrong with the other half," said Mustafa.

She went silent and looked intently at Mustafa. She smiled and asked, "You're just a charmer when you decide to talk. Is it all right if I hug you?"

"You can hug me anytime you want. You look so much like Zeina. I don't think I can face her anymore. I am not the man I used to be. I bet they are looking all over the place for me. I am sorry. I just can't face anyone I knew before the rally."

She did not know what to say. After a pause, she kept looking at Mustafa, searching for the proper words, but none came to her mind. She then said, "Lie down, Mustafa. Lie down on the sand."

He slowly and suspiciously obeyed. Michelle asked him if it was OK with him if she lay down crossways, with her head on his belly. He agreed.

Michelle started speaking. "Listen, Mustafa, I want to help you more than anything. I will help you leave, but you're penniless. If you listen carefully, we can do it, but you cannot play hard to reach. The first thing I want to do is give you money to sustain yourself for a few weeks. How much did those thugs steal from you?"

When Mustafa told her that it was $800; she told him that she would give him the full amount. He answered that he would be glad to accept it if it was a loan.

"Yes, it will be a thirty-year loan without interest, but before I can do this, you have to work at the farm and make some more money. My father really likes you and he is not suspicious about anything. With the money from working as a farmhand, he will feel that you have enough money to sustain you, and he will let you go."

In the evening, as the three of them sat down to Bertha's fried chicken, fried okra, and zucchini, Michelle, in prior agreement, asked Mustafa to say grace. He had told her that saying grace was not part of his family's routine. William gave her a strange look as if to say, *What are you trying to pull, engaging someone who is having difficulty speaking?* Mustafa lowered his head and started.

"In the name of God, the Merciful and the Compassionate. This is to give thanks, for I was unconscious, and they woke me up; I was hungry, and they fed me; I was without shelter, and they housed me; I was emotionally drained, and they nurtured my soul. I am eternally thankful to Mr. William and Miss Michelle Parker. Thank you, Lord. Amen."

"Good God, you ought to become a Baptist preacher!" Michelle said, gazing at Mustafa. "I never thought you could recite it like this. This is great, but never call me Miss Michelle again."

Her father asked if she knew all along that Mustafa could speak and that he was faking it, not talking. "No, Dad, Mustafa wasn't faking it. He was in shock, and as part of his withdrawal, he was unable to speak. He only started talking when I was about to take a thirty-five-foot jump into the pond next to the eucalyptus tree. He felt he had to speak out, since he was afraid that I would hit the bottom and break my legs. It was his concern for me that made him start."

William was looking at Mustafa, not knowing what to say. "Can you say anything else other than well-prepared prayers?"

"Yes, sir. I can say that you have the most beautiful daughter I have ever met. Her physical beauty is only exceeded by the beauty of her soul."

"Mustafa, you're doing a great job for one who couldn't speak hours ago! What about me? Don't I deserve something?" said William teasingly.

"I am sure like daughter, like father," said Mustafa.

"Oh man, even when you combine things, they sound good.

Believe me, Mustafa, your regaining speech, and Michelle's gradu-ation are the best things that happened to me this year. Welcome to our home."

Just as William started thinking that his difficult Michelle may finally have been charmed by someone, she looked at her father and said, "Dad, you think Mustafa can work at the farm to make enough money to leave here and go to see his Zeina?" Her state-ment deflated William's hopes. Even so, he was more than happy to have Mustafa work there.

Mustafa explained to William that while Zeina was his love, the two had a major disagreement and that he was not going back to her right then. Mustafa wanted to be as close to the truth as he could afford.

————

The following day, Mustafa started working at the farm, which he did for almost a month. Michelle would take him out after four, before dinner. All the while, Michelle could tell his thoughts were on Zeina. Yet it seemed he could not bring himself to go and face her. Michelle also spent time with him in the evening.

During one of those close-but-short-of-being-romantic ses-sions, he asked Michelle if she could do him a favor. Could she call Willie and check on things, and arrange for Willie to make copies of his records at the foreign students' office and have them ready to be mailed to him… without telling him Mustafa's whereabouts? Michelle made the call from a public phone in a town thirty miles away and talked to Willie.

Willie was beside himself on hearing that his friend was alive and well. He told Michelle that Mustafa had gone through a major trauma—one that he could not describe to her. He added that at the moment, no one knew whether he was dead or alive. When Willie tried to confirm that it was Mustafa she was talking about, she described the birthmark on the side of Mustafa's neck.

Willie shouted, "Yes, it is him! I need to call Zeina and Faris and let them know he is alive!"

After he made sure she was for real and the two warmed up to each other, Michelle told him that Mustafa did not want to be found, as he still could not reconcile what had happened to him with his perception of himself, and she added that he was smart enough to evade their best efforts. Willie then told her about Mustafa's accidental sighting of Zeina wearing the same kind of cap his rapist had worn.

Mustafa had not shared that part with Michelle. It was easy for her to figure out that Mustafa was either confused about Zeina, or he was trying to break up with her, having politically linked her to the rapist. Thoughts started streaming through her head.

She later contacted Willie a second time with the address of a mailbox ten miles from the phone she was using. He was to send the requested documents there. Willie agreed and said that they had found Mustafa's love letter to Zeina on the horse trail. Finally, Michelle told him that Mustafa never for a second stopped loving Zeina. His love for her was undiminished but rather confused, and this confusion was preventing him from seeing her.

"You know, Willie, I do not agree with Mustafa, but it is a cultural thing. He thinks his manhood was ripped away from him. He needs to get rid of this feeling before he can face Zeina."

Willie told her that Zeina still did not know that he had been raped.

CHAPTER 8

The evening chats between Michelle and Mustafa gradually grew deeper. Michelle wanted to probe into his psyche and tried to draw him in without being dishonest about it.

"You know, Mustafa, I do like you a lot. I don't know why. I find you very perceptive and sincere. Do you think of yourself in these terms?"

"Sincere I am, under normal circumstances; perceptive I am, only when it relates to others. I think I am less perceptive about myself. I allow deep-seated forces within me to influence and even overtake my better judgment. Yet I seem to be unable to overcome it, even when I recognize it is the case. How about you, Michelle?"

Michelle was not prepared for her question to be redirected back toward her. She thought for a while and said that she was moderately perceptive and realistic about herself and others, whether friends or foes, but she would like to be more perceptive in both.

"Like, for instance, now… If Zeina were sitting right here, would you tell the truth about what happened to you and kiss her, or would you rather I am sitting next to you and you would reveal the truth to me after you kiss me, recognizing that you are unable to reveal the same to Zeina?"

"Wow, wow, wow! This is a loaded question! You need to explain it to me in plain English."

"There is nothing to explain. I presume that if you cannot tell Zeina about what happened to you, you will not be able to go back to her. If you cannot go back to her and kiss her, will you kiss me instead and reveal yourself?"

"Aren't you asking me if I don't mind kissing you, since you know I am not able to go back to Zeina? The answer is yes, I will gladly kiss you if I knew I was never going back to Zeina, and no, I will not kiss you if I have hopes of disclosing my experience and reconciling with her. This has nothing to do with how attractive and charming you are. Before I leave here, I hope to reveal myself—not that it will change anything, but for you to know me better. It will be an unusual present: not of financial value, but of emotional value."

Michelle told him that she had her answer. "I respect you more for your honesty and loyalty to Zeina. I can feel the turmoil, and possibly the self-torture, you're in, but you're the only one who can solve this specific dilemma."

————

After Mustafa had worked on the farm for a week, William became more impressed with him. He was a very intelligent and hard worker who earned every penny. At sixty-two, William was starting to think of the things to come. While he was all set up financially, he was concerned about what would happen to the farm after he left. He confided in his office manager that he would not mind seeing Mustafa and Michelle permanently together. She happened to agree with him.

The office manager's encouragement gave him the incentive to try cementing a relationship between Michelle and Mustafa. William suggested to his daughter that the two of them, plus Mustafa, establish a routine of dining out once a week. The idea did not appeal to Mustafa, who feared he would encounter members of the search party or be seen by others who may have seen his picture in the paper. William insisted, and neither Mustafa nor Michelle could change his mind. The routine started with serious trepidations on the part of the two young people. Michelle also did not want Mustafa to be found by his Duke friends. She thought she had a better chance with him if he separated from his past.

At the first dinner, Mustafa and William sat alone, waiting for Michelle. All of a sudden, Mustafa blurted out that he needed to be on his way to Stanford University, near Palo Alto, California, to see if he could revive the same generous scholarship they had offered him a year earlier.

William was very surprised, but inwardly thankful that he had the opportunity to keep a hand in Mustafa's plans.

"I accepted Duke's offer so I could be close to my friend Faris. During that year, I maintained a straight A average. Do you think Michelle will help me follow up with Stanford, since I am in the field all day, with little time to call them?"

William smiled. "Yes, I am sure Michelle will help you with the task. My office manager can aid her in finding the right person to contact."

———

Michelle was elated that Mustafa was looking forward to resuming normal living at one of the nation's top schools.

After several attempts, she got hold of the admissions committee head. He told her that they could offer him a similar scholarship, only $6,000 shy of the first one. Michelle thought about it and was about to relay the disappointing news to Mustafa. But then she thought that instead, her father might be amenable to making up the $6,000 difference. She talked to William, and he was in complete agreement. She told Mustafa that Stanford was expecting him, and they said they would manage it one way or the other.

Within six weeks of Mustafa's connecting with the Parkers, he was ready to move on. In the latter days of his stay with them, Michelle was so attentive to Mustafa's needs that she was almost mothering him. Through Willie and the mail, she managed to collect as many of Mustafa's documents as possible. On one occasion, she almost slipped and told Willie to mail the documents to her own address.

William saw him off with a firm handshake and told him that he was welcome to come back anytime, and that he could come back as a guest or to work—next time in a supervisory job. As William was saying goodbye, Michelle came into the office to take Mustafa to the airport, surprising him with a ticket to San Francisco. Bertha accompanied her so she could say goodbye as well. Mustafa told her that he would let her know after he had completed one more thing.

He looked at William and Michelle and said, "What I am going to say is an expression of joy, which includes no lamentations. I promised it as a present to Michelle, but it is also for you, William." He waved Bertha in from the doorway and then proceeded to read a poem—his first poem in English, after having written poetry in

Arabic for six years.

Joys and Lamentations from the Wind

I am the wanderer of my mind.

I am the seeker of my truth.

I am the wise man of my kind.

I yearn to know why fate is so,

Without a reason and a cause.

So here I am with a probing pause.

I seek to know why I proceed.

I seek to know why I succeed.

As if no one has ever thought,

why one word is clearly decadent,

and another word sets a precedent.

As if no one has heard of Adam and Eve.

And as if references are impossible to retrieve.

But it is a yearning that possesses my mind,

and assumes that I am truly one of a kind.

So let me go on a journey that many have traveled.

They went forward and backward and got bedeviled.

Seeking to probe why fate is so,

without a fair conclusion.

As if some have found a scheme of perfect collusion.

And others have floated without friction or resistance.

As if they tried to buy misery,

but instead found a perfect existence.

So here I am after a lifetime of experience,

probing the failings and successes of my expedience.

Finding no discerning logic, malice, or lack of fairness,

rather, a kind pattern full of kindness.
So baffled have I become to explain the course of my life,
to give it a meaning and a cause.
Until one day when I unexpectedly paused,
after the wind blew with a gust,
and I got my sudden answer,
to be written with an obsessive lust.
It is the wind that blows,
and impacts our lives without cause.
It is the wind that deserves our consideration,
and produces our joys and lamentations.

To: Michelle and William
In your honor.
I am full of joy that the wind blew in your direction,
and put me in your kind and wonderful care.
Your eternal friend,
Mustafa

He handed the poem to Michelle. She was speechless and looked at him, quietly shedding tears, since she never had the slightest idea about his poetic talent. She hugged him tightly and said, "I wish the wind had blown much earlier and brought you to us. We thought we got a defeated man; instead, we got a lofty creature. What a beautiful poem. Although yours has been a brief visit, you are now my most memorable companion and will possibly be the one for a long, long time. Good luck and stay in touch, or I will deal with you my way."

Bertha was similarly moved and captured the young man in a hearty embrace.

While Mustafa was temporarily distracted, Michelle whispered in her father's ear, "I don't know whether to cry or to smile. His presence has impacted me in a deeper sense than ever before. He is more than just good-looking; he is beautiful on the outside and the inside. I hope one day I will see him again."

William was melancholic and said, "I was happily taking care of my herd. Now I feel I've lost a special young friend."

Mustafa answered, "I need to cleanse my soul, and I am sure that without you initiating the process, it would have been impossible."

He waved goodbye and left, carrying his duffel bag on his back, intentionally only looking forward, not wanting to look back and compound his forlorn separation from them.

CHAPTER 9

Ten miles forward, Mustafa stopped to eat one of the three sandwiches Michelle had prepared for him. In his bag, he found a note wrapped around a $3,000 bundle. It said,

I know you are going in one direction. Keep going, do not disappoint me. In one hour, I am leaving for New Haven, just to be with my friends. I badly need an immediate replacement; at best it will be a partial one. I know that it will not be as fulfilling—I hope it will be soothing.

This sum is a loan and there is another $6,000 waiting for you with Dean Andreotti of the business school to make up for the shortfall in this year's scholarship. The dean promised that next year, you will not need to make up anything. Remember that you owe me $9,800 altogether. It is a thirty-year loan with zero interest, payable at the end of the thirty-year term.

Mustafa looked at the note and nodded his head in total amazement. He smiled and pondered for a long time, with a deep sense of appreciation and admiration. It was clear that he had feelings for Michelle, but they were nowhere close to his feelings for Zeina. Michelle's and William's generous hosting did much to alleviate his sour feelings about himself in many respects, except for one: his overwhelming feeling of loss of his manhood continued to be his cultural and emotional crucifix.

Mustafa stopped at the first post office he could find to mail the airline ticket back to Michelle. He intended to keep his promise to himself to walk all the way to Stanford. He felt he still needed the challenge.

The first night he slept under an overpass, using the sleeping bag given to him by Michelle. She told him that if he decided not to fly, he could use it in the open or on top of an economy hotel mattress if he felt the hotel was not clean enough. She also advised him to go to YMCAs, whenever he found one, to shower and clean up. While minor pointers, so much of Michelle's help and advice sustained him well during the trip.

He did not always walk. He was surprised by how many people offered to give him a ride. They were mostly very gracious—many gave him food and drink, and some even offered him money. It was all positive and emotionally remedial. He was enjoying the trip, staying at motels about half the time, after he found Michelle's unexpected $3,000.

Nineteen days into the trip, Mustafa decided to head to Columbia, Missouri, to look up a friend, who was studying at the University of Missouri. As he was walking by the side of a rural street, six cars and pickups passed him. The seventh, a pickup, stopped and offered him a ride. Mustafa was well relaxed after spending two days at a hotel in St. Louis. Initially, he told them that he would rather walk. A cute girl, Imelda, with unusual tattoos, got out from the passenger seat and gently dragged Mustafa to the back of the pickup. She told him that they were heading to a camp five miles short of Columbia, but that they would be happy to drop him off in Columbia proper.

Mustafa did not resist much. He noticed something different about all four passengers, the two in front and the two in the back of the beat-up truck. They were all blondish, with a small stature, and were slightly haggard. A couple of the seven cars in the caravan looked almost brand new, while two others were junkyard vintage. Although the four in the pickup truck were young, all had unkempt teeth.

Their looks prompted Mustafa to engage with them. After he told them that he was Palestinian—and they had no idea what a Palestinian was—he took over asking them questions. He found out they were descendants of an Irish tinker community. Their main activity involved jewelry, auto thefts, and auto body repairs. He got the impression that they were an industrious group of people, but all in questionable fields.

When they got to the camp, he could hear everyone greeting each other in a warm and chummy way. What attracted his attention most was the young age of some of the married women and the loose sexual language used in greeting each other. He wanted to leave for Columbia right away. Imelda told Mustafa that she would give him a ride the following day and for him to relax and join the party later in the evening.

That evening, the party was full of fun and wildness. Mustafa sipped slowly on a glass of bourbon, watching. Despite Imelda's repeated efforts, he refused to dance with her. In the end, she gave up. She told him that he must be tired, and she showed him where to sleep in a trailer. She asked him if he needed to use the bathroom, which he ended up doing. In the meantime, Imelda took it upon herself to search his duffel bag, where she found the $3,000 bundle and pocketed it. She excused herself shortly afterward.

The following day, Imelda knocked on Mustafa's door to offer to take him to Columbia. She then took him to a motel she was familiar with, a few blocks from the university. When she entered the motel room, she sat in a chair. She looked at Mustafa, took out only a $2,500 bundle, and said, "This is yours if I and you get to have a good time together."

Mustafa told her that the money was his. She admitted to it but said, "You would not have known that I took it if I had not told you. You can get it back if you accept my conditions. And if you try to go to the police, I know how to talk to them. You will have no chance against me."

Mustafa refused and managed to grab the bundle from her hand. She ran out to the motel office and told them that she was giving a stranger a ride and that he stole $2,500 from her. The manager of the motel got involved, and between hearing Mustafa's foreign accent and counting the bundle of $2,500, he believed that Mustafa was guilty as charged.

When the police arrived, Imelda was fully prepared, as she told Mustafa she would be. He noticed her narrative was well rehearsed and most likely only changed slightly to fit this specific situation. And as forewarned, he had no chance against her.

Mustafa was soon in jail. The police offered him a public defender, whom he accepted and who was available in short order. Mustafa explained where he got the money from, and the public defender told Mustafa that his story had to be corroborated by Michelle or William. He tried hard to convince the attorney that he did not want to involve them beyond what they had provided for him, but the defender told him clearly that they were his only hope. Imelda had no record. The story she and the hotel manager presented sounded very credible.

In the end, he relented, but he insisted that the lawyer contact

Michelle, and not William, and report back on the conversation. Yet, he knew Michelle was in New Haven and her whereabouts were only known to William, so he was forced to ask the attorney to call William and ask to speak to Michelle. The public defender reported back that William was very curious as to the lawyer's interest. The attorney only told William that his call was related to Mustafa. William asked to speak to Mustafa and was told that he was unavailable.

William got mad and was about to hang up the phone when the public defender informed him that the young man was in jail, accused of stealing $2,500. William told the lawyer that he was aware that Michelle had loaned Mustafa $800, and that he had paid him $300 in wages.

After disclosing the particulars to Mustafa, the public defender, in typical lawyer fashion, decided that Mustafa was lying, especially after the attorney heard William's version about the $1,100. The next morning, the public defender told him he had struck a deal with the prosecuting attorney to have Mustafa serve one month in prison. Mustafa got mad and cussed at the lawyer and even accused him of railroading him since he was a foreign student. The two almost had a fistfight after the public defender raised his hand in a gesture to slap Mustafa.

In the meantime, the public defender told Mustafa that if he didn't accept the deal, he might end up imprisoned for one to two years. His lawyer had heard that Imelda was working on the policeman on the case, telling him that she hoped this "damned foreigner" would spend five years in prison. The public defender revealed that the policeman was interested in Imelda in more than one way, including sharing with her many of the same prejudices. Apparently, he was happy to respond to the advances of this cute and firm-bodied eighteen-year-old girl.

Later that day, the defender reported that he was sorry to say Imelda had captured the policeman's complete attention with a quick blowjob in the policeman's own office. With all the information he was hearing, Mustafa knew his case didn't look good.

Gradually, the available evidence was stacking up against Mustafa as the policeman in the case confirmed to the prosecuting attorney that he knew Imelda well, and that she sounded trustworthy to him and had no record of any kind. The policeman's fabrications became specious when he told the prosecuting attorney that he verified that the money belonged to Imelda. The prosecuting attorney told the public defender that he was in no mood for a compromise and that he was going "for the maximum."

CHAPTER 10

In the meantime, William called his daughter. Michelle was beside herself when she learned that her father did not call her first before he talked to the public defender. She admitted that she had given Mustafa $3,000 without informing William about it—not to keep it from him, but because she knew well that William would not have disagreed with her if she insisted. William was most apologetic and felt guilty about his error.

Michelle flew to Durham the following day. There, she and William discussed the matter. Then they sought the advice of their local criminal attorney, John Carpenter. Carpenter reminded William of the Secret Service experiment in which William received a stack of $100 bills that were duly recorded and logged. The bills were used by the Secret Service to trace counterfeiters who might use them as originals to print off fake ones. Carpenter told William that he himself was the record keeper of such a packet and if the bundle was logged properly, they would firmly exonerate Mustafa.

Carpenter then grew quiet, thinking. When he spoke again, he told William and Michelle that William could not divulge that there was such a Secret Service program. Furthermore, if the police department or the public defendant in Columbia, Missouri, were either complicit or derelict, they could exchange the $100 bills easily. Carpenter, being one of the leading criminal attorneys in the state of North Carolina, told Michelle and William he and they needed to be involved in person, to prove that the original $3,000 came from them. William agreed and expressed his readiness to foot the bill.

Carpenter contacted a professional friend of his, a local criminal attorney in Columbia. Within forty-eight hours, William, Michelle, and Carpenter were in Columbia, their presence unknown to anyone but the local attorney.

The four met with the prosecuting attorney and asked to see the bundle without touching it. They asked him if he could write down the serial numbers of all twenty-five bills, which he did without objection, and then gave Carpenter a copy of the list.

Once the copy was received and checked against Carpenter's list, Carpenter told the prosecuting attorney the packet came from Mr. Parker's safe. If he wanted an iron-clad proof, they could call the local Secret Service agent in St. Louis to confirm the twenty-five $100 bills came from the government of the United States to William Parker, and from William to his daughter, and then to Mustafa.

Carpenter gave the name of the Secret Service agent to the prosecuting attorney in case he wanted to verify that they originally came from the government, and then to Parker. The prosecuting attorney decided to drop the case against Mustafa without involving the federal government and said that he would file charges against Imelda instead. The prosecuting attorney apologized to the group and insisted on accompanying them to release Mustafa from jail. Before he left, the district attorney's office prepared the documents to apprehend Imelda and anyone else who was involved with her in defrauding Mustafa and attempting to frame him.

He told Carpenter that his office had several infractions to address with the tinkers, but this one had the proof he needed to charge them. He explained to them that within the hour, ten patrol cars would be heading to raid the tinkers' camp. Michelle at that point asked if she could watch the raid. Carpenter looked at the local attorney and said, "Why don't we all go? After all, you and I charge by the hour." William smiled and said that it was fine with him.

They all proceeded to jail. As the guards released Mustafa and took him to the reception area, he could not believe his eyes that he was once again face-to-face with the most generous and caring people he had ever met.

Michelle could not help herself. She ran toward Mustafa and gave him the tightest hug any lover could give another, except that the two were not lovers. Mustafa, under the circumstance of feeling guilty for his friends' troubles and in response to Michelle's hug, felt he had to reciprocate.

The prosecuting attorney looked at William and asked if Mustafa and his gorgeous daughter were in a relationship. William answered, "I wish they were. It is hard to say one way or the other. Only they know."

Mustafa and Michelle went into a corner, whispering to each other. Michelle said, "I guess the wind changed its direction since you left us."

Mustafa said, "Did it ever! But there is a consolation: you, I, and William are together again! What a great surprise and how embarrassing that I brought you all the way here. Also, not only did you give money, but I am also probably costing you twice as much dragging you over here all the way from Durham."

"Listen—you are allowed to speak about anything, including sex, but not money. This is the least we can do. It's only me, and what am I going to do with all this money? On the contrary, when we spend it on a good cause, Dad and I feel much better. Are we in agreement?"

Mustafa said, "I guess, but it is still... Never mind. I know what you mean, and you know what I mean. Let us keep it at that."

"Listen, since I'm here already, why don't we spend a couple of days together after Dad leaves? How about it?" He agreed and decided to talk about the details later.

The prosecuting attorney alerted the group that the police cars raiding the place were ready and that their group would have to be at least thirty yards behind, with one policeman and a policewoman guarding them.

When they got to the camp, the two policemen took them to an overlooking plateau. Soon after, all ten cars descended on the camp and surrounded it, and the police used a loudspeaker to call on Imelda McCarthy to surrender. When no one responded, around thirty officers went into the portable camp, and in no time, there were around sixty adults and nine children on the ground.

Imelda surrendered within less than a minute. The group and the officers guarding them came down from the plateau. Mustafa came face-to-face with Imelda. She spat on him and said, pointing to Michelle, "You fuckin' foreigner, this is your girlfriend? You think she's a better fuck than me? Well, you missed out big time." She pointed to her crotch. "This is the best pussy you could ever have."

Imelda continued to rant and rave at Mustafa as they led her away. Michelle snickered and then whispered in his ear, "This is not about money; it's all about you refusing to sleep with her. Did you tell her about Zeina, the way you explained to me?"

Mustafa, raising his voice, said, "Michelle, are you serious? I would not mention Zeina's name or yours to this filth, even if my life depended on it. Do you hear how she talks and what she says?"

"But I am not your lover. Why would you mention my name?" said Michelle.

"I have a feeling you want us to spend a couple of days together for you to torture me with statements like this one."

"Don't use this word. You know I would never think of torturing you, even if you would never mention my name."

"Okay, I misspoke, I know. Torture is a bad choice of words," said Mustafa.

Michelle smiled and took Mustafa's arm as they walked toward William. "My poor father. He can't figure us out."

"Well, by now he should know. We have not seen each other for weeks," said Mustafa.

"I know, but the way we interact with each other is confusing to him. And besides, we will be spending two to three days together. That will arouse stronger suspicions."

"Let us keep it at that—the greatest love story that never happened."

"Maybe it is the greatest love story that may happen." Michelle looked sideways at Mustafa, smiling, and then letting go of his arm to head toward her father and to hold her father's arm.

That evening, William, Michelle, Carpenter, and Mustafa had a fancy dinner together. Carpenter wanted to probe further into hard-to-get-to-know Michelle and her relationship with Mustafa.

Michelle had rebuffed the invitations of two young attorneys at

Carpenter's office. One of the two continued to be mentored by Carpenter.

To change the subject, Michelle said, "Let's pretend that this ugly incident never happened and that you never had to take Mustafa's case. Let's just enjoy each other's company, here in the gateway to the West."

Carpenter paused and said, "Not only are you a beautiful young lady, but rather diplomatic...and a little bit coy."

Michelle smiled and said nothing.

The following day, William and Carpenter went back to Durham, leaving Michelle and Mustafa behind. William found it hard to leave. He had grown especially fond of the young man, not the least cause of which was the fact Michelle was attracted to him. At William's insistence, Mustafa stayed at the same fancy hotel he, Michelle, and Carpenter had been staying at. In the morning, Mustafa found out that his room had been reserved for a week's stay, completely paid for.

When Michelle came down to join him for breakfast, he asked, "Since my room is taken care of for one week, does this mean you are staying here for a week?" Michelle told him that it was all up to him, and that if he were to behave as a true gentleman, sure she would stay for the whole week.

"You know what my prophet said? He said, 'If your woman is not in a good mood, take a walk, don't argue with her.' After what you just said, I can't figure out what you are saying, and I feel like taking a walk. I don't know why—you are neither in a bad mood nor are you my woman."

"So, make me your woman and try to put me in a bad mood, then you can take a walk," said Michelle.

"I am taking a walk anyway—you eat my breakfast in the meantime. I don't want to get used to food I will not be able to afford in the future."

"Mustafa, don't be silly. Do whatever you want. I want to enjoy your company every minute over this coming week, and I hope you will try to enjoy mine."

"You know well enough that there are two women whose company I really enjoy. I know I will enjoy yours without even trying. Can we close the subject?" said Mustafa. "What shall we do now?"

"City tour, like regular tourists do," said Michelle.

She came up with a complete schedule except for one day—the day Mustafa was supposed to visit his friend, Rami, who was studying at the University of Missouri.

Although her initial approach toward Mustafa was to check his sincerity, it became obvious to Michelle that she was falling for him in earnest. Yet she was aware of his impasse. She was honest with herself that the prudent thing to do was to go back to Zeina and divulge what had happened to him during that unfortunate evening, including the rape. But she also knew that he had a mental block about divulging the incident to someone he had a very strong romantic attachment to. It was a whirlwind of confusion.

She decided that she should not try her charm on Mustafa all the time. Otherwise, she could ruin their week together, and possibly the whole relationship. She chose to make her moves only in the evenings, and mostly over well-organized romantic dinners. She was determined to try, having discounted Zeina being in the picture. She figured that it could take several lengthy visits with Mustafa to accomplish her objective, and she was ready to be prudently patient if need be.

At the same time, she was not trying to impose her love on him. She was waiting to see if his love and care for Zeina would wane enough for him to let go and direct his attention toward her. She was convinced that Mustafa had a psychological hang-up, one that could, over time, sever his relationship with Zeina permanently. At a minimum, she enjoyed his company and thought it was worth the try.

CHAPTER 11

Their days started with breakfast, a light one for her and a moderate one for him. She asked Mustafa to describe a typical breakfast, back in Amman, Jordan. When he hesitated, Michelle asked him first to describe his dining table there. He told her that it was a table that seated four and was big enough for them, as he had one sibling only, and that the table was covered with a plastic flowery tablecloth. He proceeded to tell her that they did not eat sausage, or surely not bacon, in the morning.

She then asked him to describe his family members' interaction with each other at breakfast.

"There is not much interaction. There is nothing really to prepare—yogurt spread, cheese, tomatoes, and olives. Some people eat eggs in the morning; we don't, and we don't talk much. We eat fast, much faster than the Americans. We do not visit with each other over meals like you do here. We mainly visit with each other after evening meals."

"What do you usually tell your father after meals?"

"I don't tell him anything. After dinner is when my father used to dish out advice. I agreed with him all the time, out of respect," said Mustafa.

"And how about your mother?"

"My late mother did not say much. She was a housewife. She gave us her blessings and wished us good luck."

Michelle was trying to get closer to Mustafa by satisfying her curiosity. She was more detailed in her questions, trying to draw him in, especially for her next subject: Zeina. She asked Mustafa if she could see Zeina's picture. He said that he did not have her picture on him. Michelle could not understand why and asked if he usually carried one in his wallet. Mustafa told her that he did not and never had. She said that she thought it was strange.

"Let me describe her to you," Mustafa said. "You told me that you are five feet eight inches tall; she is the same. I think she is two to four pounds lighter than you, at 128 pounds. She has hazel eyes; you have green eyes. She wears her blondish hair short; you wear your chestnut hair long. You are both well proportioned, with your waists where they should be. You have one permanent dimple and two when you laugh; she does not. She walks from her hips; you walk from your waist. Listen, I can go on and on and tell where you have birthmarks and where she does."

"You son of a gun! You've been casing me up and down and pretending you weren't interested at all. You're a sneaky character," said Michelle.

He told her that he only observed people who meant something to him, not just anyone. He added, "For whatever it's worth, let me share with you my social philosophy. I don't carry anybody's picture, not of my mother, my father, not my girlfriend, lover, fiancé, or wife. I do not celebrate anyone's birthday, including my own. I do not celebrate Muslim holidays, nor Christian ones. I don't celebrate birthdays or anniversaries, but I do celebrate graduations and anything dealing with achievement. I want to live day by day as if every day is a celebration."

He continued, "I don't believe in having more than one opposite-sex relationship at a time, even if it were less than serious. I am six feet one inch tall, and 198 pounds in weight. I bike, jog, and play tennis. I believe I am sincere, with a moderate sense of humor and a small ego. Does this satisfy your curiosity, Miss Michelle?"

She looked at him with a straight gaze, intending to lighten the conversation, and said, "How did you figure I was around four pounds heavier than Zeina?!"

Mustafa told her that she had the advantage of having a well-endowed and sexy bosom. Michelle asked him to come closer, and when he did, she jokingly rubbed her breasts against his nose.

"You are a purist, Mustafa Makram. You want the world not to concentrate on the trappings of life, but on the essence, and in theory, I agree with you, except human beings use trappings to express their feelings and to start new relations and end sour ones. They are needed unless you have what you described: a perfect relationship, with lovers living in bliss and total harmony."

"Well, Michelle Parker, that is what I want—a partner whose smile starts my day, every day of my life. Zeina did that for me, and I feel you could as well. That is, if I am a good boy. It cannot be a one-way street."

A city tour followed that morning for four hours. Mustafa was impressed with what he saw, but more importantly, what he heard about Missouri, President Truman, and the local history of Native Americans. When it was lunchtime, Michelle took him to a unique American diner where they served hot dogs, steaks, fried chicken, and above all, pies. Especially mincemeat pie.

Both sat next to each other at the counter. When Michelle told him that the pie did not contain any meat, he wanted to sample it.

The waiter behind the counter, listening to the conversation, said, "But we use pork fat."

Mustafa gave Michelle a nasty look. She knew she'd made a mistake, having been less than fully informed. She apologized first, then she used both hands to hold his face and turn it toward her. Looking at him straight, she said, "Listen, Mustafa, I make mistakes sometimes. I'm not perfect—I'm only human. Maybe you are making a mistake by making a big deal of your incident and staying away from Zeina."

He looked at her silently, in a probing fashion, and said, "There is nothing to apologize about. It was an honest mistake. You know I love Zeina, and she is on my mind, but don't keep reminding me of her. I want to forget about my pain and enjoy our being together. I find your company soothing and calming. You are so intelligent, and you are beautiful...but you already know that."

"I don't mind you telling me these things. I don't mind you telling me I am beautiful. I'll tell you the same, but I know you don't want to be told you are handsome. It is not part of your routine cultural expressions about males."

"You are right. I will just say you are beautiful, and you don't have to say anything, not even to thank me, because you are and you know it," Mustafa answered.

At that point, with both sitting on counter stools, a good-looking young girl passed behind them and rubbed her palm across Mustafa's behind. Michelle saw it and instantly got mad. She grabbed the girl's hand, turned around, looked her in the face, and said in a loud voice that attracted the attention of other customers, "If you do that again, I will..." She stopped, realizing she was being overheard. Michelle then let go of her hand and resumed sitting at the counter.

Mustafa jumped off his stool, looked down at Michelle, and in a split second, he realized that she was very protective of him. With her face flushed and her eyes bulging, and still sitting on the stool, agitated, he hugged her tightly, put her cheek on his chest, and started stroking her hair. Michelle relaxed her head farther onto his chest.

He said, "It is OK, it is OK. We are together and I will not allow anybody to touch you either."

In a few seconds, Michelle calmed down. She pulled herself up and said, "Thank you," and then gave Mustafa a peck on the lips.

When they got out of the restaurant, Michelle said, "I don't want to go on a tour with thirty other people. Let's go by ourselves. I'll lease a limo and a driver."

Mustafa wanted to say no, but instead, he said, "Whatever you feel like."

She went to a public phone and looked up the contact information of several limousine companies. She got one for $100 for a two-hour tour. In the limo, Michelle lay down in his lap and told him not to bother her until they got to the first site. It was a twenty-minute ride, during which time she massaged Mustafa's thighs with her cheeks and head. When they stopped at the site, she raised herself, straightened her hair, and gave Mustafa another peck on the lips.

During the day, Michelle held on to Mustafa's arm and placed her head on his arm whenever she had a chance. Mustafa responded by showing greater warmth toward her. They were having a grand time and Michelle was not pressing for more than a cuddly and warm physical relationship.

Two days later, they went to a jazz club. As the barman handed Michelle her drink, it spilled some, and she swayed backward to avoid the spill, about to bump into a young man who was behind her. He grabbed her right buttock and tried to turn her around to face him. At that point, she poured the drink on the arm he was grabbing her buttock with, all in view of Mustafa. Then she pulled Mustafa forward to give him a real kiss on the lips, trying to send a message to the guy. Having witnessed what happened, Mustafa hugged her and placed her head on his shoulder to calm her down.

Fortunately, the incident caused no physical contact between Mustafa and the transgressor. She then kissed Mustafa again and thanked him.

"What for?"

"For kissing me in earnest and saving the occasion."

Mustafa looked at her. "If it is a matter of kissing this beauty, here is another kiss." He kissed her passionately on her lips.

When they went back to the hotel that evening, she was beaming. Their rooms were next to each other. She looked at Mustafa and gave him a finger kiss off her lips and said good night, smiling all the way into her room.

Near the end of their stay, Michelle and Mustafa were again touring by bus. She was clearly in a cheerful mood. An elderly lady sitting across from them asked Michelle where she was from. Michelle said, "We're from Durham."

When the lady introduced herself and then asked about their names, Michelle introduced herself and Mustafa. The lady inquired if Mustafa was from Durham, too. Michelle avoided answering directly. She told her that he was on his way to Stanford University and that she would be going back to Durham.

Mustafa looked at the lady and said, "You see, I was on my way to Stanford when I got in trouble. Michelle immediately flew over to bail me out. What more can I ask? And now she, unfortunately, is going back, but—and this is the best part—she is going to be visiting me at Stanford. Aren't you, Michelle?" He smiled.

Michelle looked at him, pleasantly surprised and nodding. Slowly but surely, Mustafa was warming up to her approaches. Not much more was going on, other than Michelle feeling buoyant all the time she was with him. She knew that he was getting more interested in her. She kept to the same routine every day and at night, ending the day with a casual kiss on his lips. Mustafa was also getting used to the routine.

———

On their last night, Mustafa suggested the two of them share a scotch. Michelle preferred wine, so they got both and relaxed in Mustafa's room, teasing each other. Unexpectedly, Mustafa got serious. He turned Michelle around to face him. He paused for a while.

"Listen, Michelle, you are a precious person to me. Without you and William, life would have been very different. I just want to be honest with you. I have become close to you, yet I have not resolved what I am going through with Zeina. It will probably take a couple of months before I decide to ask for her forgiveness or otherwise break her heart, and it all will be my own doing and my own inability to overcome my phobia about what happened to me. I don't want to end up breaking her heart and yours at the same time. I will not accept a situation where I will be duplicitous with you or her. In the end, I must face the music one way or another. Within two to three months I should know, and I will let everyone know of my decisions, or my protracted challenges and continued torment. Regardless, I want you to respect me more than anything else. I hope you don't think I am full of myself."

"I know, and I don't want you to do anything you're not sure of. I'll wait for your decision, and no, I know you're not full of yourself, and I know that you are sincerely in anguish. I know."

They said good night to each other and met in the morning for each of them to go their own way. It was not an easy goodbye. Michelle tried to convince Mustafa to take a flight to San Jose, but he said that he wanted to walk the remaining two-thirds of the trip. Both of their eyes were watery. He kissed her gently on her lips.

After he unwrapped his arms from her waist, she slowly stroked his right arm down to the tip of his fingers. She turned around with a sad look in her eyes, walking back to her room. There, she cried her eyes out.

CHAPTER 12

The only other small disappointment he had in Missouri was that he could not locate his friend studying at the University of Missouri. The rest was more than satisfying, notwithstanding the fact he spent time in an American jail. In a way, Mustafa was starting to enjoy his cross-country walk, although in Kansas it got flat and boring.

In Topeka, he told a friendly restaurant server, Stan, what he was doing, and the server expressed his deep admiration for Mustafa's undertaking. When Mustafa told him that half of the time he was sleeping in parks, Stan invited him to sleep at his place. After some hesitation, Mustafa accepted, waited for him for an hour to get off work, and the two headed to Stan's house.

To Mustafa's surprise, the house was upscale. When Mustafa asked him how he could afford such a house at a server's income, Stan told him that a very rich old customer bought it for him and shortly thereafter, they quit talking to each other. After the two exchanged views about parents and parenting, Stan offered Mustafa a joint of marijuana. Mustafa turned the offer down and attempted to lecture him about the side effects of such smoking.

Stan had heard it before and was not interested in considering any of it.

As Stan got high, Mustafa tried to fix dinner for the two. Stan would not let him. He told Mustafa that his father was still sending him $400 a month, and with his income from the restaurant, he could afford to easily buy dinner for two. They went out and Stan insisted on paying.

Afterward, Stan drove Mustafa to a fancy house. The house was super upscale, fenced in with a two-acre garden. Stan told Mustafa that the house had eight bedrooms. It was his father's house, who was living with his new very young wife after his mother eloped with an encyclopedia salesman. His father's new wife was only five years older than Stan. His father was fifty-seven years old.

When the two went back to Stan's house, Stan told Mustafa that he could be his benefactor going to Stanford, and that he would be able to provide him with $20,000 a year if Mustafa would help him kill his father. The older man was supposed to be worth $25 million, all of it going to Stan, but his will was scheduled to be modified for the full benefit to go to his young wife.

Mustafa was shocked at the proposition but said nothing as he kept probing. Stan said that his young stepmother was in the habit of visiting her mother every other weekend, and that such a time would be ideal to carry out the plan. Without saying it, Mustafa implied that he was considering his murder request. He told Stan that he needed to go in the morning to the library to research his presentation to the admissions committee at Stanford.

It was all a ruse. Mustafa wanted to research what to do about Stan's criminal preposition. When he got to the library in the morning, he decided to first consult with his confidant—none other than

Michelle. She was elated to hear from him and presumed that he just missed her and wanted to chat. When she first heard the story, she advised Mustafa to collect his clothes and leave Topeka as fast as he could.

As an afterthought, she told him that he needed to go to the police. "If something happens to the father, you will feel guilty for the rest of your days, knowing that you could have been there to save his life."

She told him not to worry about it for the time being, as she was going to consult with Carpenter, their criminal attorney, and have him advise her what to do. Carpenter told her that in this case, Mustafa was obligated to tell the authorities. Before too long, a police car stopped by the library and picked him up, courtesy of Carpenter. Mustafa's story sounded credible to the police because Stan had logged a series of violations and had been accused of several other crimes, none with enough evidence to be charged.

The police asked Mustafa if he would wear a wire, so he called Michelle again to find out what Carpenter thought. He called Mustafa and left it up to him, explaining that the danger of wearing a wire was in the possibility of Stan discovering it. In the end, Carpenter spoke with the police and convinced them that they needed to be very nearby to save Mustafa if Stan did find out about the wire. The police agreed and gave Mustafa a special remote alarm so he could alert them in case of danger.

———

Mustafa stayed at the library all day, keeping with his prior days' routine of returning in the evening. He did not arouse Stan's suspicion. He planned to go to the house after Stan left work at six.

As Mustafa was killing time reading, he looked for articles about mink farming since he was scheduled to pass through Utah, famous for mink farms. Suddenly, someone came from behind and covered both his eyes. He did not know who it was. He could think only of Michelle and Zeina. He did not want to venture a guess, lest he embarrass himself by guessing wrong.

"Do librarians do things like this in Kansas?" he decided to say.

"No, they don't in Kansas, but they do in North Carolina," said Michelle. He stood up, and they embraced warmly, with her putting her cheek on his neck. After they let go of each other, cheerfully smiling, she asked, "You are interested in mink farming?"

"I have been reading all day. I read about wheat, barley, hops, and now mink farming. I am not supposed to go back to the house till after six."

"Knowing what you're going through and your upcoming attempt to record Stan's statements and possible confession, I couldn't wait back in Durham to hear about the mission. I wanted to be close by, to hear that all was OK right away. I'll be waiting for you at the police station, per Carpenter's arrangement. A police car is waiting to take me back to the police station."

"And I am waiting for a prearranged taxicab pickup. The driver of the taxi will be another policeman."

When Mustafa got there, as expected, Stan reopened the murder-assist subject. As directed by the police, Mustafa said that he would participate in helping Stan if he would get $25,000 per year for three years, and he further told Stan that for such a sum, he would only assist and not participate in the actual killing. Stan said he would think about it.

The police had told Mustafa that they wanted to wrap it up that evening, if possible, and that they would be listening through his wire device and another nearby.

Mustafa told Stan that he was very nervous about the whole thing and that he would be leaving the following day if no decision had been made by then. Stan agreed to pay him $75,000 over three years. He asked Stan to describe the plan in detail.

Apparently, only Stan's father had the main code to turn the alarm completely off, and the code had to be entered correctly the first time. Stan's father shared with Stan another code, where the alarm could be turned off by entering a different code twice, five minutes apart—otherwise the alarm would get triggered by the slightest variation. Stan told Mustafa that he needed him to enter the code at the gate a second time to turn the alarm off completely.

Per the coaching from the police, Mustafa asked Stan about the method he planned to use to kill his father.

Stan got suspicious. "What's it to you? You just stick to disarming the alarm."

Per the police instructions, Mustafa quickly explained that he needed to know just in case he heard shots. "Would you be the shooter, or someone else?"

Stan was convinced. He said that he had already stolen one of his father's guns and added a silencer to it.

"Have you tried the gun to make sure it works?" asked Mustafa.

"Yes, I tried the gun before you arrived. I shot into my house's support wooden poles."

At that point, the police believed they had recorded enough evidence to convict Stan. Within a minute, ten policemen barged into the house and handcuffed Stan and Mustafa, the latter to conceal his participation in the entrapment.

The police contacted their colleagues at the police station informing them that Stan was under arrest, and not to be surprised when they see Mustafa in cuffs also, to cover up his collusion. When the two were brought into the police station, Michelle managed to control herself, having been coached in detail. In front of Stan, one of the police officers told another that Mustafa was being extradited to Missouri, as he was wanted there for a more serious crime. It was all a ruse to buttress the cover-up.

One police car took Michelle to her hotel, and another took Mustafa to the same hotel. There they hugged and kissed in the lobby, all initiated by Michelle, after which both headed quickly to Michelle's room. She hugged Mustafa and pushed him onto the bed to lie over him and proceeded to kiss him all over.

"I don't know what I would have done if anything had happened to you. I would have been inconsolable, being responsible for your harm."

"You, responsible? Why are you saying this?" asked Mustafa.

"Well, it was our attorney who advised you to cooperate with the police."

"I understand—you just like to blame yourself. Well, you can pay up and make up for the danger you exposed me to: you can give me the same number of kisses you have given me in the lobby."

Michelle noticed that Zeina's memory seemed to have momentarily evaporated from Mustafa's mind. They paused so very briefly in their romantic advances but resumed right away, as Mustafa had not noticed her slight ambivalence about the nature of his new enthusiasm. Some of their kisses were passionate, but right away Michelle reverted to teasing him as if his interest had not been transformed.

———

If there was a moment for the two to become intimate, that moment was the one. Michelle seemed to hesitate, with thoughts streaming through her mind. Confused, she decided not to try further despite the heavy caressing and petting the two exchanged.

Mustafa wondered about her hesitation. He did not carry forward with any attempts to become sexually intimate. He was sensitive to the fact that it could have appeared inconsistent, on one hand expressing his loyalty to Zeina and on the other indulging in the ultimate act of physical betrayal.

Michelle stayed another night, then left, all on a positive but not necessarily firm note.

CHAPTER 13

Upon returning to Durham, her father was anxious to hear about what had transpired in Topeka, and the details that Michelle conveyed pleased his heart.

"Although it hasn't been long, you now seem to feel Mustafa is part of our family," said Michelle.

"Yes, it's almost as if we've adopted him!" said William. "Of course, that doesn't mean that he can't become part of our family in a different way." He looked meaningfully at Michelle, who got the message.

On the other hand, with William's comment, Michelle felt strongly that she was tired of the cat-and-mouse game and wanted to find out if her affection for Mustafa had a future or not. She decided to try to find out where things stood…not through Mustafa, but through Zeina. She called Willie, and after relaying Mustafa's positive news, she told him that she needed to meet with Zeina. She told him that she felt, at that juncture, that Zeina needed to hear from her directly.

She wanted to check Zeina's feelings toward Mustafa. In her mind, Michelle was determined to make a decision—to go all the way for him, or to abandon her hope. She wanted to gauge Zeina's feelings closely to see if they left enough space for her to go forward, or otherwise drop the whole thing.

————

Willie got together with Faris to consult with him. "You can be sure that Mustafa is fine and recovering well from his traumatic experience," said Willie.

"That's very good news," said Faris. "I think it would be good for Michelle to relay Mustafa's news directly to Zeina if you trust Michelle and her motives."

"I have no reason to suspect anything about her character, or her motives."

"Then go ahead and connect the two," said Faris.

Willie called Michelle. "Faris supports the idea: I will check with Zeina first before letting you know if the two of you could meet."

Michelle thought that was a good idea. "Please let her know that I am not trying to establish a relationship with her unless she wishes. Only to comfort her regarding Mustafa."

Willie called Zeina and explained the circumstances, but he only told her that Michelle and her father had helped Mustafa on the way and that they had news to relay to her.

"I welcome the gesture and am available to meet Michelle at her leisure," said Zeina. "I cannot believe that she went to the trouble of finding me and wants to meet."

Willie agreed to be the conduit between the two and promised to take care of the logistics for the meeting.

————

The two Durham residents met at a fashionable bar at the invitation and choice of Michelle. Michelle was well prepared. She looked very presentable but very lightly made-up, all intentionally choreographed not to make Zeina jealous. She wore her mother's wedding ring, pretending that she was married, to give Zeina the impression that she had no romantic interest in Mustafa.

Likewise, Zeina was well dressed and very smartly made-up, looking very beautiful. Willie had described each to the other. When Zeina entered the bar, they recognized each other instantly. Michelle stood up to greet Zeina. The two looked more like cousins, much less than rival beauties. Their good looks were apparent, and it would have been a challenge to tell who was prettier than the other.

Michelle took the initiative and said as she shook hands with Zeina, "Mustafa spoke briefly about you. You look as described, tall and very beautiful."

Zeina answered with a faint smile and, "Thank you."

"I am here to tell you that Mustafa is fine, although very sad, as much as we could tell during his brief stay with my dad. He wanted you to know that he is safe; unfortunately, he insisted that I do not contact you or anybody else right away. I'm sorry. I don't have much to add, but I am happy to answer any of your questions," said Michelle.

Zeina asked her if she was still in touch with Mustafa. Michelle said that he did not want to stay in touch with her or her father, or with anyone else, for that matter, and that he only wanted to be by himself to purge the effects of his traumatic experience.

When Zeina said that he should have come back to her rather than leaving her worried to death about him, Michelle answered right away, "But he went through the worst experience of his life;

he was brutally tortured."

"Even if I were brutally raped, he would have been the first person I would have gone to," said Zeina.

Michelle was taken aback by the statement of rape. She could not tell if Zeina knew about the fact Mustafa was raped. She wanted to probe into it.

"Rape for women, I guess is the same as torture for men," murmured Michelle, trying to elicit an explanation from Zeina.

"I guess it is. Men don't get raped. Nevertheless, he should have come back to me," said Zeina. Michelle got her answer that the mention of rape must have been coincidental.

"I did not discuss any of this with Mustafa. With all the care and love you have for him, can you forgive him for acting the way he did?" wondered Michelle.

"I am not sure I will. I was willing to do it the first month he was gone, but now my feelings have changed. I felt and still feel abandoned. I was willing to forgive, but no more. Not that I don't love him; I do. I just can't forgive him. He should have come to me right away. He hasn't been behaving right. He hurt me deeply," said Zeina.

"Do you want me to ask my father to help in finding Mustafa, so the two of you can try to clear the air?" asked Michelle.

"No, you need to concentrate on your own man, not mine. This is a done deal. It was meant to be beautiful but ended up being sad and disappointing. I don't know when I'll get over it, but I will. He's still the first person I think about when I wake up and the last person I think about when I go to bed. God, help me to put it behind me and move on. I think I will, since with time, I'm getting less confused and more certain that I will not forgive him," said Zeina.

Michelle told Zeina that she had contacted her through Willie because she didn't want to interfere in her or Mustafa's personal lives. "I'm sorry I'm not able to be of help. For whatever it's worth, I hope I've helped in a small way," said Michelle.

"You have. Don't you think I want to hear that he's not in danger and doing well? I do, but this doesn't mean I want to see him again," said Zeina, with a sense of lamentation, ending in a sigh.

The two shook hands. Michelle left, convinced that the relationship between the two had ended, yet she was more saddened than satisfied that Zeina wanted it to be over. She also knew that Mustafa was still vacillating.

————

Zeina headed to the bathroom; there she experienced her first pregnancy sickness. She realized what it was. She sat on the commode and cried for several minutes before another woman heard her throwing up. She tried to have Zeina open the door, but Zeina would not respond. The woman sought help from the female bar manager. Between the two of them, listening to Zeina moaning, they managed to break the door open. Zeina had collapsed with her head resting against the wall.

————

Driving back, Michelle was disappointed and confused rather than pleased. She found Zeina to be genuine, with sincere feelings and a deep love for Mustafa. She did not know what to do. She had not anticipated feeling depressed after the meeting, but she did. She decided to cool off psychologically and to let time take its healing course without doing anything, not even contacting Mustafa.

When she went home, she felt that she needed to clear her conscience. She thought of contacting two of her close friends but decided against it. In the end, she decided to talk to her father. She thought it was an opportunity to let him know where things were vis-à-vis Mustafa and to share with him her ill feelings about her own schemes.

William was all ears. She told him that she knew about Mustafa's girlfriend and how much she loved him and was loved by him. She told William that she went and met Zeina. "I went to see her for selfish reasons, but I ended up hurting her and hurting myself. I know that she's genuinely sad and still in love with Mustafa, but she doesn't want to have anything to do with him anymore. She's deeply hurt. I don't know how I feel about myself. She is not only good-looking; she's genuine with pure feelings. I wish she wasn't, but she is, and I don't know what to do," said Michelle.

William looked at her and said, "One thing I'm sure of, and that is whether you're going to end up with Mustafa or her, or even a third person, he seems to have attracted everyone's love, but above all, everyone's respect. He sure attracted my fatherly love and respect. He is the son I would have wanted if I were to have had a son. With that in mind, I don't want you to feel guilty about wanting to have a relationship with him. You and the other girl know that, and you should not feel guilty. This is the nature of attractive objects; in this case, it's more than an object—it's a human being: thriving, throbbing, sincere, handsome, and attractive."

He then advised Michelle to take her time and when she felt like it to be honest with Mustafa and to tell him about her visit with Zeina. "Apologize to him, and don't skimp on telling him about the visit. Take the initiative and honestly tell him why you arranged to see Zeina before he inquires about it."

Michelle felt good about the conversation. Not only did she receive her father's advice, but she shared with him her feelings about Mustafa, openly and honestly.

———

Mustafa called Michelle to update her on his trip. He told her that he was in a town thirty miles east of Provo, Utah. Before he could chat further, Michelle told him that she needed to see him and that she could be there in two days. Mustafa was not given a chance to tell her what had transpired with him in between. He more than welcomed her making the trip over, although he would have preferred to wait until he reached Provo, with fancier hotels and restaurants up to Michelle's standards.

Two days later, she arrived with a small bag, barely big enough to hold two days' change of clothes. Mustafa sensed that something was different. He immediately thought that she was going to tell him about a new romantic relationship. Michelle sat at the edge of the bed, in his small hotel room, after she pulled a chair for Mustafa to sit in.

"I did something wrong, and I want to confess it to you in person. You don't have to say anything. I'll go to my room afterward, and I'll head back to Durham in the morning. I'll wait for your response for two weeks. If I don't hear from you in two weeks, I'll know then that you don't want to see me anymore, not on my terms."

She started with a deep breath. "I met with Zeina for one purpose and one purpose only: to hear directly from her that she did not want to see you anymore. That was what I hoped. I lied to her, and I wore my mother's wedding ring to give her the impression I was married, surely to someone other than you."

"I proceeded to minimize the story about how we met and how we have no contact with each other anymore. She believed what I told her. She volunteered that she still loved you, but that you betrayed her and broke her heart and that she does not desire to have anything to do with you anymore. She was very beautiful, sad, still in love but down, almost depressed. I've fallen in love with you, and I want you to choose either me or her or neither. I did what I thought I could not and would not do: being dishonest and devious. Your answer, for better or worse, may relieve me of my guilt. If you decide to let go of me, I'll be relieved, but sad and totally disappointed. It's time you decide! I'm going to leave, and you won't see me here in this town before I go."

———

Michelle left Mustafa's room without providing him with an opportunity to respond, and he did not have the chance to ask her to stay longer, nor did he follow her to her room or see her that evening. In the morning Michelle left, sad but resigned to either have a healthy and loving relationship with Mustafa or to have no relationship whatsoever.

On the flight back to Durham, she was sad and pensive. She did not know which way Mustafa would decide. When she returned to Durham, she cried on William's shoulder.

"Don't hold back, cry and cry as long as you want. You may not know it, but I cried for almost two years when your mother passed away. Like Mustafa says, 'It is the wind that produces our joys and lamentations, but it is time that heals most wounds.' Wait and see, it may not be a permanent wound," William told her.

Michelle decided to go and see her friends in New Haven. Half-way to the airport, she turned back to the farm. There, she told William the last thing she wanted to happen was to miss Mustafa trying to reach her. "I can't take it anymore; I must know one way or another."

CHAPTER 14

Willie called Mustafa and heard about what had transpired, particularly the ultimatum Michelle gave him. He could tell Mustafa was in a daze and couldn't figure out what exactly had happened. The two friends brainstormed different possible scenarios for her behavior, and none of them was more likely than the others. Mustafa hadn't called Michelle, as he didn't have an answer for her, much less for himself.

Willie described to Mustafa how he had facilitated the women's meeting. He explained that he had no way of getting in touch with him, but he assumed that Michelle would not have asked for the meeting without his knowledge. Mustafa told him not to worry about what had occurred, but it was vital to concentrate on finding out about Zeina's state of mind and her feelings about him. Willie readily agreed, and they made plans for him to visit Zeina once more.

Willie met with Zeina to ask her about the meeting he had arranged between her and Michelle. Zeina was open with Willie. She told him that whether he or Michelle end up contacting Mustafa to tell him that she loved him before and still loved him then, more than anything or anybody she had ever loved but her heart was broken and was not likely to mend, and as such, her relationship with him was over, despite the fact she grieved about the breakup every single hour.

She added, "I told Michelle that I would have sought his understanding in case I was ever raped. As an afterthought, maybe not… Maybe rape is the only thing a woman would not share with her lover."

Her references to rape and the reversal in her sentiment about it were surprising to Willie. He wondered about it but did not want to appear to dwell on it in her presence. Zeina's decision about the end of the relationship confirmed what Michelle had told Mustafa.

Willie waited for Mustafa to contact him two days later. By then, he had written down every point and argument Zeina mentioned, in order not to leave anything out. He repeated the information to him and explained that he was reading from his written notes. Mustafa asked him to drop him a copy of the notes in the mail, addressed to the motel he was staying at. He added that he had seen a sign at a mink farm for temporary work, and he was planning to apply for the job and chill out for a week.

———

After his conversation with Willie, Mustafa went to the farm but could see nobody there. He kept banging on the gate, and after five minutes of ringing the bell and knocking, he got tired and sat down for about ten minutes before a young couple drove up with a crying baby. When he made eye contact with them, he asked the woman about the job. At first, the young lady did not know what to say. She was very agitated, but managed to regain her composure after she must have decided Mustafa posed no threat. She told him that she and her husband did need help, but they had to go out, and they would interview him in about an hour, after they returned. She opened the gate for him and asked him to wait in the house, which was 150 feet farther in. She and a young man and the baby soon left the premises after she told Mustafa again to go into the house and wait for them. Mustafa did as she directed.

In no time, the police arrived to find Mustafa sitting in a rocking chair. As they barged in, they ordered him to raise his arms and lie on the floor. At first, he did not know what to do, but his utter surprise quickly faded some and he slowly lay down.

He was handcuffed and questioned about Mr. and Mrs. Sloan and their baby. The police told him that Mrs. Sloan called them and shared a story as to what she had witnessed: someone going into their residence, trying to burglarize the place. Mustafa told the officers that he was there for a job, and he had not seen a baby except the one with a young couple, whom he believed may have been Mr. and Mrs. Sloan. He added that Mrs. Sloan had the baby in her arms. When he was asked about how old the couple were, he said that he thought that they were both around twenty-one or twenty-two years old.

As Mustafa was being interrogated, he was Mirandized, a rule he was familiar with from prior experience. He overheard one officer asking another, "Did she mention her name? Are you sure it was Mrs. Sloan?"

"Hey, Chief," a policeman called to the officer interrogating him. "Robertson just checked in. The dead bodies of Mr. Eugene and Mrs. Samantha Sloan were found in the back of the house, stabbed to death."

Mustafa was horrified.

Within the hour, he could see two local television reporters outside the police station. As Officer Robertson returned to the station, he shook his head and said, "One chummy police officer—need we say who? passed the news to his favorite TV station, mainly that the suspect was a male, a foreigner, and his name was Mustafa Makram. The news was on the air before the Provo newsmen had arrived. Chief, you've got to do something about him," referring to the officer leaking the news.

The police department offered Mustafa a public defender, but first, he asked for the yellow pages. To his utter surprise, he noticed an ad for a criminal attorney by the name of Shawky Mustafa Zurzur. Mustafa figured that Zurzur must have been an Arab American. He was familiar with the first and surely the middle name, but the family name sounded somewhat strange. He told the interrogator that he wanted to call Zurzur. The interrogator reminded him that he had the privilege of only one call. In this respect, it was Mustafa's lucky day. Zurzur was there and available, and he had heard about Mustafa's being taken into custody on the news. He told him that he was about to call the police station to offer his services. Zurzur added that he was originally from Ramallah, Palestine, and that everyone in town, and even in Provo, knew who Zurzur was.

Mustafa's new attorney was at the police station in less than fifteen minutes. There, he was greeted by just about everyone. He told Mustafa not to say one word unless he advised him to do so. While in the interrogation room with Mustafa, Zurzur called several people, including the county attorney, who later drove to the police station. Based on what Mustafa told Zurzur, he was convinced that Mustafa was completely innocent. He asked the county attorney if they could have an arraignment hearing the following day. The county attorney got back to Zurzur and told him that the judge agreed to have the hearing the following day since he was going on a three-day vacation the day after.

At the hearing, Zurzur put the dispatcher on the stand. He asked her if the lady who called in the crime had a speech lisp. The dispatcher confirmed that she had. Zurzur then handed the judge an already prepared, signed statement by Mustafa, stating that the female who met him at the gate and later drove out with a young male had a lisp, and was holding on to what looked like a one-year-old baby.

Zurzur told the judge that the Sloans were in their thirties and had a fourteen-month-old baby that was missing. He also presented to the judge that Sloan's car had disappeared while Mustafa was at the house, waiting for the young couple with the baby to come back. Zurzur added that Mustafa could describe the car, and that the police should issue an APB based on its specifics. The police chief stood up to agree that his officers confirmed that the car was missing, and that Mustafa was sitting in a rocking chair when he was apprehended.

Based on such facts, Zurzur asked that Mustafa be released and said that he would host him and guarantee his availability to the law, if needed. The county attorney agreed, provided that the arrangement was put in writing. Mustafa was released under Zurzur's guarantee. As they were driving to his lawyer's office, Zurzur referred to Mustafa as "Cousin," rather than using his name. Mustafa knew that such was a habit from the old country, but he hadn't used it in the US.

"I was eight years old when my family migrated to the United States in 1948, just after the loss of Palestine and the establishment of the state of Israel. I was born and raised in a small town, Ramallah, and I took my town traditions with me to the United States.

Cousin, do you realize that everything is, in the final analysis, a commercial deal, subject to endless horse-trading? You seem to be a nice young man and I like you—us both being Palestinians—so I want to tell you I have plans to make money out of this whole affair. I am already known all over the state of Utah, but your case will enhance my reputation to new heights. I can then financially take care of that, with funds to spare. We'll embarrass the police department by presenting that if not for my legal genius, you may have gone to prison for life! I need the public's recognition as I've applied for a position to be on the Board of Trustees of the University of Utah. That alone will increase my legal practice by 20 percent, and I happen to have a huge family to support."

Zurzur took his new client to his office to get the rest of the story. There, Zurzur went to the bathroom as a phone call came through, and then his secretary came in. In the presence of Mustafa, she told Zurzur that wife number five had just called to let him know that the case against Mustafa had been dropped.

At first, he thought that the secretary was joking—not about the case, but about the fact there was a mention of wife number five. He found out in short order that there was a wife number five, but Mustafa then thought that Zurzur was married four times before.

When Zurzur saw the stupefied look on his face, he laughed. "I know you think I have been married five times and divorced four. No, it is not like that. I currently have eleven wives."

"How could you have eleven when it was number five that called you?" said Mustafa.

"Well, you still don't understand; I have eleven wives at the same time," said Zurzur.

Mustafa did not know what to say. He had never heard of any-one being married to more than four wives, which was rarely practiced but allowed by the day's interpretation of Islamic rules.

Zurzur proceeded to tell Mustafa that he was a Mormon, and that he belonged to a group that was challenging the Mormon Church's ruling that disallowed plural marriages. He claimed that he and the members of his group were practicing what they be-lieved in. When Mustafa commented that there were no Mormons in Palestine, Zurzur cited an Arab proverb: "If you cohabitate with a group for forty days, you either join or abandon them."

Mustafa immediately understood the convenience and benefits Zurzur was accruing from converting to Mormonism. At that point, Mustafa was starting to doubt his choice of attorney. Zurzur tapped him on the shoulder and said, "I can wrap this whole state around my little finger. I know how the Mormons think and act, and they trust me, although they say that I am violating the rules of the Church. The truth of the matter is that they are envious of the fact that my group and I have more than one wife. Don't you worry about it—you will have a chance this evening to have dinner with me and my wives, and my six children. And tomorrow we will discuss finding you your first wife, Cousin."

The attorney and client left the lawyer's office around six in the evening, heading to the house. Before they got there, they passed by the motel where Mustafa was staying for a week. When the receptionist asked for the balance for the unoccupied nights from Mustafa, Zurzur was quick to say, "Do you know who you are talk-ing to? Call your manager and tell him that Mustafa Makram is a cousin of Shawky Zurzur, and that I am insisting that there will be no payment for the room beyond today."

Upon calling the manager, the receptionist said that there would be no such additional payment. Then she smiled and added, "I would have done the same even if you were not accompanying this handsome young man. I just wanted to test him."

Both men picked up on the hit. Mustafa took the opportunity to try to comment on Zurzur being married to eleven different women at the same time. In an unusual form, having been shocked by a Palestinian-American being married to almost a dozen wives at the same time, Mustafa addressed the cute-looking receptionist. "I am new here. I guess you don't believe in men marrying more than one woman, as is the case with some here in Utah!"

"Are you serious? Nobody does that kind of thing anymore. It's so backward and demeaning—even just discussing it is," she said.

"I knew from looking at you and observing your demeanor how you would behave. You would frown on it and fight it if you must," replied Mustafa.

"You don't believe in such a thing, do you?" she asked.

"I...I don't even have a girlfriend," he said as he winked at her, hoping to elicit more information from her.

Mustafa and Zurzur left, with none of Mustafa's hints and implied criticism impacting Zurzur. He had heard it all, and much more. When they got to Zurzur's home, they found all eleven wives and six children sitting around a massive table, which resembled those used in medieval Europe. Nobody sat at either end. Zurzur told Mustafa to sit at one end and he would sit at the other. When Mustafa objected and asked that whoever regularly sat at that designated end should sit there now, he told him that no one sat at either end of the table except him and his guests—not any of his wives, nor any of his children.

Everyone was hospitable and wanted to know more about Mustafa, especially a couple of the children. Mustafa told them that his parents came from a village less than seven miles from Zurzur's town, but that he was born in Amman, Jordan. Wife number six asked Mustafa if he had a girlfriend. He said he did, and that she lived on a dairy farm in Durham, North Carolina. That was the first time Mustafa referred to Michelle as his girlfriend, rather than Zeina. He was concerned that the highly inquisitive and manipulative Zurzur would ask for proof. Mustafa had neither Zeina's nor Michelle's pictures on him.

Apparently, Zurzur could not help but jump into the conversation. "No, no, you can't find more beautiful and loyal girls than Mormon girls. I have in mind a couple of beautiful ones for you to consider. Just leave it up to me."

Wife number three said, "If I am thinking of the same one, she is a beauty and she is still eighteen. Yes, she is ideal for a wife."

All the while, Mustafa was thinking to himself as he didn't know what to say. Zurzur spoke again, "Oh, no, I can now think of a third prospect. This is perfect. One is eighteen, another is nineteen, and the third is twenty. You can marry the twenty-year-old girl first, and in a year, you can marry the nineteen-year-old, and the eighteen-year-old will come last."

Mustafa managed to collect his courage and said, "I thought plural marriages are against federal law."

"It is a gray area, yet to be properly tested," said Zurzur. "You don't have to officially marry any of your wives—just like me, we are married under the covenants of the Lord. Each one of my wives knows that I am married to her, and she knows that she is married to me. Even if there was a law to the contrary, it cannot prevent what is ordained by God. If you are inclined to marry all the three prospects I told you about, all at the same time, you can do that tomorrow, provided that all three agree. Do you want to do that?"

Mustafa was shocked at the question, and to deflect the question completely, told Zurzur that he was intent on marrying an Arab girl. Afraid that Zurzur would come back with the argument that he could marry the three unofficially and marry an Arab girl officially, Mustafa added, "I only want to marry legally—an Arab girl, as I just said."

———

Zurzur was keen at that moment that his family did not hear anything about a preference for Arab girls. He took Mustafa by the arm and dragged him to the billiard room. He scolded him for not being sensitive enough to know that he was insulting all his wives, as they were all fine Mormon-American girls.

Zurzur tried to convince Mustafa to get off this "Arab girl" preference. Zurzur continued to make all kinds of lurid statements. "When was the last time you undressed a girl and looked at her all naked, just as the Lord has created her? I am sure when you undress the three together, you will not be able to stop yourself. You will jump on top of one of them as soon as it sticks up with you."

"No, no. I told you, I will not sleep with anyone except an Arab girl," Mustafa reiterated.

All the time Zurzur was snickering, but also insulting Mustafa in the process. He told him, "You must be the dimmest jackass I have ever met. You don't deserve my help—I should have left you in jail. I will show you to your room and you can masturbate instead. Make sure you don't do it on yourself. There are towels in the room."

It was not an easy night for Mustafa, as he was dreading meeting the promised three prospects. The family gathered in the morning for breakfast. The eleven wives were considerate of Mustafa, asking him if he slept well and if he needed anything else. One of the eleven wives was stunningly beautiful, only two years Mustafa's junior. She gave him several beguiling looks. Mustafa was eager to stay away from her, but his host must have intentionally sat him next to her. He tried to change seats, but Zurzur would not go for it. He told Mustafa that he was their guest, and he should be seated at the top of the table. "I intentionally placed two of my most energetic wives next to you to serve you properly and without delay," he told Mustafa, in front of everyone.

After breakfast, one of the wives left, then come back in a matter of fifteen minutes. She was accompanied by the three prospects. They were beautiful, as described.

Zurzur addressed the girls. "This is the man who wants to make you his wives. You need to look at him carefully and decide if he is acceptable, and also to decide if you are willing to live with each other harmoniously as wives of the same man and as sisters. Think about it and give me your answer one week from today."

When Mustafa heard the decision wasn't due for a week, he was relieved. He was afraid that Zurzur would conduct some sort of ceremony on the spot. Instead, he thought that he could do something to resolve the problem in the meantime. His first thought was to run away, but the highway was three miles away from Zurzur's ranch—too far for a clandestine escape. He decided to consider it carefully. He took most of the day and half the night, thinking of a potential plan, but he could not come up with anything.

The third day came, and suddenly he realized that he needed to give Michelle an answer. Whether his calculations were correct or not, he convinced himself that since he was going to opt for Michelle rather than distant Zeina, seeking Michelle's help made sense. His concentration shifted to calling her at 3 a.m., Utah time, and 5 a.m. Durham time. Mustafa succeeded in making the call.

"Michelle, don't speak loudly. I am in trouble, and I need your help."

"Trouble again! What kind of trouble?" asked Michelle. Then, she prompted, "What's your answer to my question?"

Mustafa understood her inquiry well and said, "This is my answer. Isn't it obvious? Don't talk anymore but come to this address, which belongs to Shawki Zurzur, 143 FM 12, Sweet Desert, Utah. Surely not alone—with a private detective, if possible, not the police. I have to go."

———

The following day, Michelle, through her family's criminal attorney, engaged the services of two private detectives. She could not brief the two to any reasonable degree. She just told them that her boyfriend was in danger at that location. She instructed them not to wait for her but to try to canvass Zurzur's farm.

They agreed, but their shaking voices told her that the news that the site was owned by Zurzur made them very nervous. They seemed to know of his reputation and told Michelle that he was the one always skirting the law, but also had friends in high places. Yet, they knew with a high degree of certainty who in the police department was beholden to Zurzur.

Although seriously worried while she was flying to free him, she was relieved that he had chosen her over Zeina, or any other.

Upon arriving, the local private eyes were waiting for her. They explained that they used the time to alert a trusted police friend in case they needed help. Not waiting for someone on the inside to open the estate's gate, they got into the car with Michelle and parked in front of the house.

Zurzur was the first to come out. The private eyes apologized and informed him that they were escorting Michelle to see her fiancé. The fiancé aspect surprised Zurzur, especially since Mustafa had expressed his plans to marry an Arab girl. Zurzur politely introduced himself, and it was obvious he could see why Mustafa was attracted to Michelle. She was a beauty in every respect.

CHAPTER 15

The detectives had coached Michelle not to speak unless necessary, or just to resort to making small talk. She also was briefed about Shawky Mustafa Zurzur's reputation.

"What a pleasant coincidence. Your middle name and the name of my fiancé are the same! Where is he?" she asked, having escalated her relationship to Mustafa.

He hesitated for a moment—a trait he was not known for. Zurzur said, "You don't look like an Arab. He said he only fucks Arabs. He is inside. Why don't you come in?"

One of the detectives looked at Michelle. "Go ahead. We know Mr. Zurzur has a fine reputation. We'll be back in two hours to pick you both up. Don't you pay attention to this gentleman; he's a fine attorney with a creative mind," he said in a mildly sarcastic tone, trying to indicate that Michelle should ignore Zurzur's racist statement about his ethnicity.

When Michelle entered, Zurzur led her to the billiard room, where Mustafa was, all disturbed, but seemingly in good physical shape. However, Michelle could read his troubled emotional state with just one look.

They greeted one another with warm passion. Zurzur watched the two in awe, mainly at the sincerity of their hug. He waited until the kisses ended before he resumed speaking.

"I am glad you arrived so soon. Mustafa was about to get married."

Michelle looked first at Zurzur and then at Mustafa with total surprise, a look that questioned what she had just heard. Mustafa did not let Zurzur answer her curiosity. He got steaming mad at Zurzur's fabrication.

"No, no, you son of a bitch—you wanted me to get married." He repeated it in Arabic, "You son of a bitch."

"You see, Michelle, if Mustafa marries you, what will he get? One pussy. I offered him three, and one is only eighteen years old," said Zurzur, trying to insult Michelle by using foul sexual language.

Michelle didn't answer. She could tell that Mustafa had cussed at Zurzur, also in Arabic, which was rather out of character for him. The stress she noted earlier must have produced this lack of control on his part.

"Don't you speak like this in front of my fiancée! She is different—she is different than this backward, decrepit lifestyle of yours. You know, Michelle, he is married to eleven different women? All at the same time!" said Mustafa.

Michelle completely ignored Zurzur and looked at Mustafa. "Let's get out of here. Forget about your clothes—I'll buy you new ones. This man is without honor. We can wait for our ride at the gate."

As she was grabbing Mustafa's arm and hurrying out the door, Zurzur followed them and said, "You see, Michelle? We have an Arabic saying, 'Fuck and don't get fucked, and don't let your penis get lethargic.' With one pussy in five years, his penis will get lazy, and he will start looking for other pussies to revive his penis. You don't know what I am talking about now, but this is what will happen."

Six-foot-one-inch Mustafa could not take it. He dislodged Michelle's grip and turned toward five-foot-six-inch Zurzur, trying to hit him as hard as he could. As he was about to complete his action, Michelle grabbed him tight by the waist and said, "Can't you see he's trying to agitate you? He wants to create a scene, and you're accommodating him. Stop it. Stop it right now."

Mustafa held back and Michelle managed to drag him toward the gate. As the two were hurrying, Zurzur kept following them and hollered, "I bet you can't even have an erection. I was mistaken. You are afraid to fuck one single woman! You are no good. Yes, you are the one being fucked. Yes, it is obvious to me!" Eventually, Zurzur gave up and returned to his home office.

Zurzur's questioning of Mustafa's sexual prowess was not a reference to Mustafa's rape experience, as he knew nothing about it. It was intended to insult and spite defiant Mustafa. His statements hit both escapees in a completely different way. Michelle was afraid of their ramifications on Mustafa, concerned that it would bring back memories of pain and "loss of manhood."

As they exited the gate, Michelle wanted to change the subject altogether. "Mustafa, I don't care—it's all worth it. I will come to you anywhere in the world. I'm so much in love with you, and I'm pleased that you chose me over everyone else. I was afraid you wouldn't. Oh, God, it makes me so happy."

She wanted to make him feel wanted rather than rejected, as lowly Zurzur had intended to do. She said, "I hope you've forgiven me for visiting with Zeina. You have, haven't you?"

Mustafa looked at her with a curious face and said, "This is all behind us. There is no need for apologies—it is ancient history. We are now dealing with this maniac." He shook his head. "I am the one who needs to apologize to you. Ever since we met, it has been one strange entanglement after another, and in each case, you were instrumental in saving my behind. Can you believe it? Having to deal with one from a town a few miles from my father's village and having to confront him, even to confront him, physically, here in Utah! It is you who needs to forgive me for being always in trouble and dragging you into one fray after another."

Michelle looked at him, smiling, and said, "I won't apologize if you don't. Deal?"

"Deal!" said Mustafa.

After a long hour's wait, the two private eyes returned to pick them up. When they heard what Zurzur had said and done, they were not surprised. The two Mormon private eyes told the couple that Zurzur's strength was his charm, and not his legal expertise, as many in the Mormon hierarchy seemed to think. He was a regular entertainer and charmer on many of the high-end Mormon hierarchy cruise junkets. His specialty was telling Palestinian village clean jokes. The Mormons used to love them. His other persona, that of being a Mafia-like operative, was hidden from the leadership of the Church, although known to Mormons outside the ruling elite.

They also shared with Michelle and Mustafa that there were half a dozen Mormon bishops who were waiting for the opportunity to reveal the truth about Zurzur. Mustafa said that he was willing to cooperate with them, but Michelle objected. She told Mustafa that he had too much trouble as it was, and that he needed to assume a proactive role in trying to avoid future entanglements. Mustafa agreed after Michelle came up with a compromise: they would write down the details of their experience with Zurzur and give it to the private eyes for its potential use against Zurzur.

Michelle told the men that it was time for her and Mustafa to spend quality time together and asked if they could recommend a place for them to do that. The private eyes mentioned a special remote resort that was typically used by rich Mormons with plural marriages. They would go there with one of the wives whenever their wives were feuding. When they told the private eyes that they did not want to have contact with that kind of people, they said no Mormons were expected to be there, since there was a huge Mormon gathering in Salt Lake City at the same time.

Michelle and Mustafa shopped for new clothes for Mustafa and the private eyes arranged the hotel stay for three full days. Mustafa told Michelle how much he needed to unwind after having been accused of murder and then having to challenge "The premier con of the century," as he called Zurzur.

Michelle was keen to give Mustafa every chance to relax with as little bother as possible. The reservations were made for two rooms, as the resort would not have accepted two unmarried people sharing the same room.

While they stayed, Michelle arranged every activity. During the day, the two went swimming, hiking, and took hot-air balloon trips. They would picnic after the balloon ride and then visit specific Mormon temples that were open to the public. Although neither Mustafa nor Michelle was religious, he was always interested in houses of worship sites. His grandfather had once been an accountant for the Anglican Church in Palestine.

Their inquiries were general, in the sense that they sought to know about the nature of the congregations and the sources of income of the different temmples. On one occasion, they mentioned the name of Zurzur to a Mormon bishop. He signaled that he did not care for Zurzur. They, in turn, told him how to contact the two private eyes to learn about their own experiences with him. Mustafa particularly was seeking revenge.

At night, Michelle would arrange for a special meal to be served in her room. She told Mustafa that she wanted him to rest, but she really wanted the two to sleep in the same bed. Not necessarily to have sex, but to be in each other's arms. She was hoping against hope that Mustafa would take the initiative to make love to her without her pressing the issue. True to her concerns, Mustafa initiated nothing. He followed his restrictive statement to the letter. He would only wrap his hands around her and press his head around her neck all night long.

The three nights at the resort went smoothly and were energizing for both, despite the lack of sexual intimacy. Michelle did not dwell on the fact that Mustafa did not make any moves. He suggested, and Michelle agreed, to meet at Stanford in a few weeks, to spend a week together to celebrate his long-anticipated arrival. It was music to Michelle's ears. She was escorted to the airport by the two private eyes. They promised her that they would follow Mustafa for several miles to make sure Zurzur did not have any surprises for him. Once Mustafa got onto a more exposed segment of the walking trail, they turned around and left, reporting the good news to Michelle.

———

In less than two months, Michelle was at Stanford with great expectations. Soon after her arrival, Mustafa, to her surprise, told Michelle that it wasn't that he didn't desire her body, but since the relationship was getting serious, he did not want to have sex with her. Confused, she asked Mustafa to elaborate. Without answering her, he told her that lately, he could think of no one else but her. Michelle relaxed.

"I know you have feelings for me. I want to make sure that those feelings are as strong as my feelings for you," he said. Michelle tried to say something, but he put his index finger on her lips and asked her to wait. "I know it is a very strong and genuine feeling on my part, but I want to know why it turned out this way and what the future portends. I don't want to start a new phase and continue to leave victims behind anymore, especially victims as a result of my own shortcomings. I have left many in my path. Do you follow me, Michelle?"

"Oh, God, I follow you 100 percent! I don't want you to keep torturing yourself—your regrets and lamentations break my heart. I want you to share with me the joy I feel being in your life, and you being in mine. We're not perfect human beings, and we will never be. You need to learn how to forgive yourself for things that are almost beyond your control. You can't strike out your cultural norms just because you've been living in the West for three years. Culture and religion are too deep-seated to be neglected or erased in a month or two. Can I kiss you? I just want to change your melancholic mood," asked Michelle.

He looked at her with a broad smile and grabbed Michelle and kissed her on the lips passionately. She was most pleasantly pleased and surprised. "You see, you insisted on kissing me instead of me kissing you, which is even more precious," said Michelle. "Mustafa, you know that my dad has been wondering—and hoping—that you and I would be in a relationship. Do you mind if I share with him that we are?"

"You know, Michelle, if I were an American, I would want a

father just like William. He is so understanding. Although he is a rich man with a master's degree, he is still a down-to-earth farmer. He projects himself as being more understanding and compassionate than anyone I have ever met. He has been most gracious with me, beyond my wildest expectations. Sure, let him know right away. You will be negligent otherwise," said Mustafa.

She said that she would call him in the evening. Mustafa thought better of the plan. "No, Michelle. How about my flying back with you to let him know together?"

"He would love it and would love seeing you! He thinks so highly of you. That's a great idea," said Michelle.

Michelle called Bertha and told her to prepare a room for Mustafa the following Friday. She wasn't to divulge the plan to William, but put one bottle of champagne in each room, on ice, an hour before their expected arrival. When Bertha tried to probe, Michelle promised to tell her when she got back.

She wanted to share the good news with her dad and give him a chance to object if he happened to disagree.

CHAPTER 16

William was eagerly waiting for Michelle. She was all that he had, the apple of his eye and the daughter-buddy he had nurtured after his wife died. The cab arrived at the house on time, and he knew Michelle would leave her light luggage on the porch. Bertha would direct it to Michelle's room later. Michelle entered to find William waiting for her in the main rotunda.

"Tell me, how did it go? How's Mustafa adjusting over there?" he asked.

Michelle put her index on her lips, hissing at William to stop. Mustafa came in, smiling. He looked at the surprised William and said, "This time I could not let Michelle go back home alone."

William didn't know what to think, having bailed Mustafa out of trouble so many times. He had been thinking of negative news rather than cheerful ones.

Michelle asked if they could sit down at the kitchen table. There she looked at William sitting opposite her and paused. William also paused and then looked at Mustafa. She put her hand on Mustafa's hand, looking William straight in the eyes.

"Dad, I'm sure you will be pleased to hear this. Mustafa and I have started going out. That's why he's here. We wanted to tell you together, and to answer all your questions. You know, Dad, Mustafa is not American, and so he does things differently…mainly in a different sequence than we do. He told me how much he loves me and only wanted to know if I love him as much. And when I told him how much I love him, he asked that we share the news with you together right away, in person."

William put his hand on top of their two hands. He looked at Mustafa first and then at Michelle and said, "Your happiness is what makes my days brighter and my nights smoother. Nothing could have brought out this feeling than you two finding the love you have been looking for. I think it is the perfect occasion for a celebration."

Michelle called in Bertha and asked her to bring the two champagne bottles down from the bedrooms. One was a six-year-old vintage Tait-tinger Comtes de Champagne Brut Rose, and the other, Dom Pérignon Brut, was Michelle's favorite.

During their sharing champagne, and while Mustafa was visiting the bathroom, William asked his daughter if there were any marriage plans made. Michelle told him that they had never discussed it.

"Would you want to marry him in the first place?" asked William.

"Are you kidding me?! Who else would I want to marry? Sure, I want to marry him, with all my heart—that is, if you approve," said Michelle.

"Not only do I approve, but I also approve wholeheartedly!" said William. "I need a bigger family. I need grandchildren. What am I going to do with all of this? We have a grand mansion and are netting over a million a year and growing."

Michelle jumped toward her father and gave him a huge hug. "Tell me, Dad, what is it about Mustafa that attracts women like me and Zeina? I'm sure Zeina is like me. She can choose from dozens of men—so can I—yet there's something so attractive, almost alluring about Mustafa," inquired Michelle.

"Don't you think I've thought about it? I've asked myself the same question: why are you so attracted to him? I've thought about it a lot, ever since you doubted his sincerity, and later found out he was honest and on the level. After consideration, I came to one conclusion. He's very, very wholesome. He's smart, an A student, and he's hard-working. He's lighthearted, sophisticated, sincere, loyal, and squarely masculine and good-looking, and he's not imposing or aggressive. What more do you want?" William asked.

"You're right, Dad. He has almost no faults. Maybe one… another person might have reconciled with Zeina. He is different. He's too sensitive about not being up to par, especially toward people he's close to. He felt he was one thing and became another, not wanting to shortchange Zeina. On the other hand, he's all right with me. I learned about the tragic incident before we developed feelings for each other," said Michelle.

William told her to think positively and stop thinking of the past. "The future will include you and Mustafa, and I'll savor your love for each other. Indeed, I want grandchildren—as soon as possible!—but above all, only when you and Mustafa feel ready for the occasion. That will be the day."

Michelle looked at her father and said, "Mustafa needs eighteen months to get his Bachelor of Business Administration, BBA, but I'm sure he can finish in around fourteen months. What kind of schedule shall I keep in the meantime?"

"I can't tell you what kind of schedule. If you wish, you can fly to see him, or he can fly to see you, every two weeks. I don't think it would be a good idea to stay idle. What I'm going to suggest—and which I had in mind for a long time, long before you met Mustafa—is that you work for me. If you keep busy, you will enjoy your free time better, as it will become quality time. After all, Michelle, this farm is going to be yours and Mustafa's and… Excuse me, but you know very little about our operations here. Even if you decide to sell it in the future, knowing what it is all about will help you bargain for a better price. Don't you agree?" asked William.

"That's what a girl who has a comparative literature degree from Yale does—she ends up managing a dairy farm. Interesting," said Michelle sarcastically.

"Remember that I have a master's in engineering," he said calmly. "I only want you to know what the farm is about. Within less than two years, you can do whatever you want, whether to write poetry or have children. It will be all up to you."

Michelle said nothing. When Mustafa came back, he apologized for taking such a long time. He said he was reading the poems and proverbs Michelle pasted on the bathroom wall.

The three drank until Michelle became tipsy after consuming one bottle on her own. William suggested that Mustafa carry Michelle to her room, which he did. He then went down to have coffee with William, informing him that he'd removed her dress and shoes and put her in bed.

The following morning, Michelle sat next to her father at breakfast and told him that she agreed with him completely. She would start helping him run the farm within weeks after she visited her girlfriends in New Haven and Mustafa afterward.

Mustafa left two days later, but not before a difficult goodbye for each of them. It was their first goodbye since mutually declaring love for each other and after dispensing with so many emotional thorns that stood in the way. This time, Mustafa told Michelle he would finish his trip by flying to Stanford. She understood, knowing he was continually being challenged by unexpected serious surprises, and he was leery that he had cried wolf in the direction of Michelle and William too many times.

Michelle was impatient and felt lost after Mustafa left. She flew to visit her two friends in New Haven, Sara and Carol, where they were studying for their master's degrees. She was anxious to see them and, in advance, organized dinner at their apartment so she could discuss all with the two. She wanted to be deliberate, as she valued their advice. She would give them the good news first and then ask their opinions about some issues on her mind. She asked them not to be carried away by the good news. Both listened attentively.

Michelle started by telling the two that Mustafa came through and declared his love and devotion. After a brief excitement, they held back to listen to the rest, the importance of which Michelle couldn't hide. She told them that Mustafa said that the two of them would not have sex yet, specifically because he respected her so much.

"You see, this is his cultural mindset. I bet you that after living in England and here for three years, he is slightly confused. Let me hear your opinion about this. It is not that I'm dying to have sex—what matters is that it's a major issue for him."

Sara asked, "Do you know whether or not he slept with Zeina?"

"I presume not. Why would he have slept with Zeina and not with me? It makes no sense!" said Michelle.

"Yes, it does if you take into consideration one important transformation in his life," said Sara.

"You're not making sense, Sara. What do you mean?" asked Carol.

"I can understand Michelle overlooking this one, but you, Carol, without any romantic attachment to Mustafa, should have at least considered this scenario. Mustafa, between two hot love affairs, went through a traumatic experience: a rape by another man. An event destructive enough for him to abandon his first love. Doesn't it make sense that he developed doubts about his own sexual ability? After all, Michelle has already told you and me that he said, 'I am not the man I was!'"

Carol looked at her and said, "That kind of reaction is not what usually happens—not in this fashion, at least—but it sounds plausible. You know my mother is Catholic. A couple of her female cousins made it clear to their suitors that they did not expect to have sex before their weddings. He might be doing the same. You shouldn't give it much thought. I don't know whether it's religious or cultural, but it's not an outlandish request."

"You know, Carol, you and Sara are the only two people, besides my father, who know about what happened at the Goldwater rally. Do you think that Mustafa's still suffering from the aftereffects of his attack?" asked Michelle.

Sara looked at her and said, "It's a possibility, but in my opinion, it may or may not be the leading reason. I think it may not be a purely psychological reaction to his trauma. It could be religious or cultural, like Carol said."

"Did he mention marriage or anything like that?" asked Sara. Michelle said that while they talked about love and how he fell in love with her, he never mentioned a word about engagement or marriage. Sara added that not talking about engagement or marriage wasn't an indication of anything important this early. The main issue and focus should be whether he'd been damaged by his unfortunate trauma or not.

All of a sudden, Michelle got worried and went silent and pensive. Sara's emphasis caught her attention and produced additional concerns on her part. Carol wanted to soothe Michelle's concern by saying, "Listen, this could be nothing more than a personal preference. I don't think we should dwell on it. It is probably nothing, and Michelle will get to figure things out in time."

"Listen, Michelle," said Sara. "You're twenty-two, and he is twenty-two. He's not familiar with American habits and interactions. We girls know more about such things than American boys know, never mind foreign men. Why don't you simply take things at face value? If he does suggest doing things differently, just educate him, or simply ask him why. We may be making something out of nothing. I bet you're so surprised by the positive turn of events, you're expecting to find something wrong. Michelle, you're spoiling things. This is a time for celebration! I'll go and buy a cold bottle of champagne to drink right now," said Sara.

In the end, Michelle expressed her agreement with Carol and Sara. The three drank the bottle of cheap champagne, which got them to a spirited stage, but not quite drunk. Michelle then asked, "You've never met Mustafa? Oh, God, you should. He's so masculine and handsome, so well-collected and debonair. I think you need to meet him."

"Meet him where?" said Carol.

"At Stanford, when I go to see him next time. Listen, listen—don't say no. I'll take care of 50 percent of your tickets, and we can all stay in the same hotel room. We'll ask for two twin beds and put them together. How about it?" said Michelle.

Sara looked at her and said, "Don't use words like *debonair* in the future. You're a comparative lit graduate with a minor in French, while we're science students!" She laughed, then nodded. "Yes, I will go to California."

Carol agreed, and the plans for and the conversation about the trip moved their minds off Michelle's new concern. The three continued celebrating till two in the morning.

Two days later, Michelle was back in Durham. She sounded and acted in a much more vigorous form than before she left for New Haven. She shared with her father that Sara and Carol agreed to visit California to meet Mustafa. "They'll be my bridesmaids," she told him, "if we get to that stage." She could see her dad was happy that she was feeling much more relaxed.

CHAPTER 17

Two weeks later, the three met at the San Francisco International Airport and then took the bus to Stanford, where Mustafa met them. Sara and Carol immediately signaled to Michelle that Mustafa was particularly handsome, and that she had made the right choice. The three girls seemed to be floating on air and giggling all the time.

Out of nowhere, he said, "You must be the best of friends," even though Michelle had told her girlfriends that she'd already said that much to him. "You probably know everything about each other."

Michelle and Sara caught the implied meaning right away, but Michelle could tell that Carol did not. Carol said, "We know everything. We don't keep any secrets from each other, no matter how small or how unimportant."

Sara and Michelle eyed Carol, yet it was obvious that she did not know what for. When they got to the privacy of the hotel, Sara opened up. "Are you crazy? Why would you say such a thing? He now knows that Michelle has told us about the attack at the rally."

They discussed the issue of Mustafa sensing that they knew. Sara suggested that Michelle level with him by informing him that they and her father were the only ones who were told about the rally incident. Michelle hesitated at first but then said that she would tell him if the circumstances were opportune. She added that she would probably sleep with Mustafa that night. Sara and Carol were surprised. They could not figure out what sounded to them like a discrepancy: Mustafa not wanting to have premarital sex and Michelle sleeping in the same bed.

"Do you sleep in the same room?" asked Carol.

"Yes, we sleep in the same room, and we sleep in the same bed, but nothing happens. He hugs me, presses my body against his, he holds me in his arms, and he places his head on my neck all night," said Michelle.

"And he manages to control himself against your body, all night? This is weird," said Sara. Michelle asked that they both hold their horses till the following day, after which she would have told him that she shared his secret with them.

When Michelle told Mustafa that she wanted to sleep in his room, he thought it was a great idea and asked her if she could do it all three nights. That night, as Michelle came out of the bathroom, wearing a sexy nightgown, she sat on the edge of the bed and told Mustafa that she needed to speak to him. He was more than eager to pay attention to her.

"Listen, Mustafa. Since we're going out together and belong to each other, we can't have any secrets. I've told three people about what happened to you at the Goldwater rally. My father knows, and so do Carol and Sara. I realize that you indirectly said something to the effect that you knew that I've shared your experience with them. Yes, I have told them, but nobody else. Does it bother you?" asked Michelle.

"If I were to say it does not bother me, would you be kinder to me tonight?" asked Mustafa.

Michelle got confused. She did not know if Mustafa was talking about having sex. "How much kinder do you want me to be?" she asked half facetiously, trying to figure out what he meant.

"Kind enough to let me feel you, kiss you, smell you, and hug you," he said.

Michelle turned around, partially exposing her firm breasts, and said, "Do you want also to touch me?"

"I want to do anything and everything, short of violating our understanding," said Mustafa.

"Although it's not necessarily my preference, I will live by the terms of our understanding, since it's your choice. Yet I hope you'll consider my preferences before you make your final decisions," said Michelle.

Mustafa paused. She could see him collecting himself and then he looked her in the eye and said, "I did not expect to be indirectly criticized, but I am grateful for the clarification. Your preferences should have the same value as mine, so I should not have decided before consulting with you first. I was inconsiderate in the way I made the decisions about our common issues." He added, "I have always thought of myself as a liberal person, believing in equal rights between the sexes. I have just found out that my thoughts and practices are not exactly aligned."

Michelle didn't know how to answer. She didn't want to exacerbate the situation, aware that she had inadvertently cornered Mustafa. She kept looking at him without saying anything. Suddenly, he grabbed Michelle and put her down flat on the bed, with him kissing her repeatedly on her neck, in a most affectionate and animated way.

The night started with both showing conspicuous romantic feelings toward each other. They kissed, caressed, and fondled each other. Michelle was getting aroused and could feel him getting aroused, too. Mustafa, apparently to arrest the process, turned and lay on his stomach. This is when Michelle slipped his pajamas off. She raised her nightdress and began rubbing herself against his behind.

At first, things were going well, but as Michelle pushed herself harder against him, Mustafa flipped to lie on his back and pushed her up. He was breathing heavily and perspiring.

Michelle was taken aback. "What's wrong, Mustafa?"

It took him a long few seconds before he said, "I am sorry. Don't do this again—not this way. His image came to me."

Michelle tried to hide her anger but couldn't. "What image are you talking about, Mustafa? What image?" she snapped.

"The guy in Durham, the guy at the rally," said Mustafa. "He was on top of my back, just like you were."

Michelle looked at him, realizing that the subject discussed between her, Sara, and Carol was indeed true. She grabbed his head in her palms, kissed him, and apologized profusely. That night, other than Michelle sleeping in Mustafa's arms, nothing else happened between the two.

In the morning, she shared the news selectively with Sara and Carol. She told them in detail that Mustafa didn't care that she was confiding in them all the way. They were very pleased to hear that. She also told them that the two didn't have sex, but that she enjoyed being in his arms all night and with his head nudging her neck affectionately.

Michelle specifically did not want to corroborate that Sara's fears came true, and that Mustafa had indeed been impacted by his experience at the Goldwater rally.

"You can't possibly withstand such closeness to him," Sara said. "You'll most likely get on top of him in no time, even if he doesn't make any moves."

Carol was the more skeptical of the two. "You should test him by bringing up the subject of the engagement and see what kind of reaction he exhibits. You might also tell him that your engagement should take place within six months."

Michelle said that she would, though she wasn't sure she would. She wanted to find out more about Mustafa's sexual problem. She was getting more confused—not able to tell if his reticence to be sexually intimate was because he had already known of his inability, or that it was revealed to him when she was on top of his back. She decided to try to visit Mustafa more often, as she thought their closeness would be the quickest way to extract her answers.

Michelle returned to Durham, mentioning nothing to William other than the fact Sara and Carol were taken by Mustafa, and that he found the two to be friendly and charming. Within days, Michelle telephoned Mustafa and asked if he would be amenable to her visiting him once a month.

"Amenable? I would love it," said Mustafa.

Michelle's visits were refreshing for both. She was cautious not to push herself on him, and Mustafa did not take the initiative to become more intimate. On her fourth visit, Michelle decided to test the water. As she slept in his arms the first night she got there, she turned around to lie on her back and then pulled Mustafa on top of her. He did not resist, but rather went along willingly. As he continued and initiated having sex on top of her, Michelle breathed a sigh of relief.

Her relief was short-lived, though, for as the two became further excited, Mustafa started breathing heavily and perspiring, like what had happened when Michelle was on top of his back. Just as things got hot and steamy, Mustafa came out with a loud yell, "No! No!" and pulled himself off Michelle.

She immediately recognized his response. He was reacting negatively to any kind of sex, in any shape or form. Michelle got her answer, although it was not what she had hoped for. She was eager to express her care and love right away, to soothe his anxiety. She held Mustafa's head against her chest and said, "Don't you worry about anything. My love for you is all-inclusive, and I'm here for you. It will all go away with time—time is the healer of problems, tragedies, and disappointments. You're mine and I'm yours, forever and ever." She then kissed him on the lips and set his body down to hold him in her grasp.

As they did the first night, they spent two more nights together in semi-perfect harmony. Yet, Michelle could tell that he was not as relaxed as he had been in the past. When she told Mustafa not to worry, with her help he would be able to resolve anything, and that she planned to visit him more frequently, Mustafa immediately handed her a copy of his college schedule and told her to visit him any time and as often as the schedule allowed. Michelle was pleased with his attitude. She was concerned that he would become reclusive and veer toward seeing her less often.

Nevertheless, Michelle's visits were enjoyable as Mustafa was popular and Michelle was a most beautiful and sociable companion. They could barely respond to the many social invitations that were extended to them, especially when Michelle was in town.

In a way, they became closer. Talking about his sexual problem gave Michelle a wider opening to discuss other subjects. As the second school year was about to start, she crouched on the floor, looking him straight in the eyes. She kissed him first and proceeded to ask him, "Don't you think it's time?"

"What do you mean?" he asked.

Michelle said, "I think it's time that we get engaged."

Mustafa was surprised at the question, aware of his problem. "Don't you think that my persistent circumstances would become an impasse related to engagement and eventual marriage?" He grabbed Michelle's face and looked at her straight on. "I know you are an angel, but I think we should wait for my hesitation to go away."

"Listen, Mustafa, we can have sex in so many ways, but above all, I love you as you are. I'm convinced that this, and other problems—if there are any—can be resolved in time. This is what love means! It means much more than marriage, but it could and should lead to marriage. It is for better or worse, and this is all that I'm going to say: 'I want to get engaged and then get married to none other than you.' End of story."

"I do not want to be selfish, but if you are sure, nothing would please me more," said Mustafa.

Michelle smiled broadly. "I'll tell my father right away!" After the call to William, she told Mustafa that her father was elated. "You're nine months from graduating, and he proposes that we marry right after graduation. Then it will be a graduation party and an engagement!"

Michelle's mood was boosted, although she could see that Mustafa was switching between happiness and concern. She was clearly happy, for she was sure she wanted to continue to be in his life, more than ever before. Unfortunately, she also knew that he was worried that his condition would never go away.

During one visit, Mustafa suggested that they go to a cocktail gathering at his managerial accounting professor's home. As they walked to the party, Mustafa told her that the professor, Amanda, was only a few years older than him. She was a graduate of MIT and was dating one of Hollywood's top movie stuntmen. When Michelle inquired further, he confirmed that Amanda was considered the most beautiful female faculty member at Stanford.

Mustafa added that Amanda's boyfriend made $100,000 per movie. Michelle quipped that Mustafa must have been interested in her somehow, as he was keeping up with his professor's news.

He said, "No, it is just that Amanda was prominently mentioned in one of Hollywood's papers, and the article was reprinted in the university paper."

Michelle noticed that Mustafa was calling his professor by her first name. Mustafa recognized that, and he then volunteered that the professor asked everyone in the fourteen-student class to call her by her first name.

As she was greeted by Amanda, Michelle noticed how beautiful she was. Yet she was not concerned, since she had full trust in Mustafa, and after all, he had his challenges to deal with. Michelle needed to talk to her father and did not want to wait; she asked Amanda if she could use her phone to call North Carolina before it got too late. She assured her there would be no cost to her, as Michelle would use a special long-distance code to pay for the calls.

Michelle talked to her father regarding some details about the planned engagement party, hung up the phone, and returned to Mustafa. A few minutes later, Amanda announced to the gathering that Michelle and Mustafa were getting engaged and were combining Mustafa's graduation party with their engagement.

Michelle realized then that the other woman had eavesdropped on her conversation with William.

Amanda joked, looking at Mustafa, "You can invite us to the graduation party!"

Michelle was not pleased with the situation but didn't say anything. They returned to Mustafa's room, and she slept in his arms all three following nights. Nothing transpired. Michelle had gotten used to the routine, not expecting anything new but hoping for what seemed like an elusive transformation. She was determined that she and Mustafa would be in each other's lives, one way or the other.

CHAPTER 18

When Michelle got home, she told her father that she was ready to start working at the farm right away.

"You're looking distinctly chipper since you arrived from Stanford. Is there good news to share?" said William.

"Yes, I think so. Mustafa said that I can prepare for our engagement anytime I want, provided I give him two months' notice. What do you say, Dad?" said Michelle cheerfully.

"That's my girl. I say you can start working at the farm in the mornings and spend the afternoons preparing for your engagement. It's going to be one of the most glorious engagements in North Carolina," said William.

Michelle spent much of her time trying to decide about her engagement party. Her father told her that she could budget things, without his input, within a $100,000 limit. As she consulted with Carol and Sara, she found out they were not of much help. She had to resort to consulting with her paternal aunt, Rose, whom she liked a lot, and Michelle's longtime housekeeper, Bertha.

Rose and Michelle's mother were close friends, and Bertha had been working at the house since Michelle was a small girl. Rose told Michelle to give herself at least four months to prepare for a big gala. Michelle told Rose that the important thing was to realize that it was both an engagement and graduation party. She reminded Rose that Mustafa had one semester left to graduate and wanted to set an exact date. She decided on the spot and told her aunt that it would be one month after Mustafa's commencement. Bertha excitedly began creating a draft menu for the event.

Michelle told Mustafa to call his father to let him know the date of the engagement. Mustafa had warned her that his father would try to convince him to wait for a while "until he got settled," with the ulterior motive of possibly Mustafa changing his mind in the meantime.

————

Ramzi was not keen on his son marrying an American girl. But Mustafa's independence from the family, and especially from his father, had progressed considerably.

"Father, I am going to marry with every intention of accommodating Michelle's circumstances. I've put her through the wringer with my never-ending entanglements—she has always helped me out on the spot, regardless of when or where. I love and respect Michelle beyond my imagination, and I do not want to wait past her choice of date. I am determined to make her as happy as I can."

His father's initial attempts failed to dissuade Mustafa. Ramzi called Mustafa back.

"Upon thinking about it, I realize that you have made up your mind. But if you want to honor me, you must do things properly."

Ramzi could tell Mustafa disliked it, but he compromised and agreed to infuse some Palestinian traditions into the steps leading to the engagement. One tradition entailed family involvement, where prominent members of the family ask for the bride's hand. In this case, Ramzi wanted three of his first cousins in Chicago and two second cousins in Argentina to form a committee to ask for Michelle's hand.

———

Mustafa called Michelle. "I have a surprise for you."

"Is it pleasant?" Michelle asked.

"It is just different, neither pleasant nor unpleasant. My father wanted me to wait till much later for us to have our engagement. I told him 'No way,' and then we reached a compromise. He called me back and told me that he had arranged for five of his cousins to come to Durham to ask for your hand from your father. They will be representing my father and the family. Three will be traveling from Chicago and two will arrive from Argentina. My dad chose some of his richest cousins for the occasion."

Michelle laughed, and said, "I don't care whether they are rich or poor! I've already accepted to be engaged to you. There is no need for anything else."

Slowly and methodically, Mustafa convinced Michelle that it was part of his Palestinian traditions. "My father needs to feel he has been consulted about and involved in the whole affair, and not abandoned by his eldest son."

"What do these rich cousins do?" Michelle asked.

"Each set works together. The three in Chicago own around 220 limousines and eighty buses, while the set in Argentina owns nine beef slaughterhouses and twelve wineries. The ones in Argentina could easily be many times richer if they would add pig slaughter services to their business, but they won't even consider it since they are moderately adherent Muslims, albeit with a liberal outlook."

In the end, Michelle said, "I have no problem with such formality if my father doesn't object, and I don't think he will. Will you accompany me to explain the situation to my father?"

"Of course," Mustafa agreed.

When they got to the house, Michelle told William, "Everything is as good as can be, but we may have encountered a small detour."

Mustafa interjected. "I believe that my father is feeling like he is being left out of the loop. To make him feel less abandoned, I have decided to stick to certain traditions. They are different than those in the United States."

"Mustafa, please explain yourself. Don't keep me guessing. What's happening here?" William asked.

Mustafa went through the steps, one at a time, and he had to clarify the traditional rationale behind each. "The inclusion of the high number of relatives is a good sign. They psychologically act as guarantors that the groom is honorable and sincere, with the hope that when the marriage takes place, it will be permanent."

William put his palm on his mouth and laughed. "So, you want me to pretend that I'm the decision maker and not Michelle? Do you really want that, Mustafa?"

Mustafa could see Michelle trying to hold back from expressing what she felt. He motioned for her and William to go ahead and speak their mind.

"We know well it's almost a game," she said, "but so many traditions are games that symbolize hope in most cases. Just like when we sing the national anthem, we put our hands on our hearts to symbolize that our commitment to the United States is coming from the heart. Do we know if this is the case with every person who places his or her hand on their heart? We don't. It's the same with Mustafa's cousins. They're just following a tradition."

"Sure, sure, I'll go along with that. I just wanted to give you two a bit of a hard time. You look too cozy together and I fancied some feather-ruffling," said William. "But I have to warn you two—although I will try my best, I'm not much of an actor." William smiled.

———

Within days, the Chicago relatives met the Argentine relatives at the airport. They drove five limousines all the way from Chicago, one for each of the cousins. When the cars arrived, William, Michelle, Mustafa, Rose, and Bertha were waiting in front of the house, watching the vehicles go through the gate and approach them slowly. One of the limousines flew a flag that looked unusual. It was the Jordanian flag, but Mustafa could not explain the situation to William and Michelle.

When the five cousins stepped out of the car, they could see the difference between the two sets. All three Chicago cousins were seriously overweight and almost busting open their shirts below their rosy cheeks. The two from Argentina were elegantly dressed, on the slim side, and exhibited a distinctly sophisticated demeanor.

Before even greeting each other, the elder cousin from Chicago, Nijad, asked Mustafa in Arabic why Rose and Bertha were there. The tradition called for men only, on both sides.

Mustafa had already received Nijad's same chauvinistic request over the phone but decided to ignore it. Mustafa said, "It is my decision, and not yours." This was the first instance of friction between the two.

All five approached Mustafa and kissed him on both cheeks. They then shook hands with William. The three from Chicago shook hands with Michelle, hesitantly with Rose, and not with Bertha. Mustafa knew the housekeeper's attire led them to perceive her as a servant, and could see that Bertha was not offended, but rather disgusted, by the lack of attention.

The two from Argentina took Michelle's right hand and kissed it. One of them, Carlos, said, "Welcome to the Makram family." The kissing of Michelle's hand was unexpected, and the welcoming statement eased the atmosphere.

Mustafa was keeping a close watch on all the participants. Despite William's promise to control his emotions, he obviously did not like the look of the Chicago cousins at all and was probably wondering what to do with the three gangster-like, overfed guys.

Mustafa wanted an opening to deflate the crude and arrogant posture of his Chicago cousins, so he asked them about the flag in a dismissive fashion. "How about this flag? Where did you buy it, Nijad?" asked Mustafa rather sarcastically. One of the Argentine cousins asked the same.

Nijad ignored the question and grabbed Mustafa's arm, took him to the side, and whispered in his ear, "Don't you scandalize me. Your father must have told you: I had to pay the head of security $25,000 to be assigned the Honorary Counsel of Jordan in Chicago. How am I going to get my money's worth if I do not hoist it at every opportunity? Instead of praising me, I can tell from your tone that you are trying to belittle me. You are a difficult bastard."

Mustafa whispered back into Nijad's ear, "No, you are a sleazy and cheap bastard." The friction and animosity between the two continued with a sharper tone.

As they went into the house, Mustafa could tell that William and Michelle understood that the Argentine cousins were much more sophisticated than the three from Chicago. Although never having lived in an English-speaking country, they spoke far better English than the Chicago cousins. They all sat in the living room, minus Bertha, who had resumed her duties. Carlos started talking, telling Michelle, William, and Rose that what they were doing was a tradition and did not mean much, other than the cousins blessing the plan of the lovers for an eventual marriage. The Chicago three disagreed and insisted that if William were to object, there would be no engagement and no future wedding.

The two sets got into a heated argument. Mustafa, becoming sourer and angrier with each passing moment, asked everyone to shut up and listen to him. "I don't need anyone's permission or blessing to get engaged or married; I am getting engaged with or without the involvement of anybody. Michelle does not need William to approve anything, although she respects him and loves him without reservation. While she seeks his blessings, she does not need them. We are both adults and we know what we are doing. I am having this gathering to please my father. I don't want him to feel neglected. That is all, and it is the end of the story."

Rami, one of the Chicago cousins, stood up and said that no engagement could take place without William's blessing.

Mustafa stood up again. "Don't waste your time. Our getting engaged is a done deal—let me offer you some drinks. I know all five of you drink alcohol, and if you were so stuck on religious and cultural norms, you would not be drinking in the first place. Get off this subject, let me get some drinks, and let us find out how many kids each of you have!"

Mustafa saw how proud William and Michelle were of him for having taken control of the gathering. William looked at Michelle and winked at her.

Nijad, again following tradition, said to Mustafa, "You don't need to serve us. Let the fiancée serve us, not you, Cousin. You are a man."

Mustafa became even more incensed and said to him sarcastically, "Are you forgetting you are in America? I am going to follow an Arab saying, 'If you dwell within a group for forty days, either you adapt or part ways.' Are you leaving the United States anytime soon, Nijad?"

From that moment on, it was Mustafa's show, with William and Michelle devouring his every statement and move. Mustafa took his future father-in-law to the side and asked him to stand in the middle of the room, to thank the cousins and to let them know that the engagement is a done deal, no matter what. William first hesitated as he did not want to appear antagonistic, but he did in the end say what Mustafa advised him to say, only using a softer tone.

The couple went into another room to reserve dinner for nine at a very fancy restaurant. Rose was included. Michelle made the reservations after Mustafa told her that although Bertha had prepared dinner for the group, he was not inclined to give the Chicago cousins free rein to say whatever they wanted at the house. A restaurant setting would limit such talk.

The nine went out and had a reasonably good time. Mustafa made sure the cousins were invited back to the house for after-dinner drinks. To separate his feelings between the two sets, he told the Argentine cousins that he and Michelle would love to visit

Argentina sometime soon. Carlos welcomed the idea and encouraged them to plan to visit him after the engagement party.

After the cousins left, William shook Mustafa's hand and told him how much he appreciated what he did—not the least of which was the manly way he did it.

"I knew it all along. I knew that you didn't want to show it, but I knew it. You are my Sir Galahad—yes, you are," said Michelle, and then gave him a kiss and a long hug. Mustafa heard Rose say to Bertha in the background that the farm needed young blood, and that Mustafa and Michelle would certainly be it.

CHAPTER 19

Before Mustafa flew back to Stanford, he and Michelle agreed to alternate visits, with each going to see the other once a month, with a four-day stay each time. Once every three months, Michelle would bring Carol and Sara with her, and he could invite Willie and Faris over to the farm. At the same time, he was widening his circle of friends. They were all happily single except one: Frank Summerfield, from Dallas. Frank's girlfriend got pregnant, which forced an early marriage.

When Michelle came to visit Mustafa, there was no shortage of social activities. They dined with one or more friends every single night. When Mustafa flew to Durham, he was joined by Willie and Faris. Mustafa and Michelle were getting acclimated to sharing the same bed, in both places, without having sex.

On one occasion, Frank and his wife, Sandy, were having a Texas barbecue dinner for a dozen friends. As Mustafa and Michelle were mixing with their friends, Frank introduced a very good-looking woman, Amanda, to Mustafa and Michelle. She was Frank's paternal first cousin.

Amanda looked at Mustafa keenly while ignoring Michelle, and said, "We have met before, haven't we?"

Mustafa looked at her briefly and said, "Sure, sure, Dr. Summerfield. I took your managerial accounting class."

"But you didn't take my Quantitative Business Analysis class afterward," said Amanda.

"No, but I will, for I am working on research which relates to what you are teaching in the quantitative course," answered Mustafa.

"Well, I recall you were tops in my managerial accounting class—I wouldn't mind having you again. I also recall you wore very stylish men's shirts. I've never seen them worn here. Where do you get them from? I have a brother who is always looking for unique men's clothing," she asked with a faint smile.

"Well, my father handles the accounting for a French shirt manufacturer in the Middle East, and they keep sending him samples of their latest designs," said Mustafa.

She looked at Michelle and said, "From one woman to another, Mustafa really looks good wearing this style of shirt." Amanda left without sharing anything else with her.

Michelle didn't like Amanda's attitude at all and said, "I still think she looks too young to be a professor. What is she, an instructor?"

"No, as I said before, she finished college at the age of twenty and got her PhD five years later, all from Harvard and MIT. She is a whiz professor and a consultant to several computer companies in the area," Mustafa answered.

"Does she have a brother?" asked Michelle.

"That I don't know. Maybe she was asking for her boyfriend, but did not want to say it publicly," said Mustafa.

"Or maybe she was asking to charm someone she desires to be her boyfriend," said Michelle. When he told her that what she was saying didn't make any sense, Michelle said, "You underestimate what women do to be with the chosen one! Look at me! I did, and I will do anything for you to be always mine. Look at her shamelessly pretending she had never met you before—her own student."

Mustafa told her not to sell herself short. "I have been attracted to you for a long time, and it was my attraction that sealed the deal, not your persistence."

"I know you well by now, Mustafa of Palestine. You don't want to shortchange anyone but yourself. It's OK with me. Just don't carry it too far," said Michelle.

Afterward, Michelle approached Frank and asked him why his cousin was not there anymore, so curious about Amanda's hints to Mustafa. In the end, Frank told her that Amanda didn't have any brothers, only one sister. Michelle said nothing to Mustafa until later, after they went back to his apartment. She told him outright that she thought Dr. Summerfield was interested in him.

Mustafa laughed it off and said, "Listen, Michelle—half the teaching staff are eyeing her. Why should she be interested in someone six to seven years younger, and a student at that? I don't think the administration would stand for a student/teacher relationship, especially involving a student studying under her. If caught, the college administration would take action against her, whether the relationship had already ceased or was still ongoing."

"Mark my words, she's going to try, and try hard. So, be careful. Not that I'm concerned…I just don't want her to pester you," said Michelle.

"If she does pester me—which I don't believe she will, not even make a move toward me—she will be the loser for it. Like a famous poetess implied, 'In you I am separated from myself, as our souls have become one.'"

"Where do you get these words? You always charm and disarm me. They are so soothing and beautiful," said Michelle.

"Well, since you know English and French, it must be from the third language I know, Arabic," he said playfully.

Michelle went back to Durham, with Mustafa continuing to speak to her twice a day. She had given him one of several 800 phone numbers reserved for her father's marketing company, which not only marketed the Parkers' own milk but also helped fourteen other smaller dairy farms. The discussions took half an hour each, on average. Every conversation included Michelle's regular question: had Amanda contacted him yet?

Mustafa naturally answered with "No," but as the same persistent question was continually asked, he repeated "No!" several times to emphasize his belief that he did not expect Amanda to contact him.

Several weeks later, his answer—after a pause and a sigh—was "Yes. She called me to make sure I take her quantitative analysis course."

"Wow, Mustafa, give me a kiss over the phone. I deserve one because I've been right all along!" said Michelle, trying to conceal her concern about Amanda's contact.

"Shoot—I'll give you a dozen kisses," said Mustafa.

"No, I want one specific kiss as an appreciation for being right about Professor Amanda," she said mischievously.

"She wanted me to see her in her nearby townhouse. I politely turned that down and proposed to see her in her office, which she accepted."

Michelle feigned disinterest. "Go and see Amanda. It will give us more things to talk about."

But her concern was obvious to Sara and Carol when Michelle

brought up the subject the following day. The two friends were intrigued, as they were eager to find a new topic to discuss with Michelle, but they did not want it to be that kind of issue, worrying about a potential competitor. Michelle pretended to have no concerns, yet indirectly was giving herself away, transmitting serious apprehension. Both Carol and Sara wanted to soothe her feelings by asking that the three of them keep discussing Amanda's "futile approach," as Carol put it. They wanted to make sure to give Michelle as much support as possible.

Mustafa called Michelle soon after. "I was totally wrong, and I want to be as open as possible. You were right on the button. As soon as I walked into Amanda's office, she hit on me."

"What did she do?" asked Michelle.

"She asked me to accompany her to a picnic to meet some friends of hers. The picnic is going to be held at a ranch specializing in serving the best steaks in the area. She says that she is a consultant to the corporate owners of the ranch, who own sixty-two other ranches. She also mentioned that she might have a new prospect, handling market analysis for another steak restaurant chain. That business has a large presence in a different region of the country. In that case, she could possibly use my assistance," Mustafa said.

"Wow, wow, wow! She's not only hitting on you but also trying to lure you with financial benefits! She really must fancy you— wouldn't you say so?" asked Michelle.

"Fancy me, maybe, but how about if she is making the same effort toward a dozen students?" wondered Mustafa.

"No, she's not. She has her eyes on you. You recall how she noticed your shirts—that is not a sign of someone looking all around. No, she has you in her eyesight, and in her crosshairs, sort of. She thinks you're a deer, blinded and frozen by a strong light beam. In this case, it would be the fact she's a professor, and you're a student, and possibly in need of money," said Michelle.

"Don't forget how I took care of my Chicago relatives. If need be, I will take care of Amanda just as easily," said Mustafa.

This time, without getting angry, Michelle told him that she knew that, but the whole thing was intriguing and worth discussing intellectually.

"Just leave it up to me," Mustafa said. "When the right time comes, I will be crisp and decisive and make her unsuccessfully wait, and in time we will savor the results."

Michelle halfheartedly agreed without any argument.

In the next phone call, Mustafa said, "I have thought about the whole thing and have concluded that it is not much of anything. Of course, your concern is not trivial, so because of that, I have decided to act. Please drop the subject altogether until I can think of something against Amanda's advances."

Once again, Michelle acquiesced and stuck to her promise.

———

When it was Mustafa's turn to go to Durham, he asked Michelle if she minded coming to Stanford instead. When she asked why, he answered that he had plans to camp with her alone throughout her four-day visit. Michelle accepted the invitation and two days later, flew to California. Once there, Mustafa told her that his plans had changed, and he was having a large gathering with drinks and hors d'oeuvres the following day.

"I am going to formally speak to the guests. Please do not comment on anything I say, including anything you might disagree with. We can talk about it later."

Michelle again consented, but with clear trepidation and skepticism.

As the guests trickled in, Michelle saw that Amanda had been invited. Mustafa did not wait long to speak. He asked that all raise their glasses and said, holding Michelle's hand, "I know that I have spoken to most of you about our upcoming engagement in around three months. Well, I am here to announce that Michelle and I are inviting everyone here to our engagement party in Durham, North Carolina."

Mustafa could see that Michelle was totally and pleasantly surprised, even though he had not consulted with her. And she obviously understood why he had invited Amanda. This public declaration would assert to Amanda that Michelle was his one and only love.

"I don't want to think about the engagement party details. I'm just delighting in everything you said—your confirmation of love," Michelle whispered to Mustafa. "I particularly applaud the way you created the occasion to relay your message to Amanda."

Mustafa nodded and whispered back that, if possible, she should avoid socializing with Amanda at the gathering. Michelle nodded. In a matter of twenty minutes, Amanda approached Mustafa, thanked him for inviting her, and proceeded to excuse herself.

That evening, Mustafa told Michelle that he had advanced the date. At first, she was furious, but he told her that he knew Amanda would not take no for an answer. The advancement of the engagement was to make sure Amanda could not attend. On that date, the business school was having a large gathering.

"It sounds good, Mustafa," said Michelle. "But I'm not sure if you have chosen the right approach. Do you think it looks like we're getting scared of Amanda's moves?"

"No, I am not scared of anything. But since I am planning to take her quantitative analysis course, I wanted to send her a clear message in advance."

Michelle finally conceded.

Mustafa called Ramzi to inform him that the engagement had been advanced. Ramzi understood. He had no choice; he himself could not make it in the first place.

Ramzi said he would immediately contact his cousins to alert them that the date of the engagement was advanced and would also alert other relatives sprinkled all over the Americas, who had expressed interest in attending the engagement party. Mustafa asked him not to have more than thirty relatives attend, and that the large contingent of relatives needed to attend the wedding, rather than show up at the engagement party. Ramzi agreed and tried to limit the attendance of the celebration-happy members of the family.

———

Michelle immediately called Sara and Carol and told them what had transpired. They had sensed that Mustafa was that kind of guy, yet they could not help having doubts when they previously learned about Amanda having hit on him. The incident invigorated both Mustafa's and Michelle's love. She recruited her girlfriends to speed up the arrangements for the engagement. Mustafa had told her he would call Willie and Faris and explain that the engagement date was advanced to take place on a busy weekend at Stanford when Amanda would be occupied. The graduation party would now be separate.

Mustafa and Michelle sat down one evening, a week before the party, to take stock of the plans and details.

"My Aunt Rose is happy to get involved," said Michelle. "She's comfortable in her own right and told my father that she will foot the bill for all the extra costs as a result of the rush orders. She reminded him that I'm the only member of the new generation on her side of the family, and she wants to participate and feel that she's an integral part of our beautiful love story."

"I contacted my Argentine relatives and asked if they could summon all the relatives for me to thank them, explaining that in America, engagements and weddings are more a celebration for the prospective bride and less so for the groom."

"OK," Michelle said, making notes on a schedule.

"The Argentine relatives will arrive one day before the engagement," said Mustafa.

"What about those in Chicago?" Michelle asked nervously.

"I approached them to tell them how great they are, since their cooperation is necessary for my guidelines to work. I tried to boost their egos in a contrived way, telling them that they are so distinguished that they need to be less visible and less engaging for the family of the bride to feel important. Most of them liked to hear that kind of talk, especially being praised openly. Unfortunately, I think a few of them figured out my real motive."

The Argentine relatives helped and managed to control the number of family guests to stay within the perimeters set by Mustafa and Ramzi. Thirty-one cousins came to the engagement party after the Argentine cousins managed to whittle it down from around one hundred. Nevertheless, the Chicago cousins had to show off their limos: they brought six of them down to transport all thirty-one family members. Michelle noted that the contingent of Chicago cousins was all males.

"They did that on purpose, giving themselves enough freedom

to pick local females for their seedy pleasures," said Mustafa.

On the other hand, the Parkers' entourage was reserved and very respectable. Mustafa mostly associated with his schoolmates, both from Duke and Stanford. Above all, he leaned on Willie and Faris to execute his plan, and they did so with great success, even though the two were as fond of Zeina as they were of Michelle.

"Have you been able to convince Zeina to have dinner with you, Willie?" asked Mustafa.

"No, she turned down several of my casual invitations. Every time I talk to her, I sense a great sadness on her part. In the end, I lost track of her. I do not know whether she's dating or not. None of our common acquaintances see her socializing, but she's still living with her father," said Willie.

The engagement party went exceedingly well. It was blessed by a religious man who called himself a nondenominational pastor. The Chicago cousins tried to have one of them read short Qur'anic verses. Faris, at the request of Mustafa, stopped them and reminded them that for all practical purposes, the nondenominational pastor was no pastor at all. His blessings amounted to good wishes for the bride and groom only and did not conflict with the teachings of any religion.

Michelle was radiant and very poised. She acted graciously toward Mustafa's cousins, especially his sophisticated Argentine cousins. She told them that they intended to spend their honeymoon in Argentina when the time came. They, in return, promised to organize a grand tour of Argentina and to introduce the two to Mustafa's almost one hundred cousins there.

William was full of joy, especially that all hurried arrangements went as planned. Mustafa and Michelle danced extensively, radiant together. It was a night to savor and to remember.

The only strange thing at the engagement party was the presence of Amanda. Neither one of them expected her to be there after he moved the date up.

————

Soon after the engagement party, Michelle and Mustafa went back to their routine, alternating in visiting each other. Things were proceeding smoothly and lovingly between them, except for the niggling issue of Amanda.

"Mustafa, did you invite Amanda to the engagement party?"

"Yes, at the very beginning. But it was only in passing, well before I made the date change."

Michelle informed him of subtleties she thought Mustafa may have missed. "Amanda was subdued most of the time but was eyeing you with both resentment and admiration. She wouldn't make eye contact with me. When we were dancing, she was obviously quite disturbed. I told you she was interested in you."

"I'm surprised at how much you noticed Amanda's continued interest. I agree that her attention is inappropriate and not welcome. Please be assured, Michelle, that it is only you whom I love, and to that end, would you mind choosing and advancing the approximate date of the wedding? I want to relay the date to our guests tonight, in Amanda's presence."

She agreed wholeheartedly, and she knew well of Mustafa's noble motives for advancing the wedding date. It was advanced, despite Ramzi's objections. Ramzi was a classical and traditional middle-class male in Amman, Jordan. Mustafa never shared with him the presence of Michelle in his life until they agreed to get engaged. This time, Mustafa planned not to invite Amanda to the wedding.

CHAPTER 20

As if the preparations for the engagement were not challenging enough, now Mustafa and the bride-to-be and her family were getting stressed out, as they needed to get ready for the wedding to take place within very few months. The undertaking was several times more demanding than the engagement party. Mustafa was happy to see that again, Rose came to lead the cavalry. She set up organizational folders for every aspect of the wedding—for the maids of honor, the groom's best man, the attendants, and the ushers. All in all, there were twenty-two folders, each representing a specific task, person, or group. Bertha joined in and undertook the tasks that fell under her housekeeping domain.

Mustafa's choice of the advanced wedding date was intended to eliminate the chance of meeting Amanda in class before the wedding invitations went out. He managed to accomplish his plans regarding Amanda. It was a feeling of relief, giving him some breathing room.

Then his thoughts turned to two matters: his inability to engage sexually and the irritations coming from his Chicago cousins. The cousins were obsessed with showing off, and they were likely to do anything to prove they were important—a clear case of an inferiority complex. They came directly from his father's village and hit it big financially. The problem was that they didn't know the social limits of what money could, or should, buy.

During the arrangements, Mustafa spent a lot of time with Rose, who liked Mustafa as much as William did.

"I always enjoy your company, Mustafa. Has Michelle ever told you the story of my thwarted romance?"

"No, she hasn't. I'm sorry it didn't work out for you. What happened?" asked Mustafa.

"Fifty years ago, I was once in love with a young man, Samuel, whose grandfather was considered Black because he was the son of a white man and a Black woman. Samuel was 12.5 percent Black, and so was similarly considered a Black man in North Carolina."

"I take it that being Black in North Carolina at that time was a disadvantage?" asked Mustafa superficially.

Rose nodded. "Still is. Samuel was repeatedly harassed by a white supremacist group, and legally, I could not marry him in North Carolina. As I was about to move with Samuel to Montana, he was chased out of state. I never saw him again, despite our attempts to contact each other. In one letter that slipped through, he told me he was getting frequent threats not to contact me." Rose sighed. "I learned later that his letters were intercepted at the post office by a mailman belonging to the same white supremacist group." Rose put her hand on Mustafa's arm.

"Listen, Mustafa. I've become fond of you, almost as much as I'm fond of Michelle. If you ever need help, just contact me. You know that even the most passionate lovers feud from time to time. Just do not hesitate to call me and I will be fair and impartial. I'm ten years older than William, and I raised him when our parents passed away; so look at me as your surrogate grandmother. Please don't hesitate. I want you to be the happiest couple. You deserve to be, and I deserve to watch you nurture each other in full bliss. Do you follow me, Mustafa?"

He nodded and explained about the problems he was having with his Chicago cousins.

"I appreciate your telling me about them and letting me think about it. Perhaps I can come up with a solution. But I really adore your Argentine cousins. They are so fine and so sophisticated," said Rose.

"I agree with you and promise to tell you everything at any sign of trouble. I don't think there will be any, though, since Michelle is my true love, and is most accommodating."

Rose kissed him on his forehead. "I feel you're carrying a heavy load. I want you to not only live for yourself and Michelle but to make up for what I missed, having lost Samuel. You see, Mustafa, I'm living vicariously through you and Michelle. Do you know what *vicariously* means?" asked Rose.

"No, I don't," he said.

"It means I'm living through your own experiences, which I want to be wholesome, enthusiastic, and most loving."

Mustafa looked at her and said, "I am confident we will not disappoint you."

"You had better not," said Rose.

This exchange between Mustafa and Rose was the sincerest he'd had in quite a while, except for the conversations he used to have with Willie. Things were falling into place, and he was feeling very positive about himself. The successful plans so far made Mustafa feel that he could take care of any challenge, especially the one that gave him the majority of his troubles and deep regrets. He wanted so badly to be the lover he once was, especially since it involved his most passionate and glorious love, Michelle.

————

Mustafa was confident he could overcome "that problem." He decided not to spare any effort to rectify things, once and for all, and above all, he decided to take the initiative. He thought to himself and decided that he would avoid Michelle mounting him over his back. That was what he had experienced at the rally. He told her to travel to Stanford as often as she could. She said yes, except that she didn't want to neglect preparations for the wedding.

On Michelle's first trip, Mustafa bought two expensive bottles of French wine. Michelle shared them with him. She managed to drink half a bottle, but he drank one and a half. When they got into bed, he immediately took off his clothes. Unfortunately, it didn't take long—and regardless of Michelle's quick interactions—for Mustafa to doze off.

In the morning, he felt awful. On the other hand, Michelle felt great, despite the lack of real activity. She could tell that he had succumbed to the influence of alcohol. Mustafa decided to try again during Michelle's following trip.

That time he was fully ready, having decided not to touch any alcohol. In bed, he took Michelle's clothes off piece by piece and managed to make a soft frontal approach. Michelle was helping him out slowly and with special care, and things progressed farther than at any time in the past. When he almost reached a climax, he started to breathe too heavily and to perspire profusely. He tried to pay no attention to his convulsion-like reaction, yet his breathing, perspiration, and moaning increased at a very fast and erratic pace. He was trying so hard that he was exhibiting spasms.

Michelle got worried and could not withstand watching him in agony. She was concerned that he was perhaps having a heart attack or some other nasty reaction. She pushed Mustafa out and off her and asked, "Are you all right, my love? You're trying too hard. Don't worry—it will happen gradually. Don't worry about me. I'm happy as it is. Time will take care of it, I'm sure. This time you almost made it." She hugged him passionately as his head hung over her shoulder.

Mustafa skipped two trips before he attempted to have sex again. He psyched himself for the occasion. He and Michelle had just one glass of scotch each. He felt he was in maximum physical and mental shape. Again, he was on top of Michelle, and she was trying to pace their interaction. All was going smoothly until he heard a dog barking distantly. The bark was similar to what he had heard during the attack on him at the rally. From that point onward, the whole process fizzled.

Again, Michelle pushed him out and off her and asked him what was wrong. Mustafa told her that he could recall a dog barking while the man was on top of him. "At that moment, I remember smelling his oily and dirty hair."

Michelle grabbed his face and said, "Oh, God have mercy. This is OK, Mustafa. Little by little, you will get over it."

Mustafa said, "I am sorry. I spoiled the evening for you again!"

"You did nothing of the sort. It is great to have you in my arms. Let us stay in bed naked all night." Mustafa agreed. If Michelle had in mind creating the opportunity for another attempt that evening, it just didn't happen.

It was the last time Mustafa tried to make love to Michelle. He became very disappointed in himself and started to withdraw and speak as little as possible. Michelle tried every other way to revive his lively interactions to the previous level, but with very little luck. Yet, she was not discouraged. She told Mustafa that she was convinced that it would all go away.

———

Upon Michelle's arrival for her sixth visit after the engagement, Mustafa looked somewhat more animated. They spent the afternoon in San Jose, where he bought four shirts of his favorite brand. He also took Michelle to a very upscale women's shop and bought her a most gorgeous dress. Michelle was so happy that he was engaged, with a very refined and discriminating taste. She just loved the dress.

In the evening they spent hours on the couch, this time Mustafa sitting next to Michelle, whistling and humming. He was ever so slowly sipping on a glass of scotch on the rocks while Michelle drank wine. He continued whistling and humming while escorting Michelle to bed. There, he massaged Michelle's back, arms, and thighs. He did not touch her breasts or come close to her crotch and went to sleep, holding her in his arms. Michelle noticed that Mustafa's attitude was unusual. He looked more sanguine.

In the morning, after Michelle left the bedroom, he stayed behind, packing her suitcase. He carried it down the stairs slowly, again whistling and humming in a hushed way. Michelle noticed him bringing the suitcase down. She had planned for one more day together. She looked at him without speaking, totally surprised. He sat on the couch next to her and held her left hand with both his hands.

He looked at Michelle, turned serious, and said, "One of my many weaknesses is that I don't know how to beat around the bush—I may be smart, but I need to be more circumspect. This always happens when the subject is serious. This is so very serious. I think you agree with me that nothing can go on unless it maintains a modicum of balance, don't you? You are my love, and you will remain my love, and will continue till the day I die. But despite all, we cannot go on like this because there is no balance in our relationship. Sex is an essential ingredient in any loving relationship. I and I alone am unable to provide you with such an ingredient, and as such, this relationship must end. And end right away, before I cause you much more harm."

"Oh, no, this can't be! What are you doing? Why are you doing this? Are you out of your mind? What has gone into your head?!" she yelled in a high and screeching voice, screaming in fright. "You're the love of my life, and I can't do without you! Why are you doing this?"

Mustafa hugged her and squeezed her against his chest as she cried, shedding globs of tears over him. She kept crying, whimpering, and gasping for air for quite a long time. "You can't do this. You don't mean it," she kept repeating.

"If I did not love you, I would have selfishly gone on. But such a person should know his limitations. In the end, his realization tends to help him, and will save others from his inadequacies. Although my limitations developed due to unforeseen and unfortunate circumstances, they are still serious, life-transforming handicaps. Who else could have helped me overcome most of my problems more than you? And you have been patient and persistent, beyond any call of duty. I just don't want to continue deluding myself that my condition is transient. It is not, and as such, I want to save you from the consequences of my serious and pivotal shortcomings."

"If only you could feel how much I love you, you would not be saying the things you have said! I can go on and on, but you seem to have made up your mind. You will come to your senses before too long. You will. Mark my words," she said.

Through the window, Michelle noticed that a taxi had parked in front of the apartment. She immediately realized that Mustafa had planned everything and seemed to be determined.

In reaction to his preparation, she said forcefully and sarcastically, "I'm not going to humble myself. You will come to your senses. But it must come from you, once you realize that what you're doing is wrong, unfair, and traumatic. It is stupid. Thank you for packing my suitcase."

As they went out toward the taxicab, he hugged her ever so tightly, with tears pouring out of his eyes. When he let go of her, she took a step down and stopped. She then took the same step up, looked Mustafa straight in the eyes, and said, "We talked about this recently. We questioned why you were trying to decide for me. I love you and I don't want to leave. I will be happy with things as they are. While it all happened before we knew each other, the reaction was discovered after we fell in love. Have you thought about how my father and Rose will feel when they hear about this? You're not being fair to me, yourself, or them. How about Willie and Faris?" All the time, Michelle cried and wiped away her tears.

"Listen to me, my love. I have not slept for more than a couple of hours a night since I experienced this ugly inability the last time I tried. My making you so miserable has been on my mind every minute of my existence since. I just cannot take it anymore. I am so guilt-ridden—I cannot see straight nor think straight. I cannot steal years from your life trying to fix something that may never be fixed. It would be too selfish of me. You are now twenty-three, in the prime of your life, and you should be at the peak of your sexual activity. Instead, here we are trying to do the impossible. You need to be fair to yourself and recognize that the way things are is unacceptable and unworkable. If it has not damaged our relations so far, it surely will in the future," said Mustafa.

"You must have been thinking of this for a long time since you sound well-prepared and determined. As I said, I'm not going to humble myself any further. I will bury myself in my grief and disappointment. Nevertheless, you're and will continue to be my love. I forgive you, and I hope you can forgive yourself. I want you to. I don't want you to flagellate yourself with guilt—I want you to be happy. Otherwise, you will make me feel miserable. What can I say? You have been the core of my love and of my life. I don't know what else to say," said Michelle.

She turned around and tried to go down, but her knees buckled. Mustafa had to support her. He looked at her as tears again came down his cheeks and said, "I wish it was different. Perfection is for the Lord, and man is here to suffer. This is all that I have to say."

He walked her to the taxi that would take Michelle to the airport. Before she left, Mustafa kissed her on the forehead and said, "I will be in Durham shortly to pay my respects to William and Rose. They deserve to hear it all from me. Please don't let Rose know about my condition. I will tell her myself."

The taxi pulled away and Michelle continued to cry all the way to the San Jose airport. The taxicab driver had to stop three times to calm her down. At the airport, she called William to inform him that she was returning early. When William inquired, she told him not to worry about it, and that she would explain the situation upon her return.

When she arrived, she was met by her father in front of the house. She hugged William and started crying, then asked him if they could talk inside. They sat around the kitchen table, where Michelle gradually stopped crying and took a deep breath. She explained to him that Mustafa decided to end their relationship after experiencing serious convulsions during his attempts to make love to her and that it all was a reaction to what he had gone through at the rally. When William asked if they had tried to fix the problem, she told him that they both did everything possible, short of consulting a psychiatrist, but that Mustafa had consulted with his family physician.

William was more than surprised. A sense of loss descended upon him as his voice got quieter and his expressions lost clarity. He didn't try to console his daughter until much later, as he was in shock. Michelle was most considerate toward Mustafa. She told William that although she disagreed with him; she was sure he ended it because he loved her and did not want her to suffer. She told William that Mustafa planned to visit him and Rose soon, out of respect, and that she decided on the flight not to tell Rose and to leave it up to Mustafa to tell her.

———

Immediately after Michelle left, Mustafa called Willie and Faris on a conference call. He thought he was ready to tell them without hesitation, but it did not work that way. He choked before he said a word and asked them to give him a minute. He composed himself somewhat and he cleared his thoughts.

"This is more difficult than telling it to Michelle. Michelle and I have decided to call it off." He then took a long pause, without either man saying a thing. "No, I decided to call it off. I did not want to be unfair to her."

"What in the hell are you talking about? Are you serious or is this a sick joke?" said Willie.

"No, I am serious. I had to do it. There was no other solution," said Mustafa.

"What are you talking about, man? What's the problem in the first place that can't be resolved?" said Willie.

Faris interjected, "Yes, what's the problem? This makes no sense."

"I think I seriously owe you both an explanation," said Mustafa.

"Damned right you owe us an explanation, and it'd better be good. This will be your second fucking failure, first with Zeina and now with Michelle. I somehow feel you're full of yourself and can't handle love and attention," said Willie.

"There are only six people that will know about this, you two included. Promise me you will share it with no one," said Mustafa.

"In the name of God, man, get on with it. Nobody is going to tell anything about anybody. Just get on with it," said Faris.

"Here it is. Since the incident at the rally, I have lost any and all ability to engage in sex, as if it's no longer part of me," said Mustafa.

"You mean all the time Michelle was visiting with you and you staying at her house, you haven't slept together?" asked Willie.

"Not even one time, and it was all me. I thought that such a handicap would come to an end, but it has not. I don't think it is fair to keep Michelle holding out for a resolution. Nothing has changed for two years, and that is long enough for her to wait— although she said she was willing to wait forever. I cannot accept that. In time, she will forget about me, and I may get over it or keep simmering in my own juice. This is the whole story. All I want you to do is to console her, as she was heartbroken when she left Stanford. I need you to do it right away, as I plan to pay my respect in person to William and Rose sometime next week…if they accept to receive me."

"I don't know what to say. This thing is difficult to tackle, and even difficult to discuss. As far as I'm concerned, I need to digest it before I speak further. Oh, God, everyone thought you were the perfect couple! This is the strangest thing I've ever heard. I'd hate to be in your shoes. Do you have anything to add, Faris?" said Willie.

Faris said that he was as perplexed as Willie and also needed to think about it before he could speak. When Mustafa told them that he only shared his decision with Michelle this morning, Willie advised him to stay busy, to get together with friends, and that he was willing to fly over to see him if need be. Mustafa said that he felt he could handle it, but he had cried half a dozen times since Michelle left.

———

Two days later, Willie and Faris went to see Michelle. At first, it was hugs, followed by complete silence. Michelle asked them how Mustafa was.

Willie answered, "You know him well—what do you think he's going through? He's crying his heart out. He says he's barely slept an hour each night. I guess you're probably going through the same thing, so I don't need to say more."

Michelle started crying rather quietly before she said, "He is obsessed with punishing himself. He thinks this is one way he can show others that he cares…I just don't know!"

"I know what you mean. Maybe there is a wailing wall here in the United States where you and he can mope. You two can meet there and compare who is more heartbroken! For the last two days, I felt I needed to join you over there. Here is Faris—he has been dumbfounded, and he has spoken little about the subject since we first heard from Mustafa," said Willie.

Michelle said nothing much, except she kept shaking her head. "My father's very sad. He's been so fond of Mustafa and thought of him as a true son," said Michelle before she broke down, kneeling on the floor, sobbing.

Willie and Faris helped her up and tried to calm her down. It took another twenty minutes for Willie and Faris to ease out of the visit—it was getting challenging and nerve-racking for all three.

A week later, it was Mustafa's turn to visit, first Rose at her house, and then William. He had called Rose and told her that he was taking her up on her invitation to seek her help, under the conditions she had described. He quickly discerned that Rose had no clue about his sexual dilemma and his separation from Michelle. He told her that the problem was particular to him, and that Michelle was the innocent party in this affair.

He started by telling her first about his experience at the rally. Rose could barely believe what she was hearing. "You mean this happened to you in North Carolina—in these United States?!" she exclaimed.

"Yes, but the aftereffects of my traumatic experience are much worse," said Mustafa. Rose stared at him with an inquisitive look, waiting for further explanation. Mustafa told her straight out and in plain English that, as a result, he could no longer perform sexually.

Rose was quick to ask, "Had you had sex before the rally?"

When he told her that he had sex many times before, in Amman and London, she leaned back into her recliner and asked how Michelle was managing. He told Rose that he had cancelled the wedding to be fair to Michelle.

Rose was shocked at the news and kept saying that the whole thing would most likely be salvageable. Mustafa disagreed with her, informing her that he was so guilt-ridden that he could no longer sleep or concentrate on anything. Every time he touched Michelle, he felt he was misleading her. He asked Rose if the two of them could go to see William together. It would be best if he did not see Michelle then, or in the future, he told Rose.

Rose became convinced that the relationship had become irreparably severed through Mustafa's strong initiative. They headed to see William, who was most gracious toward Mustafa. Michelle had already shared everything with her father but asked him to wait for Mustafa's visit and explanation. William was most anxious to hear what caused this rupture. It was Rose who explained to William that Mustafa's rape experience caused him to lose his ability to have sex, and that he had not known about his lack of performance until he attempted to have sex with Michelle.

After he finished telling the details of the story, William entreated him to stay in their lives as a friend. Mustafa explained that as much as he wanted to be in their life, it would be more practical, especially for Michelle, for him to disappear from the picture altogether.

"I believe I have done enough damage to last two lifetimes, and for the sake of my continued sanity, I need to be less selfish. I need my actions, difficult as they may be, to benefit everyone else—I need to do no more damage even though I realize I had planned none of it," Mustafa added.

Both Rose and William went silent for a long couple of minutes. After once again repeating that he would not change anything, Mustafa expressed that having met them was the crowing experience of his life. He then excused himself and called a taxi, and within fifteen minutes, he was gone.

———

Mustafa went to see Willie and Faris. He told them how gracious William and Rose had been and that he felt good about sealing the separation. Yet, their sense of loss for him—and for them—was apparent in their demeanors. They tried to have a normal interactive and lighthearted gathering, but the situation was too raw to feel normal. The following day, Mustafa left to go back to Stanford, having advised Willie and Faris not to contact him for a month, so everyone could wind down.

In desperation, Willie decided to visit Zeina. He was hoping for someone related to Mustafa to spell out a possible solution to Mustafa's dilemma. He told Zeina about the separation. She told him that she still loved Mustafa, but she would in no way consider getting back with him. While she felt sorry about what happened to him at the rally, she did not think it was a sufficient reason to abandon her. Zeina was still not aware of the episode of the rape—she was only talking about the beating and torture. She added that she believed that Mustafa did not want to reconcile with her either.

"If I were in his shoes, I would have gone to him even if I were raped," said Zeina.

Willie did not know whether such a mention was a mere coincidence or a direct reference to Mustafa's sexual attack. As they talked further, Willie was convinced it was a mere coincidence.

Zeina told him that she was concerned about Mustafa and wanted to think of a way for his friends, especially Willie and Faris, to help him out. Willie was at a loss about how to respond to Zeina since he did not want to share with her the cause of the rupture between Mustafa and Michelle. All along, Willie pretended that he did not know the cause of the split.

———

Zeina was keeping a secret from everyone: she had given birth to a daughter who was now eighteen months old, called Zeina Junior. While Mustafa was no longer the subject of Zeina's romantic interest, she knew that she wanted her daughter to eventually connect with her father.

On her own, Zeina decided to contact Michelle. Michelle was completely surprised that Zeina contacted her at all, having previously lied to her about the nature of her relationship with Mustafa. When the two met, she was gracious in her approach to Michelle. Zeina was quick to let Michelle know that she was not indignant about her misrepresentation. She added that although both had a romantic relationship with Mustafa, she was totally over it and did not hold the slightest grudge against him.

On the other hand, Michelle made it clear to Zeina that she still loved Mustafa and that she was not offended by what had transpired between the two of them, although she would have strongly preferred that the relationship had continued. Zeina expressed her relief that Michelle felt that way. Zeina told her that she had a special reason for not telling her why she wanted to help Mustafa as much as possible, and that such a reason had no romantic angle.

Zeina said, "I will tell you what my motives are if you tell me what caused the rupture between you and Mustafa. But in all sincerity, if I don't tell and you don't tell, it would be best for both of us."

Zeina told her not to worry, and told another lie, that she already had a baby with another man, who was still in her life. When asked if she would cooperate with Zeina to help Mustafa, Michelle said yes. At that point, both women had lied to each other. What Zeina kept from Michelle was very important: primarily that Zeina Junior was Mustafa's daughter.

CHAPTER 21

Now it was Michelle's turn to be consoled. She called Sara to say she was arriving in New Haven in the evening. When Sara tried to ask questions, Michelle asked her to wait until she listened to her upon her arrival. Michelle also asked Sara to make sure Carol was there.

Michelle arrived at Carol and Sara's apartment, looking chagrined and dejected. Her two friends could tell that something was wrong. Sara sat on the couch facing the two and asked for three glasses, which Carol provided. They were both anxious to hear what was wrong. She gave each a miniature scotch bottle and Michelle proceeded to pour hers into the glass. She took a gulp, breathed deeply, and started talking wistfully. "It is over between me and Mustafa. The wedding is off. I still love him, and he loves me, but it's all over," she said.

"Why?! What happened all of a sudden?" asked Sara.

"You recall when he said that he had decided not to have sex until much later, maybe not until we marry. He thought it was all voluntary. I think subconsciously Mustafa knew that what happened at the Goldwater rally had affected him, but he underestimated the effect. Consciously, it was a different story. At any rate,

I don't believe that he had any idea as to the severity of the impact. It was severe, in my opinion. We tried to make love several times, and in each case, he kind of ended it by having a bad reaction, either by hyperventilating and convulsing, or by losing his excitement altogether. We tried and one time he almost made it, but a dog barked outside his apartment during our attempt. That brought to his mind a dog's bark while he was being sexually attacked. It stopped the whole thing."

Sara and Carol didn't know what to say. Sara asked if the relationship was salvageable, to which Michelle answered that it was not. She added that Mustafa was obsessed with not harming or shorting anyone.

"He seems to like flagellating himself psychologically. I tried and tried to let him know that I was willing to marry him under any circumstances, and that I would dedicate my life to making him whole, but he would not budge. He feels that by ending the relationship, I'll go through severe emotional pain at first, but in the long run, I'll fare much better and will lead a normal life," said Michelle.

When Carol asked if Michelle would be seeing him in the future, she started crying. "No, he told my father that he should see no one—not me, not William, and not Rose. He thinks this way, everyone will heal faster. He told Willie that he was crying more than once a day. I don't know… It's not easy. I hurt, and when I hear about him hurting, the hurt is all compounded," said Michelle, sighing and wiping her tears.

Sara looked at her. "I've been reading Islamic proverbs. There are a few verses that I really like. One of them says, 'After every predicament, there is a resolution.' And then there is another: 'Do not begrudge what is beyond your control; it may yet prove beneficial,'" she added.

"Those are really consoling sayings. I wish life was like that," answered Michelle.

The three visited for three days. Michelle felt better at the end, but sadness was still showing all over her face. She went back to Durham to hug her father and tell him that it was the two of them. "Like before Mustafa showed up." She asked William to suggest that Rose spend two days a week with them. "After all, she was supposed to be busy preparing for the big wedding, and now she's mostly idle," said Michelle.

William picked up the phone, and in response, Rose said yes—wholeheartedly.

———

Mustafa prepared to call his two sets of cousins, the ones in Chicago and his favorites in Argentina. He dreaded having to call either, for exactly the opposite reasons. He expected the ones in Argentina to be upset while empathetic. On the other hand, the Chicago set might take the chance to gloat at the whole affair. They were the envious type.

Finally, he called his cousins in Argentina. It was a disappointment to them, as they liked and thought highly of both William and Michelle. They particularly liked Michelle's behavior and appreciated her beautiful looks. They suggested Mustafa take the first plane to Buenos Aires. Mustafa thanked them and politely declined.

When it came to calling Nijad in Chicago, his reaction was totally different. He told Mustafa that he deserved what was coming to him as a result of getting engaged to an American girl. "They are loose, secondhand girls," said Nijad, referring to the fact that

American girls are more likely to have premarital sex.

Mustafa got mad. "I am trying to let you know about what has happened. I am not in the mood for a lecture of any kind." Nijad told him that if he were not busy with a huge delegation from Saudi Arabia, he would take the first flight to teach him a lesson about marriage and family life.

Nijad added, "Listen, Cousin, this delegation is staying here for a month. I will come to visit you after they leave. I will have a nice surprise for you." Mustafa did not want Nijad to visit, but he could not dissuade him.

———

Mustafa started attending Amanda's quantitative analysis class. His mood and demeanor had changed since she saw him last, and she noticed his withdrawn attitude. After the third session, Amanda asked to see Mustafa after class, which they did. She told him that he did not look good. He did not bother to answer her.

"What's wrong? Something must be wrong! You don't look like the Mustafa I knew," she exclaimed. He again said nothing.

As he was leaving, Amanda asked him to say hello to Michelle. He answered, "There is no Michelle anymore. I chased her away, as I always do, chase all the good ones away." She said nothing and managed to hold back from asking any more questions.

It did not take Amanda much longer to ask Mustafa to talk to her after class. She asked him if he was available for coffee. "I am available, but what is this about, Dr. Summerfield?" said Mustafa flatly.

"I'm worried about you not participating in class. Some of your classmates are also concerned. One of them even thought that you're depressed and may be prone to do something to yourself." When he said nothing in reply, she also said, "Stop calling me Dr. Summerfield. Call me Amanda, like everyone else in the class."

"But you are not hitting on anyone else. I just wanted to send you a message," said Mustafa.

She answered him, "First, I'm not hitting on you. But second, for the sake of argument, suppose I am hitting on you. All you need to say is 'No.' Do you suspect that I have plans to force myself on you? I think I don't need to say any more. OK? Good luck and goodbye."

As Amanda was leaving, Mustafa stopped her and apologized by saying that there was so much on his mind, especially with Michelle gone. He told her that having a cup of coffee with her might be just what he needed.

"Listen, Mustafa, you're an A student. There is no doubt about that. In the accounting class, you used to be the most engaged student. The class was alive because of you. Here, most of the students are barely paying attention except for a couple of them who keep staring at me. I want you to be involved and engaged, just like before. How about it?" said Amanda.

Mustafa told her that he would give it a try, except that he wanted to resolve his problems. When she asked him if he was talking about Michelle, he answered, "This is not about Michelle. I do not think she would come back to me even if I asked. This is about the reasons behind my asking Michelle to leave," said Mustafa.

"What reasons? Did you have a fight with her father?"

"No, it is all about me and nobody else. I am the source of the problem."

"Listen, Mustafa, I can be of help. I have resources other than myself, but I need to know what kind of a problem you're talking about," said Amanda in an exacerbated tone.

He paused briefly, looking at Amanda dismissively. "I know you—pushy and oversexed. Do you really want to know? I think that when I explain everything, you will stop hitting on me. I think I'm going to be straightforward, just as I was with Michelle when I told her it was all over." He sighed. "Amanda, I am not the man I used to be. Something happened on the way, and the reason I am here at Stanford is that I wanted to get the hell out of Durham, where it all happened. The long and short of it is that while I was at a rally for Goldwater, I was attacked by three racist thugs, and one of them raped me."

"Holy Jesus, you don't mean…" said Amanda before he interrupted her.

"Yes, I mean he stuck his penis into my ass. I was lucky—there was a two-star general that literally saved my ass. Within seconds, the general pulled him off me and attacked the attacker and prevented the other two from raping me as well. They already had their pants down and their penises out, waiting for their turns."

"This is shocking. You hear about such things, but I can hardly believe that it happened to you, someone I know!" said Amanda.

"And to add insult to injury—this is where you come into the picture—since then I have been unable to have sex with anyone, including Michelle. She did not want to end it, but I had to. She thought there was hope and I didn't, nor do I now."

Amanda stood up, looking straight into Mustafa's eyes, and said, "I have an idea. I'm leaving. I'll call you." Mustafa did not have a chance to say anything after that.

Two days later, she called Mustafa and got together with him. She had consulted a psychiatrist friend of hers, Dr. Stonewell, who advised Amanda to instruct him to start masturbating regularly for a couple of months. After that, Stonewell intended to meet with Mustafa to gauge his progress and decide what to do next.

"You masturbated when you were younger, didn't you?" inquired Amanda.

"Actually, I have never masturbated. I guess I was lucky—the girls in Amman were willing as long as they protected their virginity."

"Wow! You must practice. Girls do it, too—it's not that hard. I did it when I was much younger, but I don't anymore," said Amanda.

"Well, I guess you don't have to do it. You have your stuntman now," said Mustafa.

"My stuntman is no longer. I got tired of his games. Can you believe it? Talking about penises, he used to hide his penis in his ass and then would ask me to find it, as if we were playing hide and seek. Let's say this—he did one stunt too many for my taste. I had to unceremoniously kick him out the door. It's been six weeks and I don't regret ending that childish relationship one bit."

Two weeks later, Amanda checked with Mustafa after class. He told her that he had not even tried. She was annoyed at him and advised him to start right away. A week later, Mustafa was still reluctant to start, which exasperated Amanda.

"Do you want to be cured, or do you want to stay neutral all your life?!" asked Amanda. "Why don't you buy the latest edition of *Playboy* and check those gorgeous naked models out?"

Mustafa procrastinated further and Amanda was becoming furious with him for not even trying. One evening, she called Mustafa and asked if he had at least bought a copy of *Playboy* magazine. He had not. She called Stonewell, who, in turn, called Mustafa, and tried to impress upon him that masturbating was necessary as a first step.

Amanda called Mustafa and told him she was coming over to see him. When she got there, she asked if he had a bathtub. She filled the bathtub with water and added bath gel to it. She took Mustafa by the arm and led him to the bathtub. He followed her instructions to lie down on his back in the bubbly bathtub. He did and was, to his surprise, followed by Amanda within minutes. Amanda told him that his body was invisible to her under the bubbles.

"Now, slowly start masturbating. I can see nothing," said Amanda. Mustafa hesitated, embarrassed at the whole scene. He started masturbating and then stopped. Once again, Amanda got mad. She ordered him to put his hands behind his head and not move. She dipped her right hand toward his crotch while she continued to repeat her instruction until she got hold of his limp penis. Mustafa tried to shift.

Amanda yelled, "Don't move a thing! I am in control and will remain in control." It took her twenty minutes of methodical but escalating effort before Mustafa ejaculated.

"I am sorry," said Mustafa.

"You don't have to be. I enjoyed it but not enough for me to reach a climax. I was at least two steps removed. It was most comforting and marginally enjoyable. We know now that you're not impotent. I'll relay this to Dr. Stonewell," said Amanda.

————

In the give-and-take between Mustafa and Amanda, so many

barriers were removed. While the conversations pertained to a medical or psychological condition, the subject of sexual activity was prevalent, and totally intertwined in most of Amanda's statements and actions. Mustafa, on the other hand, was oblivious emotionally but responsive physically. Yet, he was the one who reignited Amanda's interest by vividly describing his own traumatic rape. Instead of discouraging Amanda from pursuing her sexual attraction, all Amanda did was add another objective to her sexual desire for Mustafa. Her natural curiosity, although removed from her specialty in this case, encouraged her to find an answer to a friend's problem, and possibly kill two birds with one stone.

Amanda relayed the news of their course of action and its productive results to Dr. Stonewell, with one embellishment. She told Stonewell that Mustafa had masturbated without anyone's help. Amanda went back to encourage Mustafa to try to masturbate on his own, in her presence. He failed again. The whole exercise was very new and strange to him.

Alternating between her sexual interest and her genuine desire to help Mustafa, she said to him, "Listen, Mustafa, I can help you do it, but it's best that you masturbate on your own. It is not only your lack of impotence, which is important, but also your will. You need to be willing to have sex."

As this verbal exchange between Mustafa and Amanda became routine, the two were conducting conversations about the subject with very little reticence. Mustafa tried a third time, unsuccessfully. At that point, Amanda started taking her clothes off, piece by piece, until she was naked. She pulled in a chair and sat in it and spread her legs, making her crotch clearly visible to Mustafa. He could not help but admire her shapely and sexy body. She looked most inviting. She then asked Mustafa to start masturbating, which he did. In a matter of ten minutes, he ejaculated!

"I would have been most disappointed if you had not ejaculated. I have never failed to arouse any man I was interested in. It pleases me that you're one of them," said Amanda.

Amanda then asked Mustafa to take her seat and expose his crotch. She went into the bathtub and masturbated and did reach a gratifying climax. She told Mustafa that she could not take it any longer. His body was too appealing and irresistible. She asked him not to share what had taken place with anyone; otherwise, she would be fired. She also told him that she had only one month left with Stanford, as she was leaving to join a large brokerage firm as head of research. Otherwise, she would not have pursued a relationship with him.

Without Mustafa noticing it, step by step, their sexual acts progressed. She helped him masturbate, and he helped do the same. Within three weeks, they were having sex. It was hot and passionate. Both were engaging fully, except that Amanda was more motivated.

During one of their sexual encounters, as Amanda was massaging Mustafa, she told him that she wanted him to be one of her three assistants at the new firm. At first, he turned down the offer. Then he shared with Amanda that he was working on a new quantitative stock analysis software, and he would accept her offer if she would fund his research for a twenty-eighty split in his favor. Amanda said that she would do it for a 10 percent cut if she approved his topic and his methodology. Mustafa made a formal presentation in one of the classrooms, exclusively for her benefit.

"You son of a bitch, and you didn't mention a word about this to me before! I think you have a sneaky hidden side to you!"

"No, I don't. You forget that I was trying to avoid having anything to do with you outside the classroom. I kind of reversed

course. Thanks to your help, we now have a healthy physical relationship, but one that may contain the seeds of its own destruction,"
said Mustafa.

"I know, Mustafa, that you want to emphasize the physical. I
also know that you Middle Eastern males have a hang-up about
having a romantic relationship with an older female. To tell you the
truth, I like younger men, so here we are. But why are you saying
that our relationship contains the seeds of its own destruction? I
don't understand."

"Because I am still in love with Michelle. I want to go back to
her if she will take me back after this. I don't want to hurt your
feelings, but I am going to try," said Mustafa.

Amanda asked him to wait for a couple of weeks until she quit
her job at Stanford University, after which she would be free to
find his replacement from among some of the students who had
shown interest in her. When Mustafa questioned if that was her
"methodology," using the same academic term she used regarding
his quantitative research, she said, without any hesitation, that it
was.

She added that partly because universities punished such interludes, she was quitting academia altogether. Her answer was to
Mustafa's liking, as he knew he did not love Amanda and she did
not love him, but both ended up enjoying having sex with each
other.

CHAPTER 22

Mustafa was seriously thinking of calling Michelle. He first called Willie and consulted with him, who asked him not to rush into revealing his reversal and volunteered to help. When Willie could not come up with an acceptable approach, Mustafa told him that he had decided to contact Rose, since she was most considerate and wise. On top of that, she had asked Mustafa earlier to consult with her at will, whenever he felt he needed her input.

When he called Rose, she was cautiously but pleasantly surprised since Mustafa had emphasized to William and her that a clean break would make it easier for all involved. He started by reminding her about the advice she gave to contact her whenever there was a problem. After they hesitantly greeted each other, Mustafa asked her if she was ready for some good news for a change. She told him that she was craving good news.

"I think I may have fixed my problem," he said and then stopped.

Rose exclaimed, "You mean 'the problem'?! The problem that caused everything to fall apart?!" Mustafa confirmed that it was.

Rose said she had more than a hundred related questions and wondered if he had the time.

"If you trust me, you will understand that what I am saying is the truth. All the answers are here, in and around Stanford. I don't want Michelle to know anything about it until you can confirm it, which, in my opinion, will require that you meet two people: one of whom is my professor, and the other is my psychiatrist."

Rose understood the implications. She wanted to make sure that her trip was necessary, and that there was no other way. In the end, Mustafa told her that she had to trust him without the need to ask any further questions. Rose grudgingly, and with some faint optimism, agreed to fly to Stanford ten days later.

Mustafa called Willie and Faris on a conference call and told Willie again and Faris for the first time that he believed he was cured. Faris was most pleasantly surprised. The subject of returning to Michelle was the logical next item. Mustafa was concerned that, like Zeina, she would adopt a negative and rigid posture. Willie disagreed. He told Mustafa that Michelle would not return on her own, or that she might play hard to get, but that she would eventually reconcile with Mustafa if he did not behave "like an asshole" once again.

Mustafa assured his friends that he would do anything to have her back. He explained to them that he loved Michelle beyond their wildest imagination. He also expressed his opinion that he owed her, and that he needed to rectify things by making her feel emotionally whole and secure. Willie and Faris could not agree more, heartened by Mustafa's words. He shared with them that Rose was planning to be there in ten days to validate that all the necessary prerequisites were in existence for a possible reconciliation.

————

Four days after he talked to Rose, Mustafa was surprised by a visit from none other than his Chicago cousin, Nijad. He had hoped that Nijad would not be able to make the trip. They kissed formally and Nijad introduced his four assistants who had accompanied him. After Mustafa confirmed that he was alone, Nijad dispatched one of his assistants, and in no time, he was back with a young girl wearing a headscarf. Nijad introduced her as Fatima, his niece. Mustafa shook hands with her, addressing her as Niece Fatima.

Nijad looked at Mustafa and snapped at him, "Why are you addressing her as your niece? Now that you broke up with your used American fiancée, you need a decent and young wife. Fatima is going to be your wife! Did you not just break up with that American bitch, Michelle?"

Mustafa was shocked at what he heard about Fatima first and the insults Nijad hurled at the absent Michelle. "I am not going to marry a young girl like her," said Mustafa.

Nijad looked at him and said, "Why not? You prefer older women—used women—or would you rather have a virgin, firm and as sweet as they come?! Are you crazy?" Nijad went to Fatima and pulled the scarf off her head. "I am not supposed to do this. Look at her beautiful hair—never touched by another man."

"Listen, Nijad, don't torture the girl. I don't care if Fatima was Miss Universe. I have a fiancée and I am going to try to reconcile with her. Do you understand? End of story!"

"You miserable creature. You are nothing but an arrogant piece of shit. You are a pussy, not a real man," said Nijad.

Mustafa looked at him and said, "Get out of my apartment, you ignorant bastard, and never come back here again."

Nijad became furious and was about to hit Mustafa. Instead, he looked at one of his assistants, asked him to take Fatima back to the car and come back. One of the henchmen held Mustafa down while the other two were directed to look throughout the unit. In the process, they ransacked it and ended with a prize—Mustafa's diary.

When the assistant came back to join the other three, Nijad looked at him and said, "Number three," and left. The assistants shut the door, closed the drapes, and all four took out their extra-wide belts and started whipping Mustafa. Unintentionally, one of the assistants got too agitated and a buckle hit Mustafa behind his ear. The prong pierced his skull while the frame fractured the skull. Mustafa fell unconscious.

————

In the evening, Amanda called Mustafa but could not reach him. She wanted to check on him, expecting that he would have called Michelle after she last saw him. In the morning, she called him again but still got no answer. She decided to drop in, wanting to know whether she was still in the picture or not. When she got there, the apartment door was slightly ajar. She knocked gently. There was no answer. She knocked harder, but to no avail. As she took two steps into the living room, right away she could see Mustafa lying on the floor unconscious with coagulated blood on the carpet.

She tried to wake him up. He responded faintly, but could not get up on his own, so she immediately called for an ambulance. As she was waiting, she located a copy of Rose's ticket. She accompanied Mustafa to the emergency room. Within one hour, the attending physician told Amanda that they suspected some internal damage but were not sure.

Amanda immediately called Willie, whose name had been given to her by Mustafa as the person to contact in case of an emergency. Willie knew who Amanda was. She told him that she had found a copy of Rose's ticket.

"I'll call Rose and tell her the news about Mustafa," Willie told Amanda.

All the parties were shocked and convinced that the attack must've been a burglary. None of them had any idea who could have assaulted Mustafa like that.

———

Rose drove to see Michelle. She sat her down and held both Michelle's hands in her hands. Rose said that she had been hoping to bring good news, but that the news had gotten dreary. "I was supposed to come here to let you know that Mustafa has worked out his problem with the help of a psychiatrist."

Michelle didn't let Rose finish. "If you're trying to reconcile us, it's not going to work. He must apologize and be sincere. He must be remorseful and repentant. I'm not going to accept his doctrinaire ideas anymore. He likes to flagellate himself, and in the process, he doesn't mind hurting others." Michelle started crying. Despite her hesitation, she said that she still loved him with all her heart.

"Hold off, Michelle—you didn't allow me to finish. I said I was hoping to bring good news, but the good news is now overwhelmed with terrible news. Mustafa has been severely attacked and is in the hospital with a badly fractured skull," said Rose.

Michelle resumed crying and said, "But why? What was it, burglars? Oh, my God, oh, my God. If it isn't one thing, it's another! Oh, my God, I'll fly over right away. I knew we would reconcile someday, but this? This is unbelievable!"

Rose asked her to calm down. "I was supposed to go there by myself to meet with the psychiatrist who treated him, to make sure that he was totally over his phobia. We can go together. Call your father right away," said Rose. When William heard the news, he said he would accompany them, if need be.

CHAPTER 23

Willie had always harbored a suspicion that Zeina Junior was Mustafa's daughter. He never confronted Zeina about it, and he never shared his doubts with anyone else. Suspicious, he called her and told her about Mustafa. She was in shock and asked Willie if he could visit her at home. She had something to share with him.

When he got there, Zeina told Willie that Zeina Junior was Mustafa's daughter. What she had told Michelle about being in a relationship was nothing more than a fabrication, just to put Michelle's mind at ease and to confirm that she was no longer interested in Mustafa.

"You know, I already was 90 percent sure Zeina Junior is Mustafa's baby," said Willie.

"Really?" asked Zeina. "Well, in that case, I believe it's incumbent upon me to fly over with the child and introduce our daughter to her father, if the circumstances are conducive."

"Yes, I think that is a good idea, and I also think you should do it right away," said Willie. "Perhaps it would be good for me to proceed there as well."

"Why don't we travel together since we're going to the same place?"

Willie agreed and intended also to check with Faris. Zeina then relayed some news about the Qatari ambassador. "He's giving a speech at Duke, and I'm supposed to be there. I met him through Mustafa. He called me last week to see if his two-year-old son could come to play with my two-year-old daughter. Other than planning to attend the speech, Ambassador Farouk Fakhri and his wife have planned a get-together with me and Zeina Junior."

Willie thought it would be a good idea if she immediately called the ambassador to let him know about Mustafa and tell him about her plans to go to visit him at Stanford.

"I will right away," said Zeina.

She told Willie after the call that the Ambassador thanked her and expressed his serious concern about Mustafa and promised to call her back. Within the hour, he did and informed Zeina that Hassan, his younger brother, and Mustafa's once high school classmate, would be flying to check on Mustafa right away.

Willie took the initiative of coordinating with all the parties wanting to visit Mustafa at the hospital. They included Rose, Michelle, Willie, Zeina, Zeina Junior, Faris, and Hassan. They all stayed at the same hotel, next to the hospital, where Willie arranged to have them get together before visiting Mustafa. When they arrived, Zeina and Michelle hugged each other, and everyone kissed Zeina Junior.

Rose was impressed with Zeina's demeanor and looks. Willie overheard her comment to Michelle, "Mustafa knows how to pick them."

"No, it was me and Zeina who picked Mustafa. He sure knew how to attract us," said Michelle.

———

Rose suggested that Willie advise everyone not to press Mustafa about the details of the incident. When they arrived at the hospital, they had to ask for permission for the whole group to enter the room briefly. Then, two at a time would alternate. The attending physician told them that he had instructed Mustafa not to speak, but that he could put his answers in writing.

"Rose, will you be the first to enter the room and let Mustafa know who else is here to visit him?" Willie asked.

Rose agreed. When she told Mustafa that Michelle was there to see him, he took Rose's hand and kissed it gently. He spoke without sound, just moving his lips. "I'd like to see her right away."

Rose immediately went out and told everyone that Mustafa wanted to see Michelle first. She entered again with Michelle but stood discreetly near the door to give them some privacy.

Michelle could not hold back and started crying. Mustafa waggled his index finger at her, telling her not to cry. When she got close to him to kiss him, he gestured that he was OK. He lip-spoke and said, "It is all over. You and I will be together forever."

Michelle took his hand and said, "For as long as we both live." She didn't kiss him, per the instructions of the attending physician, but Mustafa smiled broadly. Rose and Michelle left, but not before the young woman gave him a finger kiss.

As they exited, they saw Amanda and Dr. Stonewell arriving. Rose could tell that Michelle did not like the fact that Amanda was there. Rose whispered in Michelle's ear while pointing toward them. "These are the people with whom you're supposed to confirm Mustafa's rehabilitation."

"With Amanda Summerfield?!" exclaimed Michelle.

"Yes, Dr. Summerfield and Dr. Stonewell. I didn't know she's this good-looking," said Rose.

"Yeah, she's good-looking, and she keeps looking at Mustafa," said Michelle sarcastically.

Michelle didn't say anything more, but Rose noticed how she observed closely the events around her. The only soothing words came from Dr. Stonewell.

He spoke to Rose and Michelle. "Mustafa had mentioned that you two and Mr. Parker could be privy to his diagnosis. I'm convinced that Mustafa's psychological condition is mostly behind him. Physically, he is OK. He has, in the past, failed in all his intimate sex acts due to his unfortunate experience. I assume you know the details. All sexual experiences for the coming six months should be slow and easy."

CHAPTER 24

After everyone else went in to see Mustafa, Zeina said that she and Zeina Junior planned to visit him the following day. Everyone wondered why but did not have a clue.

Hassan commented, "Don't you think Mustafa would rather see you today and again tomorrow for a repeat? If you like, I will go in with you and the two of us can alternate attending to Zeina Junior, if need be."

Zeina and everyone else noticed Hassan's attention on her. She said, "It is OK today. You can come in with me tomorrow. Before I see Mustafa by myself, I would like to share something important with everyone this evening." Hassan just nodded his head approvingly.

In the evening, as they gathered to go out to dinner, Zeina asked Willie to take Zeina Junior away for a while. She then addressed the group.

"On one occasion, Michelle and I lied to each other to spare each other the pain of our circumstances. She told me that she was married and not interested in Mustafa. At the same time, I told her a lie too. I told her that I was in a relationship and that Zeina junior was the child out of that relationship. Well, now that Mustafa may have faced death in the face, I must tell the truth. He doesn't have any clue. The truth is that Zeina Junior is also Mustafa's child. He needs to know it, and you, all his friends and family, need to know it. This changes nothing as far as my relationship with Mustafa—he is and will be the father of my child, and maybe a friend in the future, and nothing more."

Michelle walked slowly toward a sofa and gently sat down. Rose followed to console her.

Hassan went closer to Zeina and said, "I had no clue, and I know this was not easy. You had to do it and it looks like you revealed it to all those involved at the same time. It is over. Can I get you something to drink? Anything?"

"My throat is very dry," Zeina said. "I would not mind having a glass of water. And would you call Willie and Zeina Junior back?"

As Hassan left the room, Zeina asked everyone not to discuss anything in front of the little girl, as she did not know yet that Mustafa was her father.

———

Rose excused herself and took a disoriented Michelle by the arm. The two left for the hotel. There, she tried to soothe Michelle's feelings. She told her that she thought that Zeina Junior was very cute, and that she had taken the best from each parent. This small talk did little to help Michelle's bewildered feelings.

Rose resorted to using reverse psychology. She told Michelle that above all, she needed to worry about Mustafa. Michelle looked at her with an inquiring face.

Rose right away said, "Yes, how do you think he will feel that he has a two-year-old daughter he never knew existed? He is already traumatized by all that has happened to him. Let's hope he won't suffer any further damage as a result of his head being bashed. Who knows how he will react when he hears about Zeina Junior, on top of all the trauma? Please, Michelle, direct your compassion toward Mustafa, not inwardly toward yourself!"

Michelle looked at Rose and said nothing. She then nodded her head approvingly and said, "I do realize you're right. I just need to wrap my head around it and accept it. It's not easy."

Rose answered, "I know well that you'll come to the right conclusion. Your late mother was no less prudent than your father. She was wonderful."

"Yes, I agree, but you're the only one who expresses her thoughts in a timely fashion—not like my father, who keeps his wise thoughts to himself until something happens," said Michelle.

"Be fair to your father, Michelle. He is a man. He can't share the girls' talk, like your mother could and I can," said Rose.

The two women agreed to spend a few more days in the area until Mustafa's prognosis improved. Michelle said that she wanted to lease a bicycle in the morning, for biking always helped her clear her head. In the meantime, she wanted to be alone. Rose told her not to be too hard on herself, and that what had transpired was part of the challenges of life, including Michelle's life. But it was nowhere near as challenging as witnessing her Samuel being chased out of North Carolina and never hearing from him again. Michelle said she understood that fully. She just needed some time for herself.

———

In the evening, the group did not get together like they did the first night. Rose knew fissures were surfacing in quick succession. She asked Willie to call everyone and say that he realized they wanted to have dinner alone but to insist that he wanted the group to get together for an after-dinner drink. The group did, but this time with the addition of Amanda and Dr. Stonewell. Rose was convinced that overall, everyone was well-meaning, but because of the nature of Mustafa's challenging circumstances, Michelle, Amanda, and Zeina did harbor different kinds of suspicions toward each other.

She was right. By the time everyone had two drinks, they were feeling much better about each other. Dr. Stonewell asked Rose if she could stay behind, as he had something important to discuss with her. To Rose's surprise, Amanda also stayed behind.

Stonewell told Rose that Mustafa had confided in him that he trusted her judgment the most, and that she needed to know that he was treating Mustafa gratis and that he was mostly advising Mustafa's friend, Amanda, on what to do in general terms. He added that they brought back Mustafa's sexual desires with the help of another female.

"You mean Mustafa was having a relationship with another woman, and she revived his sex activity?" Rose inquired.

Stonewell tried to explain that there was no relationship, just sex.

"A prostitute!" exclaimed Rose.

"No, it was another woman who doesn't want a relationship but is after sex. First, she helped Mustafa masturbate, then the female in question forced him to have a couple of remedial blow jobs, and third, she had sex with him three to four times. Once she was sure he was revived, she got out of the picture. I hope Michelle doesn't look at it as pure sex, and instead accepts it as some sort of treatment. I do know well it isn't easy to accept as a treatment," said Stonewell.

"Well, guys, this is difficult to fathom—even by me, who's not directly involved. It's going to be hard to explain to Michelle. She just found out that Mustafa has a baby girl whom he knew nothing about. It is too much for her to accept all at once. I need to think about it. Thanks for letting me know," said Rose.

CHAPTER 25

Rose suspected that Hassan might be of help. She called and met with him, asking Hassan if he minded being the one to ease the news to Mustafa about Zeina Junior when Mustafa's condition improved. Hassan immediately agreed. He said he would do anything reasonable to help Mustafa. Rose impressed upon him that she needed to solve a series of problems, which needed handling in proper sequence. She added that Mustafa getting to know that Zeina Junior was his daughter would be the foundation, to start with. The rest needed to follow systematically or otherwise things might get messy and remain unresolved.

Hassan talked to Zeina and asked if she minded allowing him to take the forefront of the Zeina Junior situation with Mustafa.

"I would like to take the opportunity to inform Mustafa that Zeina Junior is his daughter. It is my and Rose's opinion that it might come best from an impartial third party."

"No," Zeina said. "Since I was the one who kept the information from him in the first place, you telling him would put me in an awkward position."

"But he is the one who disappeared without telling you. He is the one who caused this concealment to take place in the first place," said Hassan.

In the end, Zeina changed her mind.

The following day, Hassan took Zeina Junior by the hand and visited Mustafa, who was gradually improving, at the hospital.

"This little girl certainly has a few Arabic features, doesn't she?" asked Hassan as they observed Zeina playing in the hospital room. "Do you know who her father is?"

"No, and I don't think that Zeina wants to share such information with me," said Mustafa.

After a few minutes of watching Zeina Junior inspect the view from the window, Hassan called her over and lifted her to sit on the bed. "I'm thinking of trying to find out the ethnicity of Zeina Junior's father," said Hassan.

"No, you should not do it," said Mustafa.

"Why not?" Hassan leaned back so he could view both at once. "I swear… If I did not know better, I would think Zeina Junior was your daughter. She has similar features."

Mustafa seemed to pick up on Hassan's intended implications but said nothing. Hassan then asked Zeina Junior to lie next to Mustafa and the resemblance became even clearer to Hassan.

"Hold on to the girl for a minute," said Hassan. He proceeded to the nurse's desk to ask for a hand mirror. He gave the mirror to Mustafa. "Now look into it and compare your features to those of Zeina Junior."

Hassan knew that although Mustafa was still not fully recovered, there was no way he could deny the strong resemblance.

Mustafa's surprised reaction gave Hassan hope that he had aroused some suspicions in his friend's mind.

"I'm going to take Zeina Junior back to her mother, and Zeina will be visiting you this afternoon," said Hassan.

Hassan talked to Zeina and asked her not to bring up the subject of Zeina Junior with Mustafa right then since he was in a fragile condition. "I think that it is best that Mustafa starts either realizing—or at a minimum, starts suspecting—that Zeina Junior is his. I'll pick you up and accompany you to the hospital."

"Yes, I agree," said Zeina. When she arrived to visit Mustafa, the encounter was slightly tense. Zeina took the initiative and held his hand.

He said in a hushed voice, "I am sorry."

"Don't worry about it—it's water under the bridge. How are you feeling?" said Zeina.

He said that he was feeling great since everyone was visiting. She told him that she was working at the medical center as an international patient coordinator. The atmosphere of the meeting eased gradually, fully observed by Hassan, yet he said nothing. Zeina Junior took to Mustafa, watching her mother holding his hand all the time she was there.

As the Zeinas were leaving, Zeina said, "I am teaching Zeina Junior Arabic because her father is an Arab." Hassan noticed she did not give Mustafa a chance to comment as she left in a hurry. Hassan waved goodbye to him and caught up with Zeina in the lobby.

"How do you think this initial meeting went? Do you think it was a good idea to comment about my daughter being taught Arabic?" Zeina asked.

"I very much liked the added touch. If it's OK with you, I am going to play devil's advocate and wonder to Mustafa as to who Zeina Junior's father could be," said Hassan.

Zeina didn't mind. "Yes, that sounds like a good way to handle it."

————

Hassan visited Mustafa by himself. When the opportunity presented itself, he popped the question: "Zeina told me that Zeina Junior is studying Arabic because her father is an Arab. Do you have any idea who that could be?"

"No, I don't know," said Mustafa.

"Do you think Zeina could be hiding something? Maybe you're the father—man, there is a strong resemblance here. Don't you think so? Listen, Mustafa, you're the one who abandoned Zeina. I think she got mad at first and then got used to raising her daughter by herself. You were nowhere to be seen," Hassan said. He thought for a moment and then said, "Listen, Mustafa, let me handle it! I think I know how to find out. I'm going to try to seek Rose's help without letting Michelle know."

Mustafa seemed puzzled but didn't object. Hassan left the room to put his plan in place.

"So, Rose, will you participate in the ruse?" asked Hassan.

"Yes, definitely. Remember, I'm the one who wants to resolve all the outstanding issues by telling Mustafa about his daughter as a first step," said Rose.

Rose called Hassan within days and said, "I went to visit Mustafa and told him that Zeina was being secretive. I said she would not answer anything about Zeina Junior directly, yet I suspect that the little girl is his baby, although not 100 percent sure."

Hassan visited Mustafa the next day. "I asked Zeina point-blank, and while she did not answer directly, she refused to say it was not yours."

"Do you think Michelle knows anything?" Mustafa asked.

"No, I don't think so. I will try to handle it and approach Michelle through Rose, if and when we make 100 percent sure that Zeina Junior is your baby."

Mustafa had no idea that the whole setup was a ruse for his benefit.

———

In the end, it was Rose who went to see Mustafa. She put her hand on his, looked him first in the eye, lowered her face, and said, "Zeina Junior is your baby, no doubt."

Mustafa said, "I am very concerned about Michelle's reaction. I don't want to lose her, and certainly, I want to embrace my daughter, but how can I do that without Zeina admitting to it?"

Rose looked at him and said, "Listen, leave it up to me and Hassan, and we'll keep you abreast every step of the way."

Beyond the ruse, Rose wanted to make sure that she could placate Michelle. She met with her and tried to discern her feelings and was surprised when Michelle told her that the issue was not a problem and was a situation that she could live with. Michelle had simmered down a lot after factoring in that Mustafa did not have the slightest clue that he had a baby daughter.

Rose persisted, trying to resolve the second issue concerning Mustafa. Now Michelle surprised Rose again. She told her that she decided to visit with Mustafa and let him know that she knew that

Zeina Junior was his daughter and that such did not alter her love for him in the least—that it was a non-issue. She also told her that she knew who attacked Mustafa. "See me tomorrow night for dinner," said Michelle.

Michelle went to see Mustafa. She ran toward him and gave him a passionate hug in bed. There she whispered in his ear that she knew that Zeina Junior was his and that he had not known a thing about it. "If Zeina doesn't mind, why don't we entertain Zeina Junior occasionally, while waiting to have one of our own?"

That was music to Mustafa's ears. By the time Michelle left the room, she and Mustafa felt like they were through the clouds, as if nothing new had been revealed. She told him that she would be taking care of him at the farm.

———

Rose and Michelle sat facing each other in the hospital cafeteria. Then Michelle began the story of what she'd learned.

"Willie told me that Carlos had called him and Faris and told them what he knew. They, in turn, informed me that Carlos had heard through the Makram family gossip that Nijad considered Mustafa a prized catch and was determined to marry off his sixteen-year-old niece to him. Mustafa not only rejected the offer but mocked and insulted Nijad. As a result, he and his men attacked Mustafa harshly and caused his skull fracture. Carlos described them as 'a bunch of crazies,' and he warned Willie that Nijad may still resort to further violence."

Rose could hardly believe her ears. "Of course, my primary concern is Mustafa's safety! We can leave the issue of Zeina Junior for another time."

Michelle continued. "Yes, definitely, but it's mostly resolved. So, Willie told me that due to Nijad's dubious associations, it will be hard to figure out exactly where the danger is coming from. See, Rose, Nijad is the perpetrator. He set up this plan after Mustafa defied him by not agreeing to marry his niece. Additionally, Mustafa's life may be in danger, as Nijad is resourceful and associated with criminals. I'm planning to talk to my father and arrange to move Mustafa to the farm, where he can be protected from outside elements."

Michelle could see that Rose was flabbergasted by all the news coming her way. Some of it was good news, but other issues were problematic.

"When I told Hassan about Nijad, he said that he will accompany Mustafa to Durham, instead of heading back to Washington, DC. You and I know he has an ulterior motive, as he wants to be close to Zeina," said Michelle.

"Hassan and I have met and decided the best way to approach Mustafa—you and Zeina should go together," said Rose. "This way Zeina can confirm that Zeina Junior is his daughter, and you can express your lack of objection…or even better, your full approval."

"I've already told Mustafa about Zeina Junior, but it would be ideal for Zeina and me to approach Mustafa together instead of Hassan. It will add credibility to the whole scenario," said Michelle.

Both Michelle and Zeina liked the idea and arranged to carry it out, with one addition. They agreed that it would be also an opportune time to formally introduce Mustafa to Zeina Junior.

———

Zeina and Michelle went into Mustafa's hospital room, each

holding Zeina Junior's hand. Zeina took the lead by confirming what others had told him.

Michelle said, "I think the lucky person in this affair is Zeina Junior! From now on, she will have a father and two mothers." She stopped herself. "Oh, I'm being presumptuous here. But Dad and I are planning to move you to the farm to recover. Is that all right with you?"

Mustafa nodded, not expressing the slightest objection.

Zeina said, "Hassan is also planning to go to Durham and spend a couple of weeks with you. He has been invited by Michelle to stay with her and William. I think it's a great idea."

Mustafa merely nodded again, bewildered by all the plans and arrangements that had been made about him and around him.

Zeina told Zeina Junior that Mustafa was her father and asked her to kiss him. Surprisingly, the little girl indicated that she already knew. She touched his face with her index finger and then touched her own face, spotlighting that they were both brownish, unlike her blond mother. She then touched her mother's arm and said, "White."

That was the most unexpected and surprising statement of the whole visit to the Stanford area. All three adults looked at each other with utter surprise, yet with great satisfaction. Zeina Junior's easy reception of the news was most gratifying.

———

In the meantime, Rose was still looking for the right circumstances and atmosphere to relay to Michelle that Mustafa had sex with another female, albeit as prescribed by a psychiatrist. Dr. Stonewell would have been satisfied with Mustafa's successful masturbation, but he, after the fact, modified his prescription to include sex after Mustafa failed to masturbate on his own to cover up for Amanda's going all the way.

CHAPTER 26

Rose, having failed to convey things to Michelle while at Stanford, made sure she went back to the farm. Rose decided not to tell Michelle until Mustafa returned to Stanford. She didn't want to risk creating a scene. She was afraid she could not put Mustafa's sex experience into proper context.

William was thrilled to see Mustafa together with Michelle and to see him at the farm. Michelle introduced Hassan to William, who was happy to have the farmhouse full of guests. In the heat of Mustafa's recovery and the surfacing of revelations about Zeina Junior, everyone had forgotten about who caused the harm that led to Mustafa's hospitalization.

In their search of Mustafa's apartment to check for missing items, Willie and Faris could only make a cursory search, not being familiar with his apartment. While it seemed to them that nothing was missing, there was at least one important item, totally and understandably missed by Willie and Faris: Mustafa's diary, which included every detail up to his recent attack, recorded daily. It described explicitly the treatment of and his revival from sexual inactivity, naming Amanda as his partner.

———

Nijad was pleasantly surprised to receive the diary, which had been scooped up by one of his henchmen just before they bashed Mustafa's head. Nijad wanted vengeance, feeling that Mustafa looked down on him and his side of the family. Nothing could have hurt Nijad more than Mustafa treating Fatima the way he did. She was good-looking; she was young, and she was a virgin, according to Nijad.

Reading through the trophy diary, the name Shawky Zurzur stood out. Nijad felt Zurzur would be a prime contact for the two to join forces. Mustafa's scorn for Zurzur was expressed prominently in the diary.

In no time, Nijad contacted Zurzur. When he first called Zurzur, he pretended he was trying to reconcile matters between him and Mustafa. But before long, the two agreed Mustafa was their common enemy. Nijad ended that first phone call without discussing anything important.

He waited for two weeks before he called Zurzur again. After sharing with him a few racist and highly insensitive jokes, which were well received, Nijad broached the subject of potential cooperation. In the process, Zurzur proposed Nijad should visit him in Utah so the two could talk openly and at length. Nijad accepted the invitation. Zurzur told him that he may have a special present for him.

When Nijad got there, even he was shocked at the fact that Zurzur had eleven wives. The subject of the eleven wives was a starter to discuss plural marriages and the like. The whole tenor of the conversation was most pleasing for Nijad. In the end, Nijad intimated that he would go for an unofficial marriage arrangement if Zurzur could provide him, at fifty-five years of age, a twenty-year-old wife.

The two harmonized, which gave Nijad the opportunity to open the subject he was there for.

"Did you know that I want to take revenge on Mustafa? I'm having trouble getting close to him, so having someone else commit the act would be preferable. I would, of course, finance the whole operation."

Zurzur's eyes lit up. "What are you thinking of? I may be able to help you with that."

Nijad casually told him, "I will pay you $10,000 as an advance, and $15,000 at the end of the operation." He watched Zurzur's face carefully and could see the money was music to his ears. Nijad had learned all he could about his cohort before he arrived and understood well the situation Zurzur was in. Zurzur's business was not doing well at the time, and he did not know why. He had no clue that the two private eyes who helped Mustafa defy him were making headway in spreading the word about Zurzur. Nijad heard they were both Mormons, ex-state and ex-FBI agents, and were well connected within and outside the Church.

"In addition, of course, is to revive the charges of rape against Mustafa and to undermine his relationship with Michelle," said Nijad.

"Oh, no, reviving the rape charges is impossible. Mustafa has been exonerated, and the accuser is still in prison," Zurzur said.

Nijad pretended to think the matter over. "Well… To start, I could live with Mustafa being at least threatened with the charges being revived. I want you to make his life hell on earth, regardless," he told Zurzur. "I will allot a total of $50,000 to fully accomplish my objective."

Zurzur admitted that he did not have the tools to interfere in Mustafa's personal life. This is when Nijad showed him Mustafa's diary.

"You can blackmail Amanda Summerfield and involve her in our plan," said Nijad.

Zurzur was very pleased with the trophy. "With such ammunition, I can easily do something damaging."

At the end of the meeting, the two talked as if they had been cooperating for a while. Zurzur promised to start working on the plan within two weeks.

———

Zurzur flew to North Carolina a week later and started following Michelle. On the third day, he confronted her at a shopping mall. She was shocked to run into him. He asked if she could have a cup of coffee with him, but she refused. He then said, "I am here for one thing and one thing only: to give you Mustafa's diary."

He took the diary from his pocket. It was familiar to her since Mustafa used to read her selections from it. Her interest was piqued, and she accepted Zurzur's invitation…provided they had coffee specifically at the mall.

While they sat, Zurzur read several pages from the diary that described Mustafa's relationship with Amanda. He could see Michelle's face getting flushed and angry the more he read.

"Give me the diary," said Michelle.

"I cannot give you the original, but I had copies made of the whole diary. I'd be willing to give you the pages that relate to Amanda."

"I want the pages that cover this specific time," she said, writing the dates on the back of a receipt.

From his research with Nijad, Zurzur knew that was the interval that covered the period from her separation to the day Mustafa was attacked. Zurzur accepted and did so. He pinned his hopes on the premise that the detailed descriptions of Mustafa's sexual activities with Amanda would suffice to scuttle the relationship with Michelle.

———

Michelle called Rose. "I used the first public phone I could find at the mall. I want to see you right away, but I don't wish to see Mustafa first."

Soon the two were together. Michelle handed the copies to Rose, which didn't take her long to realize what those copies covered. When she asked Michelle where she got the copies from, her niece told her the details of her encounter with Zurzur.

Rose had heard of Zurzur and knew of his shenanigans. "I need to read the whole thing before I can comment," she told Michelle, "but please do not say or do anything before you hear me out. I have some details you may be interested in."

After Rose read all twenty-two pages, she paused and looked Michelle in the eyes. "I've known about what's in these pages. I was going to tell you about them, but every time I tried, something popped up. I also talked to Dr. Stonewell about them. I need you to read one paragraph—just one. This paragraph will either convince you one way, or nothing is going to convince you of this fact: Mustafa did what he did because he had to, and not because he wanted to. Read this paragraph again."

I could hardly get sexually aroused even when Amanda took off her clothes and sat opposite me with her crotch exposed. Her posture made me feel awful and diminished. Dr. Stonewell had called me the prior day and said that I failed to masturbate. He said that I had two choices: either to be able to reach a climax or forever stay impotent. This is when I had to swallow my pride and respond to Amanda. But what is the use? I am in a catch-22 situation. If I manage to reverse my impotence, I may still lose the woman I want to share my love with, Michelle.

The two women looked at each other and Michelle spoke. "You obviously want me to be considerate toward Mustafa. Do you think he would be considerate toward me if I were to behave the way he behaved under similar circumstances?"

"I don't know the answer, since neither of us can duplicate the circumstances," said Rose. "Who would want to be raped to know the answer? And who would want to go through what Mustafa has gone through in less than two years? I really don't think even he could give us a convincing answer. He experienced extreme circumstances and probably had extreme reactions in some instances. You need to be the final arbiter of your own decisions. All I can say is that I respect him and even love him. So does your father. The rest is up to you!"

"Let me think: one rape, separation from Zeina, one holdup and attack, one false accusation of rape, one near-death experience by his cousin… What else?" asked Michelle.

"Michelle, stop it. Don't torture yourself this way. If you love Mustafa and think of what he has gone through with Amanda as a onetime exception, you need to strongly consider forgiving him. Don't torture yourself, and torture me and your father in the process!" snapped Rose.

Michelle looked at her aunt and said, "Oh, God, do I love him.

Mustafa told me that I am the light that starts his dawn. He's the light that starts mine. I must love Mustafa above and beyond. You are right. I'm inclined to forgive him—actually, he is forgiven."

Rose hugged Michelle and said in a very emotional tone and constrained voice, "That is the way, girl. Well, you're mature way beyond your age, and you're a truly a loving person. Can we just forget about our problems and have a slow and delicious meal in your gorgeous cellar? If you allow me, I know what to select: champagne, Château Margaux, and sixty-year-old port for after dinner. Shall we invite Zeina?"

"What a great idea. I would love to see Zeina and her daughter, and I think Hassan would like that too--Mustafa, as well. I guess we need to get used to the new reality," said Michelle.

———

Rose arranged the seating and placed Hassan next to Zeina, with Zeina Junior sitting between Mustafa and Zeina and Michelle sitting on the other side of Mustafa. Bertha outdid herself with a glorious dinner, and William insisted she join them at the table for this special occasion. Rose and William sat at opposite ends of the table, and Mustafa took the opportunity to coach Zeina Junior. He told her that while he was her father, he did not live with her mother and that he would be living with Michelle in the future.

Zeina raised her glass as she was joined by the others. Michelle held Mustafa's hand in a sign of approval and kissed him on his cheek. Mustafa continued to say that he had already chosen his best man, and it was Hassan.

Hassan said, "It will be an honor. How about if Zeina accepts being one of the matrons of honor?"

Everyone was taken aback, including Mustafa, as they all knew that what Hassan proposed was unheard of. Rose looked all around the table and said, "This is up to Michelle, who I am sure will think about it. It is unusual, but nothing is wrong with it. After all, Zeina Junior will be in Michelle's life as well."

William interrupted the conversation by proposing a toast to new and old friendships. After that, they thoroughly enjoyed a group dinner and reminisced about recent events.

———

Zurzur was working on the second proposed action against Mustafa. He contacted two Utah police officers, ones that he used to provide companions for, and ordered them to somehow think of a way to implicate Mustafa in some kind of malfeasance.

Within one week, the two came back to him, but with nothing to recommend. Zurzur reported his challenge to Nijad, who insisted that he find something.

"I promise you another $10,000 up front once you do."

Zurzur, being desperate for the money—he owed some to a couple of dangerous gangsters—accepted the challenge. He convinced one of his younger wives to accuse Mustafa of rape while he was staying with them.

———

As Mustafa was recuperating at the farm, he received a copy of the charges. Both William and Michelle were with him when he opened the envelope. Understanding the nature of the charges, Mustafa dropped into his chair. He handed Michelle the document and she gave it to William. None of them could believe the trumped-up charges.

Only then did Michelle share with the two men that she had been approached by and had coffee with Zurzur at the mall. Mustafa looked at her and said, "Are you out of your mind? And you have not told anyone?" William stood up and said that it was the first time he had heard about such a meeting.

Michelle put her face in her hands as Rose came in. She said, "God, this is becoming so complicated. It's a maze that changes hour by hour. Mustafa can't make a single move without getting in trouble, and now I'm doing the same thing!"

Rose asked Michelle to sit down and stop whining. Rose sat and looked at Mustafa. "I'm the one who told Michelle not to share Zurzur's visit with you. What you don't know, Mustafa, is that Zurzur has your diary, and he shared some of it with Michelle. We suspect he got it from Nijad. His purpose in relaying the information was to break up your relationship with Michelle. Can you guess which dates they chose to let her review?"

William stood up. "What dates? Will someone clue me in? This is starting to sound too entangled. What's this about, Rose?" He sat back down.

Rose looked at Michelle. "If the truth is what makes people free, this is the time. I wasn't sure if you would want to continue with Mustafa after you read about his affair with Amanda."

William jumped up again and asked, "What affair?!"

"It's not what you think," said Rose. "The whole incident was no more and no less than making sure that Mustafa was not impotent. The arrangements made for his treatment stopped as soon as Dr. Stonewell ascertained that Mustafa was sexually potent. Michelle is convinced that the whole thing was medical in nature."

Rose stopped and said, "I'll let Michelle finish and express her thoughts."

Michelle looked at her father and said, "Dad, it is all in Mustafa's diary—how he didn't want to participate in the therapeutic care at first, and then listened to Dr. Stonewell and obeyed the doctor's plan of treatment. His actions were done grudgingly, even though the regimen did work. Yes, he even mentions how he was afraid that it would ruin our relationship. Do you understand the dynamics of the whole thing?"

"I do understand everything consciously, but subconsciously I think I may have trouble with this scenario," said William.

Mustafa looked around and then said, "Allow me to speak. I want to say my peace and let everyone think about it deeply and carefully. I do not believe that I have loved, or will ever love, someone as much as I love Michelle. I thought that by walking the length of the United States, I would help myself by forgetting about and relieving myself of my trauma. What transpired and may still transpire is ten times more challenging, and most of it happened when Michelle has been in my life. I know that she loves me as much as I love her, but she may not want to take the risk of what lies ahead. The call is hers, and I will abide by her decision since I have already caused her enough trouble to last a lifetime. I will confine myself to my room and wait for her decision, and if I do not hear anything by tomorrow morning, I will know what that means."

Rose nodded at Michelle to speak. Michelle obeyed her aunt and said to Mustafa, "I know my dad knows what happened and what it means: it means that I don't want you to go to your room, for my mind is already set. For better or for worse, we'll continue to be together and fight it out together. Ours is a done deal. Let's think about what to do with these trumped-up charges!"

William said that he was very OK with Michelle's decision, and that he would have been heartbroken if it were otherwise. Rose said that she was heartened because she knew well that Michelle would decide to continue, and Mustafa would do the same. "I can see it in their eyes and feel it in every move they take," said Rose.

William called Carpenter, who asked to meet with all four of them, Mustafa, Michelle, William, and Rose. Once they were in his office, Carpenter advised them that this was a new charge, and legally it had nothing to do with the dismissed charges. He added that the only way to dismiss it was to successfully challenge its valid-ity. Carpenter was sure that Mustafa would eventually prevail, but Michelle was disappointed to hear him say that he might not prevail if Zurzur managed to bribe the judge. William explained that his associate criminal attorney in Utah told him that Zurzur had done it once before.

In short order, Carpenter contacted the same Utah criminal attorney who helped in releasing Mustafa against the murder charges. He advised him to challenge the charges but to prepare for a protracted fight. The court decided on a million-dollar bail. Wil-liam told Carpenter that he was willing to put up $100,000 and post bail through a bailsman.

———

When they were once again congregated at the farm, Mustafa said, "Michelle, I feel bad about involving your family once again in my troubles. Please, give me some space and let me think about it."

He walked into the dining room but came back very quickly. "Why not contact my cousin Carlos? He can afford this very easily—and he is not from the corrupt side of my family."

Mustafa picked up the phone and called Carlos.

"It's about time you called me," said Carlos. "You should keep in touch all the time."

"I'm sorry. Let me explain what's been going on." Completing the explanation, Mustafa said, "William is willing to foot the $100,000 to bail me out."

"Nonsense," said Carlos. "I will put up the sum. With $12 million in the bank and $148 million in other reserves, $100,000 means very little to me."

Mustafa immediately relayed the information to Michelle and William, explaining that Carlos was going to put up the money. William was not happy, but when Mustafa told him that Carlos had $12 million sitting in the bank, William relented.

By the evening, all four felt somewhat relieved but still anxious. They were unexpectedly joined by Hassan, who had been visiting Zeina all day. He told the four that his brother, Farouk, the Qatari ambassador, and his family decided to drop in for two days the following week, and that his wife and child would be spending their days with Zeina.

William was quick to speak up. "Please let me offer my hospitality to host the ambassador and his family."

"The whole family, plus one security guy, will be staying at a hotel," Hassan said. "Mustafa, I mentioned to my brother, Farouk, that your cousin, Carlos, is in the slaughterhouse business. Farouk asked for Carlos's contact information, as Qatar needs to build several slaughterhouse facilities."

Mustafa later called Carlos again and relayed the possible business prospect, to which he responded enthusiastically.

"I certainly don't mind meeting the ambassador in the United States," Carlos said. "At the same time, I will get a chance to see you two to discuss the problems being instigated by Nijad."

Within days, both Farouk and his family and Carlos were in Durham. They agreed that Carlos would send two of his architects to Qatar to investigate helping the Qatari government build slaughterhouses.

CHAPTER 27

All the parties met again within a few days to finalize the details of Nijad's downfall. The conversation opened with the problem of the charges pending against Mustafa in Utah.

"When I met with Nijad the first time, he proposed a business deal that required $7 million of investment on my part," said Carlos. "The deal had been negotiated and everything was ready to go until I found out it was all a scam that involved criminal elements. Because of that, and because of his treatment of Mustafa, I am intent on stopping him, and stopping him once and for all."

"Keep in mind that Zurzur may be a conduit to reach Nijad. The diary that Zurzur possesses must have come from him," said Michelle.

Carlos made note of the revealed link between the two and Mustafa affirmed the same. "There are also the two Utah private eyes who helped me and Michelle in the past. They appeared to be very professional, and I know they dislike Zurzur," said Mustafa.

Carlos promised to take all of that into consideration. Then Farouk said, "Why don't we use my good ambassadorial offices to introduce Carlos to the FBI? Let me call the FBI and arrange for you to meet with them."

Carlos flew back with Ambassador Fakhry to DC, where Carlos met with two FBI agents. He right away identified Nijad as his cousin and expressed his suspicion that Nijad was cooperating with other gangsters. The meeting lasted two hours. In the end, the agents told Carlos that they did not seem to possess any evidence that either Zurzur or Nijad had violated any federal laws. It was a big disappointment to Carlos.

He went back to Durham to inform the group of the disappointing news and to encourage them to come up with an effective plan. No sooner had Carlos gotten back than one of the FBI agents called and advised him that one way they could entrap Zurzur is to try to have him sell them Mustafa's diary, and to make sure that he sent it in the mail. The agent also told Carlos for the plan to work, someone had to offer Zurzur much more than Nijad was seemingly paying him for his services.

The group agreed that Michelle was the perfect candidate. She needed to impress upon Zurzur that she was still interested in the original diary and did not want partial copies, and that she was willing to pay a hefty price. Then Mustafa said, "Michelle, how about if William contacts Zurzur, pretending that he is against our relationship, and wants as many points as possible to use against me to end this 'damned love affair.'"

Michelle jumped in. "I do not like it at all. It's too negative and maybe ominous."

"I agree," said Rose. "It sounds eerie, although perhaps more effective than Michelle making the contact."

"I don't want to say you two women are superstitious…" said Carlos. "Maybe Mustafa suggesting this approach is proof that his trust in his love for Michelle is strong enough to withstand anything, even the infamy of being duplicitous."

"I agree with Carlos," said William. "If Michelle doesn't object, I'll gladly do it." Jokingly, he added, "After all, I can approve any sum requested on the spot. I don't need to check it out with any-one!"

Carlos said, "No, this is my idea. I want Nijad caught because he has been trying to stick it to the family. I am not the only one he tried to swindle, and after all, Mustafa is my cousin; William, not yet your son-in-law yet. Like they say, let the tribes pay for their own mistakes."

William said nothing, silently showing his agreement.

"I am allotting $50,000 to accomplish the mission," said Carlos.

Rose jokingly said, "If that's the case, I'll volunteer!"

Everyone laughed, and any tension regarding the discussion dissolved. Farouk said that his wife and daughter were having lots of fun with Zeina and Zeina Junior. He extended a dinner invita-tion which included his wife and baby, Zeina and Zeina Junior. He told Mustafa, "With your permission, I would like to invite Zeina and your daughter to spend a week with us in Washington, DC."

Mustafa said, "Actually, you only need to check with Zeina. She has been Zeina Junior's mother and father from the start." Farouk nodded and everyone took notice, especially Michelle.

———

Two days later, William called Zurzur with a convenient pretense. After he introduced himself, he openly told him that he was no longer in favor of Mustafa's relationship with his daughter, and that he was about to kick Mustafa off the farm. He added that he had several arguments with his daughter, and if it weren't for his sister, Rose, he would have convinced Michelle to leave Mustafa.

William continued, "Listen, Mr. Zurzur. I heard Michelle talking to her friend in New Haven and she mentioned that she has copies of Mustafa's diary, where he confessed to having side affairs in the meantime!"

"Yes, she does have some copies. But there is juicier stuff that she hasn't seen. She has only around twenty pages."

"No, no, twenty pages will not cut it. I want to analyze every bit of that diary, and I want to expose Mustafa to Michelle and Rose. He was all the time lying about his background. I want to expose that angle too, on top of his betrayal of my daughter," said William.

"I can send you a complete copy of the diary," Zurzur said.

"No, that is not good enough. I want the original," said William.

When Zurzur asked him why the original, he told Zurzur that was what his attorney advised him. "You have a good attorney," said Zurzur. "I met him at a conference in Utah. Give me two days to think about it. By the way, how much are you willing to pay?"

"Well, I'm surprised that you're asking for any money at all," William said. "But if it's that important to you, I think $10,000 is fair."

Zurzur said he still wanted to think about it for two days.

William knew that since it was the original, he was asking for, Zurzur most likely had to check with Nijad. William's lawyer told him that Nijad would make sure he had a complete copy of the diary before selling the original.

Zurzur called William two days later. "I've decided that this is more valuable to you than $10,000. I think $100,000 is more reasonable."

William pretended to be shocked. "I may be able to pay thirty, but not seventy."

Again, Zurzur told him to wait two more days. William's lawyer was right on the button when he told William that Zurzur would have to check with Nijad again.

When the phone rang two days later, Zurzur made a final offer of $70,000, provided William would pay in advance.

William agreed to pay seventy but said that it was out of the question to pay in advance, and the two items to be exchanged must be verified through some kind of procedure. Zurzur asked about the kind of procedure. This time William told him that he did not know and would get back to him later.

William asked Farouk to check with the FBI.

Farouk relayed to William that they suggested having William convince Zurzur to cross state lines while carrying the diary. "As the diary is stolen property, it will come under their jurisdiction if transported in this fashion, and especially if it was sold," Farouk added. "The FBI agents said that the Denver airport is a possible venue for the exchange."

When William spoke with Zurzur next, he proposed to him what the FBI had suggested. The meeting took place. William checked Michelle's copies against the original pages of the diary. He then checked specific markers relayed to him by Mustafa, and upon verifying that the original was real, he handed the cash to Zurzur. He barely walked fifty feet before four FBI agents surrounded him. They were all young females, which managed to confuse Zurzur's two security men.

William went back to Durham feeling like a real hero. Farouk and his family had left, but all the others, having received the news in advance, were waiting for him, including Zeina and Zeina Junior. It was a glorious evening with the group having dinner in the cellar. What was particularly different at this dinner pertained to Zeina and Hassan. As they cheered William's success, Hassan and Zeina exhibited very warm exchanges. Mustafa looked at Michelle and Michelle looked at Mustafa, both with clear satisfaction at what had been developing between the other two.

————

Zurzur did not understand what was happening at first. Despite his many criminal activities, he had never given any thought to the possibility of being played. He tried from the start to claim that the money was his, but the FBI was more than ready. They had advised William to make copies of every single $100 bill, four to a page, for a total of 125 pages. When the FBI showed Zurzur the copies, he knew it was all well-orchestrated as he recognized he had been had, in proper order.

As was the case with many of the FBI's operations, they dangled the possibility of a reduced sentence for Zurzur. His bail was set at $500,000 since he was also being accused of organizing the attack on Mustafa, an attack that was related to transporting the diary across state lines and attempting to sell it. Zurzur did not have the money and contacted Nijad to bail him out, knowing he was putting him in a bind. In guarded language, Nijad told him he could afford to foot 10 percent of the bail, $50,000, but he wanted to think about it to be sure he could make such a contribution clandestinely without getting implicated. That was fine with Zurzur, who nonetheless made sure that Nijad knew that without bailing him out, he was taking a risk of Zurzur cooperating with the FBI!

————

Mustafa and Michelle were sleeping in separate rooms due to his fragile condition. That evening Michelle went to his room in her nighty, snuggled next to him, gave him a kiss, and asked, "What do you think about your ex-girlfriend's new affair?"

Mustafa teased back, telling her not to criticize the mother of his child.

"I have to confess that Zeina Junior is so cute, and you should be proud of her and of your past relationship with Zeina, which produced such a beauty," said Michelle.

"I am very proud of you, but I expect compounded pride when we have another Zeina Junior, one who will resemble her mother," said Mustafa.

"I keep saying it—you're a charmer," said Michelle.

He told her that he was feeling much better and that in a couple of days, he wanted to go and swim in the pond where she attempted to jump naked.

"What are you planning to do? Do you want to get rid of me? To jump in a four-foot-deep pond?" said Michelle.

"No, I have a surprise for you, but none that I can share with you now," said Mustafa.

"I am so happy you're here in my arms. Poor soul, you have gone through a lot. It's time for me to try to unwind with you! I'll just hold you in my arms all night, and I care less about the surprise," said Michelle.

As everyone was waiting for news about Zurzur's interrogation, Mustafa and Michelle went to their favorite pond. She was wearing a revealing bikini, while Mustafa was wearing swimming trunks. She wanted to go into the water, and at the same time drag Mustafa along. He stopped her, carried her in his arms, and kissed her repeatedly and passionately. He then placed her down on the sand of the pond, took off her top and then her bottom, and made love to her passionately and romantically, several times over.

Michelle was involved in every move and every breath. Above enjoying the part, she indulged herself in buttressing the fact that Mustafa was back to normal and more sexual. "Don't get out of me—I want to feel you all the way. It has been a long time coming. Now I know what I was missing. In the past, I was resigned to living with you, regardless; I'm afraid now I can't live without. Let's do it again," said Michelle.

Mustafa responded immediately, with the same strong passion he exhibited through and through. "You think if you were to sue those thugs who attacked you, you could convince the judge that what they have denied you all those years was much more than average lovemaking?" asked Michelle playfully.

"Sure, I can, and we will make love in front of the judge and the jury. If we perform like today, they can't help but award us big bucks," said Mustafa, snickering. "But even this may backfire. What happens if the jury gets impressed with our lovemaking but decides that it is all your doing, not mine?"

"No, no, you must have made passionate love to Zeina as well," said Michelle.

"Would you believe it? I only made love to Zeina twice. This is why I never thought she would get pregnant, and no, it was not as passionate. On one occasion we were interrupted. This is why we are here. Nobody comes to this pond to interrupt what we are doing. You see, Michelle, our eyes must savor each other's bodies and our minds must savor each other's minds. Passionate love follows. Didn't you see me looking at your gorgeous body and my thoughts surfacing, recalling your moves and your expressions?" said Mustafa, minimizing the quality of his love making with Zeina.

"You know, Mustafa, I don't think this is a put-on. You really mean it, and it is so beautiful. Have you ever thought of writing?" asked Michelle.

"Writing poetry, sure, since you mentioned it. We now must take care of three challenges. The first is Nijad, the second is Amanda, and the third is Zeina," said Mustafa.

Michelle raised her torso, looking at Mustafa lying on the sandy ground with total surprise. "Nijad, I understand, but what about Amanda and Zeina?" she asked with a strange look. Mustafa then explained to her that he was still working on a stock quantitative analysis program that had so far proven two-tenths percent more accurate than anything on the market. Amanda was his coach in promoting the program to the investment world. As far as Zeina was concerned, Mustafa said that he wanted her and Hassan to get married, since he wanted Zeina Junior to have an ideal stepfather, and one who could teach her Arabic.

"Why haven't you mentioned those before?" asked Michelle.

"Both subjects are relatively new. Plus, at the same time, I was continually getting in trouble and distracted. You were always busy trying to bail me out."

Michelle looked at Mustafa amusingly. "Can I ask you a question? Please don't take it the wrong way. Is it in the genes?"

"What are you talking about?" asked Mustafa.

"I'm talking about Palestinian genes. Is it in your genes to be constantly in trouble and turmoil?" said Michelle, smiling.

"Yes, it is, and it is also in the genes that we make love every day. But next time you have to strip naked in the house before you walk to this pond," said Mustafa playfully.

"Your thoughts about Zeina are noble, and Hassan is handsome, educated, and rich," said Michelle.

"No, Farouk is rich, but Hassan is almost penniless. He is not allowed into Qatar because he criticized the sheikh of Qatar in the papers. In retaliation, the Qatari government froze over $10 million worth of assets—all that he owned," said Mustafa.

Michelle was surprised. Mustafa told her that he was anxious to make money, to help support Zeina Junior, and that he did not want Sammy, Zeina's father, to keep on supporting her.

"What about Amanda? I'm not comfortable watching you associate with her, said Michelle.

"What options do I have? I'm only a month or two from presenting my program to three different investment firms, all courtesy of Amanda," he said.

"Well, I'll have something for you to consider soon, but I don't have anything right now," said Michelle.

CHAPTER 28

When the two returned to the farm, Bertha asked Michelle if she planned to take a nap in the afternoon. "You know better. I don't take naps!"

Bertha slyly said, "You were at the pond, weren't you? I guess you went up and down several times… That is, in the water."

Michelle understood the insinuation and said nothing but gave her an astute smile.

When the group finally received the news, it was discouraging. Nijad seemed to have promised Zurzur lots of money for his silence, but for an unknown reason, he could not bail him out through a bailsman. He needed to pay the total sum of $500,000. Although Nijad would not, Zurzur was still not singing despite having sold Mustafa's diary to William.

Rose alerted everyone that they needed to regroup that evening to prepare for a thorough conversation at dinner. The discussions, which included Mustafa, Michelle, William, Rose, and Hassan, were animated. There were a dozen suggestions, but none were adopted by the group. Finally, all agreed that there was little to be done against Nijad without Zurzur's cooperation.

Mustafa suggested that each one should think of something that would cause Nijad serious legal problems.

Michelle jumped in and said, "We've only been considering two jurisdictions, Utah and federal. What about Nijad's home state of Illinois—what's his record like there?"

They were all surprised that they had not thought of this. "Does anyone have contacts there?" asked Rose.

"I could ask Farouk to give a speech to the Palestinian-American community of Illinois. While he's there, he can establish contacts and check on Nijad," said Hassan.

"I can contact my criminal attorney, Carpenter, and have him check the court records of Illinois about Nijad."

Everyone was very happy to finally get the ball rolling. The following day, they put their thoughts in motion. In no time, Carpenter let them know that he had found out that Nijad had been sued tens of times.

"But somehow," said Carpenter, "he has managed to either win or to have the lawsuits dropped. I smell something fishy—there is no way that thirty-three lawsuits were dropped by the courts. Let me do some more investigating."

It was a pleasant surprise for everyone to hear back from Carpenter that same day. "The plaintiffs in twenty-two of the lawsuits were Arab Americans, and three of the Arab American plaintiffs were prominent Chicago businessmen. I'd like your permission to look into these three."

"Definitely!" said William.

"And make sure they're invited to attend my brother's speech, and are included in the dinner afterward," said Hassan.

———

Hassan's brother, Farouk, paid special attention to the two of the three who attended his speech. He also found a way to extend their time together.

"I'm on a mission to connect Qatari business interests with business interests in the different Arab American communities. I need some local help in the process. Is this anything you can assist me with?"

Both were more than happy to help. Farouk met with the two for breakfast and asked about Nijad.

One of them said, "I'd advise you not to deal with Nijad. He's dishonest, and a gangster."

"I am glad I asked you, for he is one of the candidates on my list to do business with," said Farouk, having made that story up. "Could either of you give me some details about the man's dishonesty? I want to make a record of it and eliminate him from any future consideration."

The two gave Farouk several examples, with one particularly interesting legal transgression. "Nijad provided the sexual services of one newly recruited eighteen-year-old girl to a businessman in Wisconsin. The businessman turned out to be a sadist and a torturer. The girl managed to escape and returned to Michigan, where she hid and initiated a lawsuit against Nijad and the businessman. Nijad ended up paying her a large sum of money to shut her up."

Farouk reported the incident to Carpenter, who in turn thought the FBI may be interested in it due to its nature, being an interstate crime.

"I'm sure the FBI will be disinclined to do any early research into the situation, so I will instead engage the services of the two private eyes who had helped Mustafa and Michelle in Utah," said Carpenter.

In no time, they located the teenager, who had moved to California. Unfortunately, Carpenter reported that after the FBI visited her, she relayed the news of their visit to Nijad. On his own, he gave her another considerable sum of money so she would refuse to cooperate with the FBI.

———

The news about Nijad's staying outside the grasp of the law was frustrating to all. Down in Argentina, Carlos was always in the loop, but his participation was not known to Nijad. Carlos tried to invite Nijad to visit him, but he turned the invitation down. Carlos knew well that he could control matters much more easily out of Argentina as he was well connected, all the way to the president of the republic.

Carlos again proposed that the whole group get together in Durham, and also include the two private eyes, Carpenter, Zeina, Amanda, Willie, and Faris. Amanda's inclusion did not sit well with Michelle.

"Carlos wants to include everyone mentioned in the diary, despite the fact that Nijad is aware of their association with Mustafa," Hassan explained to her. "Carlos believes that Nijad will contact some of them, sooner or later."

William's fourteen-seat table in the cellar managed to accommodate everyone. Carpenter managed the meeting. "Can you all identify yourselves?"

When it was Zeina's turn, she said, "I'm Zeina. Mustafa and I have a child together. Hassan and I are dating." It was the first public announcement of the relationship between the two.

When it came to Amanda, Michelle and Mustafa were tense

about her potential answers. They thought she would talk about her relationship with Mustafa, but she did not. She said that she had been Mustafa's professor at Stanford and that she was still working with him, consulting on his efforts to sell his research to potential investment firms.

"Now, let me be clear," Carpenter said when the introductions were finished. "I want to entrap Nijad in the most legal way possible. I will not accept any talk of using illegal methods."

Carlos interjected and said, "We can use American legal instruments in America and Argentine legal instruments in Argentina. I can control things better out of Argentina, all the way to the United States".

"That goes without saying," Carpenter said. "But remember that Nijad, in the final analysis, will have to be prosecuted in the United States." Both agreed and left it at that.

Amanda asked, "Is Nijad's contact information and address available to the group?"

"Yes, I have those details and can make them available to anyone interested," said Carpenter.

"Yes, I want them," said Amanda, surprising Carlos.

"I think everyone should consider any and all potential legal methods to get to Nijad, provided you check with me first. Then the group will connect through a conference call within one month," said Carpenter.

———

When Michelle and Mustafa left the house in the evening, Michelle whispered in Mustafa's ear that he had to perform again. When he asked why, she said that Amanda's presence reminded her that he had a debt to pay for his relationship with Amanda. He looked at Michelle with a darkening face and bulging eyes. Before he said anything, she commented, "What's wrong? Why are you looking at me like this? I was joking! Don't take it seriously."

Mustafa spoke slowly but firmly. "You keep reminding me of this weird relationship in my life. It came about due to a tragic and traumatic experience, plus its aftermath. I would rather forget about it, but you continually bring it up. I have never loved Amanda; neither did I have any desire to have sex with her. It is something that happened, all prescribed by a psychiatrist. I want to forget about the whole thing, but you keep mentioning it, sucking the air out of the room. You need to understand I will never touch Amanda again, even if my whole life depended on it—not only my sex life."

Michelle tried to soothe his feelings, but to no avail. He told her that he was going to his room alone and not to bother him. That was the first time Mustafa's anger had surfaced. It was civilized, but critical and firm. Michelle felt bad. She left for her room to bury her disappointment and harmful attitude under the bed cover.

In the morning, this time it was Mustafa who went into Michelle's room. He found her curled up in bed. He asked her to get up, freshen up, and for the two of them to go for a walk in the fresh air. Michelle hugged him for a long while, apologized, and got ready.

During the walk, Mustafa told her that Amanda was working on her own and no longer at Stanford. "She is consulting at seven different investment firms, and she has a new boyfriend, a twenty-one-year-old student who has just graduated from Stanford. I hope this eases your mind. She was not after Mustafa Makram—she is after young and firm bodies, and she is easily able to find them around with ease. And by the way, I will say it again: she was nothing more to me than a masturbation facilitator. Do you get it, Michelle?"

"I got it, loud and clear. Even when you speak with an accent and use foul language, I got it," said Michelle.

Mustafa apologized for his choice of words. They snuggled together, walking quietly for several minutes. He stopped and said, "We have been concentrating on Nijad. I think we need to think of cementing Zeina's relationship with Hassan instead. They complement each other well, and they will be great parents to Zeina Junior. Zeina has been a single parent for too long. I think it will make me feel better if they hook up permanently."

Michelle looked at him. "With or without Hassan, Zeina Junior now has a father and two mothers, and two local grandparents, Sammy and William. There is a possibility she may be your only child. I want her to be mine too, if Zeina allows it. I know both of us want children, but what about if we can't?" exclaimed Michelle, trying to solicit Mustafa's opinions about life without children.

"Then it will be the two of us, except when Zeina Junior is with us. And who knows? Zeina and Hassan will probably have children of their own and we will be their second parents, just like you want to be Zeina Junior's second mother," said Mustafa.

He told her that Hassan's biggest challenge was the fact he was almost penniless and did not have even a work permit.

Michelle said, "I thought that his brother Farouk could secure a work permit for him."

Mustafa contacted Farouk. "Did you know that Zeina has publicly confirmed her relationship with Hassan? Under such circumstances, do you think you would consider getting involved in helping him?"

"The only reason I did not try earlier to get Hassan and Zeina closer was because I was considerate of your feelings," said Farouk. "Now, knowing where you stand, I will try my determined best. I am more than capable and willing to support Hassan financially 100 percent."

"I think that Hassan would be too proud to accept help as a married man," Mustafa said. "How about if the family could start a business for Hassan? Then you could have a lien against his frozen assets."

The idea was welcomed by Farouk, who said that he couldn't get involved to help Hassan in Qatar, but he had friends in Saudi Arabia who would do such a transaction, with a hefty collateral against Hassan's frozen assets. He promised to start working on it right away.

Mustafa told Michelle about the newly proposed arrangement. She loved it and suggested that the two of them, Hassan and Zeina, have dinner together without anyone else.

Michelle said that it would be nice to start working on this basis—couple to couple. She also suggested that they start having Zeina Junior visit to give Zeina and Hassan time together. Rose and William also said they wanted to take care of Zeina Junior.

———

Amanda had already arranged three presentations for Mustafa to demonstrate his quantitative stock analysis program. Having secured Nijad's contacts, she—without telling anybody—was planning to go after Nijad in a big way. Her interest in young men notwithstanding, Amanda was a principled and determined person, yet very adventurous. She felt bad about Mustafa's serious beating by Nijad's men.

Amanda called Mustafa. "The presentation dates are set over three days in New York."

When he arrived, Michelle was with him. She accompanied both of them to the three presentation dates.

The first investment firm said that they had tested Mustafa's abbreviated program and were impressed with it, but they had to test the real program before they could assess it. Amanda said she was sure Mustafa would not mind. However, he did mind a potential investor having unrestricted access to his program. Instead, he countered by offering to spend three days with them demonstrating the program, but not to provide unrestricted access to it. The firm accepted and a date was set.

The presentations at the other firms went just as well. Mustafa told them that he was willing to demonstrate the complete program, since he had agreed to do the same at the first firm. There were no objections.

Within a month, Amanda, Mustafa, and Michelle were back in New York, but this time for an extended ten-day stay. Amanda could see how proud Michelle was of Mustafa's demeanor and command of the meetings. She kept expressing her pride and continuously encouraged him. Amanda was also very impressed with Mustafa's knowledge and mastery of his software.

Two of the companies relayed that they were ready to make an offer after confirming that Mustafa's program enhanced returns by at least two-tenths of 1 percent. Mustafa called the third and they accepted the opportunity to make their offer at the same time the other two did. They offered $5 million, $8 million, and $10 million. The $10 million offer came with a stipulation that he would not work with any other investment firm. Mustafa turned it down and finally accepted the $8 million offer. Amanda's cut was 10 percent, amounting to $800,000.

When the three went back to New York to sign the legal documents and receive the payment, Amanda said right away, "Now I have the financial tools to fight Nijad."

"What?" asked Mustafa. "I didn't think that you were so intent on going after Nijad. It sounds a little strange."

She didn't answer him, and the three spent a pleasant time together without Amanda elaborating on her statement about Nijad. They returned to North Carolina and Amanda began putting her thoughts into action.

———

William was not in on the prospects of Mustafa achieving a windfall at this young age. When Michelle sat down, she shared the news with William and Rose, who were overwhelmed and pleased beyond bounds. Mustafa said that he and Michelle were going to visit Carlos in Argentina, but before embarking on that trip, he intended to loan Hassan $500,000 to start a business. He then said, "If Michelle approves."

His statement quickly elicited surprised looks on William's and Rose's faces. Michelle maintained a blank look without saying a word. Everyone was still thinking about how to get to Nijad.

CHAPTER 29

Amanda organized her plan of attack as if she were preparing a lecture for her class. She set up two binders, one describing the operation and another containing the relevant documents. She kept the first one in her desk, but the second was in her safe.

She started trying to contact Nijad, but he refused to take her calls. Ever since Zurzur was entrapped in Denver, Nijad had become very careful. Two weeks later, he cautiously called her back, and she asked to get together with him. He suggested they do business over the phone. She rejected that idea on the pretext that either phone might be wiretapped.

Reluctantly, Nijad agreed to meet with her in Chicago. She was picked up in one of his limousines and driven to a bakery. Nijad was not there, but two of his assistants were. They interviewed Amanda, which turned into an interrogation. When they were satisfied, they drove Amanda to a second location at the beach. There, they kept her waiting for an hour before Nijad showed up.

When he looked at Amanda, she could tell that he was very impressed with her youth and looks. Her reaction was the opposite of Nijad's. She saw a man, sixty to seventy pounds overweight who was bursting at the seams. He seemed like he had high blood pressure, and his breathing was wheezy.

Yet, she was determined and had set her mind to carry through regardless. His looks were only a minor impediment. She told Nijad that she wanted to cooperate with him—a spurned woman who had been dumped as soon as Mustafa managed to revive his sexual functions. She described what she had to do to accomplish that, appearing to consider her actions to be necessary but distasteful.

Nijad told her directly that he did not trust anybody, and that she had to prove that it was not all a trap. In the evening, she slept with Nijad to his full sexual satisfaction, including giving him a blow job. Furthermore, she mustered to reach a climax herself. To Nijad's self-centered and tribal mind, Amanda convinced him that she was desperate to take revenge on Mustafa, resorting to sleeping with a man she did not know before, nor did she then.

Amanda's plan included the pretense of needing money. She did not want Nijad to know anything about the $800,000 largess. Their relationship progressed as Amanda performed perfectly. She became like a mistress to him. Nijad, in appreciation, gave her close to $10,000 a month. Amanda always mentioned how much those payments helped her.

Before Mustafa and Michelle left for Argentina, Amanda asked to visit with them. She flew to Durham and the three had dinner at a fancy restaurant. She managed to arrange dining at the chef's table, in the kitchen, in case any of them was being followed. She told them that she wanted to put them into the picture, and for them to relay it to the other members of the group. Mustafa and Michelle thought they were ready for Amanda's news. Right off the bat, she said, "I want you to know that for the last six weeks, I've been sleeping with Nijad."

They were stunned. Mustafa leaned backward, putting his two hands on his head, and stared at her, repulsed and angry. It was obvious that he did not know what to say. After staring at Amanda, Michelle held Mustafa's arm with her two hands, also dumbfounded.

Amanda said, "I planned the whole thing. To me, Nijad resembles my stepfather, who raped me at the age of thirteen and kept abusing me physically and sexually until my mother reported him to the police. Nijad did the same thing to you, Mustafa, short of raping you, and I intend to make him pay for what he did to you. It's true we had sex behind Michelle's back, but my motives were noble. I intended to help you and to hand you over to her in perfect body and good spirit. I'm like you, Mustafa. Every time Nijad sleeps with me, I see my stepfather. He sure brought up bad memories."

The two kept totally silent. They did not know how to respond. "And you want us to tell this to William, Rosa, Farouk, and Carlos?" asked Mustafa. "How can we also share it with Carpenter? It makes no sense to me. Why would you go to such lengths? You sound obsessed. It makes no sense," he said again. "I cannot deal with it. I must give it serious thought because there is something off here. I know what I am thinking, but I don't know what Michelle is thinking!"

Michelle said, "I'm not able to think. This is very strange. Did you consider what will happen if Nijad discovers your duplicity? He will probably kill you. No, no, this isn't right."

Amanda looked at them and said, "I'm going to do it—just don't betray me. You must tell the others before Nijad tries to check on things. You must especially tell Carlos right away, as Nijad thinks he's on his side."

Michelle looked at Mustafa and said, "I have an idea. Let's all three of us try to meet with Carpenter before we tell anybody else."

The following day, Carpenter made time for them and heard the full story. "You're on your own, Amanda. I'm advising my clients not to participate in the scheme, but at the same time for you not to share your plan with anyone." Carpenter shook his head. "Be careful. You're dealing with a gangster. I suggest you contact the two Utah private eyes directly to help you out. They were very dependable. I know you recently received $800,000, and that amount should provide you with ample money to pursue ten cases of the kind at the same time."

Amanda asked to meet with all present, in Durham. She told them in a more gentle and circumspect way that she was associating with Nijad to extract incriminating information from him. She added that she knew that some of them might disagree with her, but it was too late.

When Rose tried to argue against her plan, Michelle stopped her and told her that they had already consulted with Carpenter. "His advice is for everyone else to distance themselves from Amanda's plans, and for Amanda to make her own decisions. She has in fact already done that, and it is too late to back out now."

Within hours, Amanda was on her way back to California. She got a call from Nijad asking her if she could make the trip to Chicago over the weekend, and that he missed her. Amanda reminded him that she had previously told him that she did not plan to exclusively go out with anyone, including him, and that she had a local date over the weekend. Nijad offered her an additional $10,000, but she answered that he was missing the point and forgetting that her association with him was for the purpose of taking revenge on

Mustafa. She added that she was not selling herself to get rich.

It seemed as if Nijad was becoming infatuated with Amanda. The following Monday, he called to tell her that he was willing to fly over to California and still would pay her $10,000. Amanda snapped at him and said, "I'm not going to sell myself, neither in Chicago nor California. If we become real good friends and I happen to need money, I may borrow some from you, but listen to this carefully: this is not sex for money. We are friends since we have a common enemy."

"Mustafa must have really spurned you to get under your skin!"

"I am no different from you. You are after Mustafa because you were insulted and belittled. I was belittled and trivialized because the way he dropped me was totally demeaning."

Through all this give and take, Amanda was sure Nijad believed that she was genuinely interested in exacting revenge against Mustafa.

"We can rendezvous next week, do you agree?"

"It won't work that way," Amanda said. "I think we should spend two days a month together, alternating between Chicago and California."

Nijad had no choice. He accepted the arrangement for the two to get together the first weekend of every month. When he was scheduled next to fly over to see Amanda, he asked her to have a bottle of Johnny Walker, Black Label, ready for him. She recalled when she was with him in Chicago, he was drinking the same constantly. *Could Nijad, with all his rosy cheeks and protruding belly, be an alcoholic? That may be an angle to get at him with.* But she could not think of anything specific.

They had agreed to have dinner before going to the hotel.

Amanda could see that Nijad was irritable.

"Zurzur's incarceration is annoying, mostly because it is denying me his services as a potential effective operator. At the same time, his charges will potentially cause the FBI to associate the two of us together," he said.

"That's quite a problem," said Amanda. "What are your choices?"

"I don't really have a choice. I can either bail him out or not. I can attach some conditions to my paying off his bail. You will like this: in return for the $500,000 bail, Zurzur will be assigned to arrange a kneecapping of Mustafa."

Amanda nodded and kept eating. After thinking out loud for quite a while, he told Amanda that he decided to bail Zurzur from prison.

When they arrived at their rendezvous hotel, he brought a foldable bag with him from the limousine. In the room, he immediately showed the contents to Amanda. He told her to take $10,000 and deliver the balance—$100,000—to a certain location yet to be determined. Amanda knew straight away that he was using her for his own purposes, beyond anything that had to do with Mustafa. She took the opportunity to further buttress her contrived hate for Mustafa.

"I'm not your carrier. Do you want to plan something for Mustafa, or shall we forget that we have ever met? There will be no more sex until we come up with a plan. This meeting is over. You can take your $110,000 and shove it," she said.

Nijad tried to calm her down, but she would not take no for an answer. She told him she was checking out and it was up to him to stay or to leave. Both left, but not before Amanda was sure Nijad had seen this aggressive side to her. He returned to Chicago empty-handed.

———

In the meantime, Michelle agreed to go with Mustafa to their pond, a preferred venue for their sexual activities. Michelle had an ulterior motive. She wanted Mustafa to loosen up and not associate her jokes and sarcasm with his experience, especially his traumatic experience of rape.

"Listen, Mustafa. I want you to listen to me through and through. The other day you got mad and slept by yourself because you thought I was hinting at what had happened to you at the Goldwater rally. That wasn't the case. I don't want you to stay uptight. Women get raped by the thousands every day here in the United States—you seem to think you're the only one. You are not even unique among men. I'm not trying to trivialize your feelings. Please, honey, loosen up and don't be suspicious about my jokes and comments. We are supposed to possess some intellectual thoughts. Don't shut me up. I don't want to feel constrained or be afraid to express myself. Do you agree with me?" asked Michelle.

Mustafa apologized. "There is a saying that those who count the lashes have a milder feeling than those being whipped. I know what you are saying, and I may be uptight, but I am the one who was whipped, and you—although most empathetic—are counting the lashes."

"Wow, what words of wisdom. Yet, based on what you just said, I guess I can't help it, I'm destined to count the lashes and you'll continue to recall the fact that you have been whipped, which brings me to what I wanted to say: you are a very attractive man in every respect, and I mean in every respect. I have been attracted to you from the very beginning, although I tried to make you a con man to deny my feelings for you. So does my father. He said more than once that he found in you the ideal person to be his surrogate son. What I'm wondering about is how come you attract people like Zurzur and Amanda. He has been crooked all his life, and she uses sex equally to achieve her noble or her devious objectives, almost with the same commitment and vigor!"

"What do you want me to do, psychoanalyze myself? I don't want to do such a thing. All you need to do is to shake me up when I behave in an uptight and self-righteous way, and I will probably listen to you and change my course. One day, the changes you produce in me will become permanent. Do you think I slept at all the other night when I lectured you? I don't think I even closed my eyes one time. I kept thinking of you and the unintentional hurt I caused you. Now, I don't want to dwell on what you said or what I said today. I want to be a genuine hillbilly from North Carolina, when in the mood all what they say, 'It is time for sex.'"

Mustafa and Michelle made love repeatedly and ran into Bertha as they returned. She said, "Is there any water left in that pond? I think you guys have splashed it all away."

CHAPTER 30

Nijad's feelings for Amanda were getting stronger by the day. Despite the fact he was married, it was routine for his cousins, and even his nephews, to ask him about his sexual triumphs. When a nephew asked him if he was going with a certain girlfriend, he answered that he was no longer associating with such uneducated people.

When he was asked why, he said he only went out with women with doctorates—mentally referring to Amanda. The nephew told him that he was not even a college graduate. Nijad said that he surely was, going into his bedroom and fetching a doctorate diploma he had bought from a university diploma mill for a mere $300.

———

Before bailing Zurzur out of prison, Nijad passed word to him that Amanda was working for him, and for Zurzur to cooperate with her. Zurzur got out to find that his so-called wives had carried out a coup. They called a couple of advocacy organizations that managed to involve the police and immediately convinced a judge as to their mistreatment.

The judge issued a ruling to the effect that Zurzur had kidnapped the young girls and was keeping them against their will. Almost immediately after his release, a Utah arrest warrant was issued for him.

Zurzur was out of the jurisdiction of the state of Utah at the time. While he was not sure about Amanda, he contacted her to help him out. She said that she could not meet with him but would try to help hide him from the authorities. She suggested that he come to California, and she would lease a furnished apartment where he could hide. If he could find a way to Colorado, she would facilitate his reaching California. Zurzur managed to take a bus from Kansas, where he had been in a federal prison, and reached Colorado.

There he was met by the two private eyes out of Utah. When Zurzur saw them, he knew he had been had. To start with, he was outside the state of Kansas, in violation of his bail terms. The two private eyes impressed upon him that they could easily take him back to Kansas, where his sentence would be increased, and his bail would be revoked for good. Without the slightest argument, Zurzur agreed to cooperate. He informed them that he did not know the whereabouts of Nijad, nor had he initiated any criminal activity with him.

———

Nijad waited for Amanda to call, and when she did, he set a date with her in Chicago. She accepted his invitation, concealing her plans, having arranged for the private eyes to be in Chicago. It so happened that Zurzur had called him before contacting Amanda, and the two men had arranged that Zurzur would be escorted from Colorado all the way to California by a couple of bodyguards.

As the bodyguards arrived to accompany Zurzur, they saw the two private eyes apprehending him. When Nijad heard about it, he knew that Amanda had betrayed both of them. He made sure she was met in Chicago by three of his assistants. They knew what to do before handing her to Nijad. Later, she knew she was in trouble as she was locked in a secret apartment where he raped her whenever he had the chance.

Having satisfied himself sexually, Nijad contacted the private eyes and proposed a swap.

———

The private eyes already suspected that something might have happened to Amanda when she did not show up in Colorado. That prompted them to change their plans and keep Zurzur instead of handing him over to the authorities. They informed the group after they received the exchange offer. It was a shock and a challenge to everyone, and for the first time, they felt the stakes had gotten significantly higher.

A meeting was held in Durham. The first thing Mustafa had to forget about was attending his commencement at Stanford. Michelle had intended to take pictures and shoot some clips to share with Mustafa's father, figuring it would be the perfect present, in addition to pictures of the engagement event, before their anticipated but not yet planned wedding. She was visibly shaken at the news of Amanda's kidnapping.

Carpenter spoke with a somber tone. He told the group the

plan had become much more serious, and now they were involved in causing direct danger to a human; namely, Amanda. He reminded them that while it was her naïveté which led to her kidnapping, every member of the group had a role in it. He did not think any of them was liable, but every one of them would be forever affected if anything were to happen to her. He recommended that an exchange be arranged as quickly as possible. Everyone agreed.

On top of the glum mood and sad faces of everyone, Mustafa felt responsible for the situation. None of it would have happened if it were not for him surfacing into their lives. He felt that he had to address the entangled mess they were in. It must have been the cumulative effect that hit and depressed him.

He looked at Michelle and said, "The circumstances that brought me into everyone's life were beyond my control, but if I had not appeared on this stage, no one would be in this mess. I alone cannot solve this situation, but my actions after we free Amanda may relieve you of my bad luck. It looks like the longer I hang around, the more pain I inflict on everyone, notwithstanding that I love each one of you—Michelle above all. In this case, it is better to concentrate misery in one person than to spread it around and destroy everyone's life more than it has already been damaged."

Michelle stared at him. "What do you think you're saying? Here we go again—you're trying to flagellate yourself to feel good. Like I told you once before, you have a Jesus complex. You want to be the sacrificial lamb of God. Let me tell you something, Mustafa Makram: Jesus was crucified to save humanity. If you crucify yourself, you'll ruin the lives of everyone here. Can you see the difference, or perhaps you just can't resist? You want to feel good about yourself regardless of what happens afterward! I've heard this song before. I didn't say much then, but I'll be damned if I'm going to keep silent this time. Stop moping and help us think of something to free Amanda. Many of the best ideas in this fight came from you, and you damned don't know how much we appreciate your contribution."

Michelle stood up and left. Rose spoke next. "This time I'm afraid I'm 100 percent on her side. You should not have said this. You're just piling on when we need the least thing to cheer us up. I mean it, Mustafa. Stop it and stop it altogether."

She continued. "Don't you understand? You're one of us now, so you can't just disappear. We will worry about you wherever you are, and you'll worry about us. Don't be a crybaby, always inflating everyone's supposedly fragile feelings. Permanent grief is not a substitute for a genuine resolution. This is what we are looking for, and this is what you should be working toward. You owe Michelle a big apology, and more so, you owe her a promise that you'll not do this again. This is your home, and we are your family."

Hassan excused himself and said that he would like to talk to Mustafa in Arabic. "What in the hell do you think you are doing? Man up, Mustafa. Men confirm their adulthood in tough times, they don't withdraw. You are embarrassing me too. What do you think everyone is thinking about you, including Zeina, who felt a great sense of loss when you disappeared? She may think now that she could have been altogether wrong! Keep sitting at this table, do your duty, participate with everyone else, and don't go after Michelle yet. She will simmer down overnight."

Mustafa stayed put. Right away, to change the subject, Hassan reverted to the subject of Amanda. The gathering slowly went back to normal. Mustafa excused himself and said that he was going to call Carlos, and they talked at length. They agreed that Carlos needed to interject himself into the picture right away.

———

In the evening, Mustafa went into Michelle's temporary room. She was dozing off, having secluded herself since she gave it to Mustafa. He woke her up, and as she opened her eyes, he said, "I am here to apologize for having been a jerk. You and Rose made me realize how inconsiderate I have been, and suddenly I agree with both of you. You have been my compass and I have been misguided. I hope you will forgive me."

Michelle got up to hug him. "You have been through a lot. I didn't mean to give you a hard time. I want you to see the glass half full; you will feel better, and you will make everyone else feel better. You don't need to apologize—I can't stop loving you no matter what. Rose adores you and thinks the world of you, and also thinks I'm so lucky."

Michelle kissed Mustafa passionately. He kissed her on her forehead and said, "I think you were right. I wanted to torture myself by leaving and separating from you. It would have been a death sentence for me. I do owe you a sincere apology."

———

Carlos called Nijad and told him that he wanted to help in facilitating the exchange. He asked Nijad to give him a couple of days. He also contacted the private eyes and asked them if they could assemble half a dozen private detectives, to be ready for the exchange. The additional private eyes would jump into action only if the exchange did not go as planned.

When he called Nijad back, Nijad said that he did not trust

anyone, since he had been betrayed twice before. At that point, Carlos said that he would fly to the United States and handle the exchange himself. Nijad again told him that he didn't think he could trust anybody. Carlos was ready for Nijad's hesitancy, and he knew how to jar his lack of confidence. He told Nijad that he was so confident about a smooth exchange that he was willing to transfer to him, unencumbered, $1 million right away, to be returned to him upon the completion of the exchange.

Nijad seemed to feel good about the offer, and he immediately accepted the new terms. Carlos was glad that Nijad had not done too much checking up before agreeing. He didn't realize that Carlos was the third richest man in Argentina, with a net worth of $160 million. Nijad thought Carlos was worth one-tenth of that. Obviously, a man of such lesser means would not risk so much of his wealth unless he were sincere.

The following day, Carlos transferred the $1 million to reach Nijad within twenty-four hours. Carlos had to involve the chairman of the board of the bank to complete the transaction. Based on the recommendation of the private eyes, a rendezvous site was chosen. Carlos's instructions were clear that nothing should take place than a clean exchange. He did not want a single complication to intervene. He asked the private eyes to have Mustafa meet Carlos, for the two to be on the same side, and for the exchange to appear tribal in nature, totally detached from American legal constraints.

On the third day, everyone involved showed up. Carlos and Mustafa approached Nijad. The three exchanged kisses, Middle Eastern style, all to Mustafa's dislike but with his full acquiescence. The exchange was completed without a hitch. Amanda hugged Mustafa and Carlos. She looked as if she had been tortured, and in a sense she was totally abused. She whispered in Mustafa's ear that

Nijad had raped her on nine different occasions—brutal sex, with her being handcuffed all the time—but she managed to survive.

During all of that, one of the private eyes was snapping pictures. He had three super high-definition cameras all set up. As soon as Zurzur shook hands and hugged Nijad, he told him that he expected someone would try to betray him again. When Carlos heard that, he said that he would be willing to fly Zurzur and Nijad back with him to Argentina until they felt safe to return to the United States. When Nijad told him that they did not have their passports, Carlos said that it was OK, and that he could get them into the country for one month.

———

Mustafa accompanied Amanda to Durham after he contacted Hassan and asked him to gather the group. Mustafa and Amanda entered the cellar with Mustafa wrapping his arms around Amanda. It was the moment feelings got publicly settled. Michelle realized that Mustafa's hug was that of care and concern. Above all, she was happy that things turned out successfully—it finally helped Mustafa get rid of his guilt about his liaison with Amanda. Michelle hugged Mustafa and kissed him ten times. Hassan approached Mustafa and told him that he made him proud; William did the same.

Carpenter said that he would take care of informing the FBI. Mustafa told Carpenter that Nijad and Zurzur were on their way to Argentina, accompanying Carlos on his private plane. Carpenter said that he would instead speak to Carlos the following day.

Michelle said, "I don't want any more meetings. I want to go to the pond, for me and Mustafa to relax." Mustafa knew what she was hinting at. Hassan, for the first time, kissed Zeina in public.

Rose said that she needed a vacation and that she was going to go to her house for two days to unwind.

That evening, before Michelle started her romantic interlude, Mustafa told her that he was going to let Carlos handle Zurzur and Nijad, and that he was going to concentrate on cementing a closer relationship between Hassan and Zeina.

"And we should prepare for our wedding."

Michelle said jokingly, "I think I changed my mind; I would rather continue making love to you by the pond. We don't need to get married."

Mustafa answered, "How about if we get married at the pond, and wait for all the guests to leave, after which we can get naked and make love all night?"

"No, that's impossible. It must be tonight." They headed to the pond where they engaged in sex all night.

In the morning, Bertha saw Michelle's scratches and said, "Well, this is what happens when you do in the pond what you should do in the bedroom."

Michelle just smiled, then asked Bertha, "How come you're always waiting for us when we come back from the pond?"

Bertha answered, "Because I can tell when you and Mustafa are headed there. I just wait for you to see how well it went." Michelle smiled and said nothing.

Carlos called the following day and suggested that Amanda fly to Argentina, to relax and be safe until things got finalized. Amanda accepted the all-paid vacation. When Mustafa called to check up on her, she told him she was housed in one of Carlos's twelve wineries.

"It's fabulous, Mustafa," Amanda said. "I'm being wined and dined every evening and am dancing every single night. I take different tours during the day."

"I'm glad to see you're having a favorable vacation to help you forget recent events," said Mustafa.

"Well, I couldn't help myself. I called Carlos to suggest a plan of action. But this time he told me quite firmly that from now on I have to pretend that I've never met either Zurzur or Nijad. He's planning to take care of everything himself. I don't know why I can't continue to help," Amanda complained.

"If you were smart, you would have done as I did—anticipated Carlos's course of action and carried it out before he suggested it; in other words, you should have sidelined yourself a long time ago," said Mustafa.

———

Two weeks into Nijad's and Zurzur's visit, Carlos told them that the Argentine government was not willing to renew the special permit for their stay and to prepare to leave the country as soon as possible. They said they would go to Switzerland, but Carlos told them that the Argentine government insisted on sending them back to the United States. When Nijad asked if Carlos intended to fly them in his private plane, he said that they will be flying in a private plane belonging to the Argentine government. Every word Carlos conveyed had been orchestrated with the Government of Argentina. Nijad and Zurzur had no choice but to do what the Argentine government ostensibly wanted.

Carlos further relayed to them that they would be flown to a small rural airport, to avoid being recognized. Before they left Argentina, Nijad checked to find out if the American government was looking for him, and his associates said that they were not, but there was an APB for Zurzur. Nijad asked Carlos if he could impress on the Argentine government if they could fly each separately and each to a different airport. Nijad did not want to be entangled with Zurzur, since he was facing serious charges and having jumped bail. Carlos later told Nijad that he had secured his request.

The two government planes took off five minutes apart and each headed to a different airport. It was no sweat for two sets of FBI agents to meet each plane separately. In fact, Nijad and Zurzur were told where each was heading in advance. It was all a contrived undertaking on the part of Carlos.

As planned, the two were apprehended upon arrival. Carlos, who was intricately involved in the setup of their arrest, had asked that the two be denied contact with the outside world lest they order retribution against Amanda or any other person. The FBI told Carlos that they could easily do that since Zurzur's attorney was waiting for him at the Kansas prison, but they had to allow Nijad one phone call to his yet-unchosen attorney.

Carlos waited for Nijad's monitored phone call to take place before he and Amanda boarded his private plane back to California. A new apartment was leased for her, without disclosing the address of the apartment to anyone. From California, Carlos headed for Durham, specifically to the farm, where he met with Mustafa, William, and Michelle. The others were summoned for an evening meeting. Rose, Hassan, Willie, Faris, and Zeina joined the group. There and then, Carlos told them that Nijad and Zurzur were in prison, albeit in different prisons. It was the greatest surprise the group had ever heard. Hassan hugged Zeina and Mustafa hugged Michelle.

Carlos took the helm of the meeting and summarized to the group what he wished would happen and described his contribution to help reach a conclusion, in the hope of giving everyone the peace of mind they deserved. He told them that Zurzur and Nijad would be tried separately but most probably at different times. He said that he would pay all expenses for everyone to attend the trials. Michelle reminded Carlos that most would be there as witnesses, and the only two who might need help were Willie and Faris. Carlos continued to say that in the case of Amanda, he would compensate her for temporarily abandoning her consulting practice. And since Amanda was expected to be a key witness, he would offer twenty-four-hour security until things were completely safe.

He also described the main charge against Zurzur as kidnapping, fraud, and transporting stolen property across state lines. In the case of Nijad, he was also charged with kidnapping and fraud, but above all the feds were interested in Nijad cooperating by providing names of individuals operating in the Italian, Lebanese, and Jewish mafias, all for a slightly reduced sentence. Carlos thought that neither Zurzur nor Nijad would be sentenced to less than twenty years, under the most optimistic circumstances.

CHAPTER 31

The same evening, Mustafa took Carlos to the side and asked him if he could be of help in the case of Hassan. He told him that Hassan had no money to his name, and that it was Farouk who was supporting him financially. Mustafa was thorough in describing Hassan's feud with the Qatari government and the ensuing freezing of his assets. He was totally open about the subject, telling Carlos that Hassan was reluctant to pursue marrying Zeina, being almost penniless. Carlos promised to help and said that he would talk to Farouk, as he was heading to see him regarding the proposed construction of the two slaughterhouses in Qatar.

In DC, Carlos told Farouk that Argentina had just renewed the beef export agreement with the United States, and there, Carlos met with US Deputy Secretary of State Lawrence Brightbill and planned to have lunch with him while visiting Washington. He asked Farouk if he minded Carlos discussing Hassan's case with Brightbill. Farouk told him that he welcomed such an effort, as he was denied by the Qatari government to undertake any effort on behalf of his brother.

Carlos did as he promised. He emphasized to the secretary that Hassan had only criticized the government but had never taken any action against it. Brightbill promised to investigate the matter. Before long, Carlos and Farouk invited Brightbill to visit William's farm in Durham.

Brightbill was hoping not to go there empty-handed. He had contacted the foreign minister of Qatar and asked if the government would unfreeze Hassan's assets, with all other outstanding issues to be kept unresolved. He explained to the foreign minister that Hassan's prospective bride was an important conduit to raise funds in North Carolina. Brightbill was rationalizing his request based on his hope for William potentially raising money for the party.

Within days, the Qatari government agreed to release Hassan's cash and financial assets, which amounted to slightly more than $3 million. That was tens of times more than the $2,500 he was receiving monthly from Farouk. When the floor was given to the secretary to address the group, plus William's friends and guests, Brightbill mentioned how he had been successful in unfreezing $3 million of Hassan's assets. Hassan and Zeina, who were totally out of the loop, were most pleasantly surprised—so was everyone else.

———

When Michelle questioned Mustafa, he told her that he was waiting for the two of them to go to the pond before he would tell her. She said he was a big liar, and it was she who always wanted to go back to the pond but that it was him who was in a trance, sometimes because he was tense about some events and other times because he was too giddy about the successful course of events.

He told her that the pond was on their property, and there was no reason not to go there at night. "Like tonight," he said. They did and had lots of intimate fun all over again.

The following day, Mustafa talked to Rose. He told her that ideally, he would love to have a double wedding—his and Michelle's and Hassan's and Zeina's. "Can you imagine Zeina Junior attending both her mother's and her father's weddings at the same time? Wouldn't it be great?" said Mustafa.

Rose agreed to see what she could do after she explained to him that combining weddings was unusual.

"Hassan has asked me if I could be of help and start planning his wedding to Zeina. I'm thrilled to be asked, but before I say anything, you'll need to discuss your idea with Michelle. Have you bounced your idea off Michelle? For many reasons, not the least of which is Zeina's prior relationship with you, this is vitally important," said Rose.

Mustafa told her that he had not but would in the evening. He did just that, and Michelle loved the idea without the slightest hesitation. She then teasingly reminded him that he had not formally asked for her hand, and that he was taking her for granted.

"If I thought for a moment that our lives would not be together, I would have left and ceased to speak to anyone in the group. The mere thought of it would have been devastating, and the only place where I could bury my regrets would have been a vast and desolate desert," said Mustafa.

"I'm afraid that your ability to be descriptive isn't good enough. I want you to go down on your knees tonight, in front of everyone, and ask me if I would marry you. In the meantime, I'll leave you to ponder my potential answer."

In the evening, as requested, Mustafa addressed the group and kneeled in front of Michelle. "I am here on my knees, asking Michelle if she will marry me. I hope she will accept, if only first with some reservations, and later out of charity."

Michelle laughed. "Now I accept out of the deepest love a woman ever felt toward any man. I also have a surprise. I talked to Zeina this afternoon, and she confirmed that she and Hassan have agreed to join us and have a double wedding."

Everyone in the room clapped and was most delighted with the announcement. William then spoke and said that he had never imagined meeting someone like Mustafa and feeling so close to him and to be so admiring of his character. William then invited Rose to speak.

She said that Zeina and Hassan called earlier in the day and asked her also to arrange their wedding ceremony. "I told Mustafa before that I live vicariously through happy events like the ones announced this evening. Nothing is as sad as losing a lover, as I lost Samuel, and nothing is as gratifying as helping in nurturing a love affair. Today, I am blessed: there are two that I'm involved in."

CHAPTER 32

Michelle and Mustafa agreed to wait till after Zurzur and Nijad were put on trial for them to wed, provided that the two trials were scheduled within one year, and subject to Zeina's and Hassan's concurrence. Hassan and Zeina agreed.

The first casualty was Nijad's honorary consulate. He was dismissed from his position as Honorary Counsel of Jordan. While he savored not having to continue dishing out money to the different Jordanian officials, the loss of the exploitation of the title was a major blow to his ego and his operations. He had been using it as an entrée to connect with the Chicago and Illinois officials, pretentiously on behalf of his government but actually to influence the officials for the benefit of his illegal operations.

An article was published in the local paper in which Nijad's association with the Jordanian government, on one hand, and the local mafias, on the other, were mentioned. The Jordanian government was quick to ask the State Department to intervene, hoping it could have Nijad extradited to Jordan, instead of incarcerated. Even that request cost Nijad under-the-table payments. The Jordanians represented that he was an important agent of theirs and his incarceration would compromise their national security.

In no time, Farouk told the group that the Jordanians and Americans reached an agreement to send Nijad to Jordan. Farouk talked to William and told him that he could not interfere directly. He asked William instead to seek the deputy secretary's help in stopping the transfer to Jordan after Farouk would have confirmed seriously damaging pieces of information. Farouk could not. He contacted Carlos and told Carlos what he was trying to confirm, that Nijad had bribed a couple of Jordanian security officials. They managed to give him a fake identity, with inflated operational importance.

Carlos went to work right away, and he in turn managed to grease the palms of other security officials. He asked them to check whether the identity the Jordanians had presented to the US State Department was Nijad's or a made to order one. As everyone was waiting anxiously and desperately, they all got into a glum mood and very much froze their activities, including their romantic interludes.

In a matter of three days, Carlos secured the answer: it was all a convenient setup to save Nijad's skin from prison in the United States. Carlos relayed the news and more. It turned out that Nijad was a Jordanian agent, spying on the Palestinian and Jordanian Americans in the United States. Farouk contacted Amanda, who contacted the two private eyes. They were requested to check with some Arab Americans in Chicago—ones that were known to Farouk—to inquire from them as to Nijad's local spying activities.

The inquiry produced results. The private eyes found out that Nijad was very active in the field of spying for the Jordanians in the United States. He was nowhere active in being a regular security agent of the Jordanians, as the Jordanians had relayed to the Americans. Furthermore, he was responsible for the apprehension of one Chicago Arab American dual citizen by the Jordanians. The information was relayed to William, and he, at Farouk's request, took the initiative to contact Deputy Secretary Brightbill. The State Department investigated the matter and found out that Nijad had not been to Jordan for at least eleven years, totally contradicting the credentials they had received from the Jordanians.

Initially, the State of Illinois insisted that as part of the settlement, he would serve five years first in Illinois. When Illinois checked with Amanda, Carlos advised her to insist on ten years before any extradition. He also advised her that she and others could object to his extradition later on. The ten years were secured as the federal government impressed upon the Jordanians that Nijad could have received a forty-year sentence.

Furthermore, it was stipulated that Nijad would serve in Jordan's most difficult prison, Al-Jafr, another five years. A $5 million collateral of Nijad's money was placed in escrow to guarantee that the Jordanian government would abide by the agreement. It was partially secured from his Mafia sources in the hope of limiting his testimony against them. Nijad was amenable to the arrangement. The government allowed him to have a say in where to serve in the United States, as his life was in danger. He chose one federal prison where the three mafias of his peers had very little influence. In addition, Nijad agreed to pay Amanda $3 million. Mustafa and Michelle had much less of a claim and decided not to go for any.

Michelle, Mustafa, Zeina, and Hassan were elated. It made their prospects to get married soon much more probable. Amanda was equally pleased since she was not anxious to testify about her sexual relations with Nijad. In the process, Nijad came through and passed complete information to the feds about his Mafia connections, notwithstanding they helped out financially. As to Zurzur, he turned down the government's offer and opted for a trial. The federal government sped up matters to impress upon Zurzur to settle. The trial was scheduled to take place in seven months. As much as everyone hoped for a settlement, the trial started after only a one-month delay.

It was true that Zurzur was an attorney with thirty years' experience, but he was no more and no less than a fixer. What he forgot to take into consideration was the testimony of seven of his wives. The court was surprised that his "harem" included one attorney and one physician. It happened that the testimony of those two was most damaging, especially the testimony of the physician. She described how Zurzur forced her to write prescriptions for his criminal friends, without having examined them. The attorney described how he made her back-date documents. By the time the seven wives finished testifying, Zurzur's potential sentence was up to sixty years. His attorney advised him to seek a settlement and to accept anything twenty-five years or shorter. In the end, Zurzur agreed to settle. It was twenty-five years, with no possibility of parole. In addition, Amanda was awarded $1 million, to be secured from the sale proceeds of Zurzur's ranch.

No sooner was the Zurzur case settled than Michelle got together with Zeina again and asked her if she wanted to help Rose arrange the two weddings. Zeina asked her if Rose alone would mind taking care of both, and for each couple to split the cost fifty-fifty. Upon hearing Zeina's request, Rose said that she would be glad to arrange every detail, and Carol and Sara were thrilled to be of assistance on Michelle's end as dual maids of honor.

When Carlos was informed about the advanced date of the wedding, he contacted Rose and requested that he be allowed to pay for both weddings. He authorized her to spend up to $100,000. William objected and insisted on paying for Michelle's share. Mustafa had to speak to him to let him know that in Palestine, the groom paid for the wedding costs. Then, when William insisted and reminded Mustafa that the wedding was taking place in America, Mustafa asked him to be considerate since Carlos was instrumental in closing the book on their challenges. William grudgingly accepted, and Farouk relayed his desire to pay for Hassan's half. Mustafa again had to intervene to convince Farouk that without Carlos, everyone would have been still mired in the evil actions of Nijad and Zurzur. Farouk also relented.

Mustafa went to see Michelle to tell her the good news. She told him that she was so satisfied that it required the two of them to visit the pond.

Mustafa asked, "The real pond?"

"Yes, Mustafa, the real pond. This is grand, don't you think so?" said Michelle.

Mustafa answered, "It is big if it is final. It seems that if there is not one thing, there is another."

"What's the big deal? We'll have great sex, regardless. I want to be naked with you caressing me," said Michelle.

"You know what my problem is, Michelle? Every time I think of you, I see you naked," said Mustafa.

"Wow, listening to you it feels like you see me wrapped in thick bear skin. Let's see which one you see tonight, at nine!" said Michelle.

After the two finished their improvisations, they went to see Zeina and Hassan and told them what had transpired in between. The four went to see Rose and gave her full latitude in managing the weddings, provided Michelle's friends Carol and Sara were both her maids of honor. Rose wanted to produce something special. She readily agreed to include Sara and Carol. She spoke to William and told him about Carlos's $100,000 budget. She added that she expected to spend even more, and that she would be ready to pay for all additional costs. That started a new argument about who was to pay, and they finally agreed to split the cost of things beyond Carlos's budget.

Rose wanted a very special wedding—one not only to represent the backgrounds of the brides and grooms, but one to reflect the trials and tribulations of the group. Rose looked hard and could find very little to reflect on the themes that led to this occasion. Finally, she found a North Carolina Black song and dance troupe. Their main theme and act were about slavery and freedom. When she contacted the manager of the troupe, she asked him if he could modify his act to suit the story of Mustafa and Michelle, which naturally included the story of Hassan and Zeina. He was more than amenable, for the handsome sum of $10,000.

Rose told him the whole story, and even gave him three of Mustafa's poems. When his scriptwriters finished telling a story of the trials and tribulations that had ended with joy and love and bounced it off Rose, she was beside herself. She was almost mesmerized when she saw the rehearsal of the final version. She shared the news with no one.

Four months later, it was time. Sara and Carol were captivated as William escorted Michelle, and next to him, Sammy escorted Zeina down a very long walkway in front of the farmhouse. Mustafa and Hassan walked from opposite sides, heading toward the brides. Per Rose's guidelines, the two sets stopped twenty yards from each other. They paused and unexpectedly, the troupe appeared between them, from nowhere. They first went slowly to describe Mustafa's heartbreak having to leave Zeina, followed by a description of his trials trying to reach Stanford. In the end, the musical reached the date of the wedding. The song ended by saying that they will sing no more but would let the events make their own music. Each groom and each bride approached each other and exchanged their vows. They shared the most passionate kisses. The music resumed, but this time it was all dance music.

They danced all night, including Willie, Faris, and Amanda, who was there with her new twenty-one-year-old boyfriend. It was a glorious occasion where everyone danced till two in the morning. After all the guests were gone, Michelle insisted on going to the pond in her wedding dress, and Mustafa in his tuxedo. They spent the rest of the night there, till dawn.

Michelle and Mustafa enrolled at Oxford University, she to continue studying comparative literature while he went for a doctorate in economics. Zeina and Hassan settled in Durham after they bought a business in the area. William got used to traveling to England to see Michelle and Mustafa once a month. Rose joined him every other month, and Carol and Sara visited with them once a year. Zeina Junior accompanied William and Rose to visit Michelle and Mustafa. She often stayed for a month, twice in the summer. Amanda got married to a student five years her junior and kept cooperating with Mustafa as he refined his stock analysis program further.

Two years into their marriage, Mustafa and Michelle had a baby girl—they called her Yara, a *baby butterfly* in Arabic. Rose moved in with Mustafa and Michelle and enjoyed babysitting Yara. Mustafa, Michelle, and Rose moved back to Durham to join William at the farm after the two graduated with doctorates. Mustafa planned to continue with his research and Michelle to pursue teaching college around Durham.

Wagih Abu-Rish is a Palestinian-American author and activist who writes with conviction about issues related to social justice and equal rights. A former foreign journalist, Abu-Rish's global and comparative perspectives again come to bear in this novel, his third, on gender role, intercultural and romantic challenges.

www.ingramcontent.com/pod-product-compliance
Lightning Source LLC
Chambersburg PA
CBHW020058310726
48970CB00002B/379